PRAISE FOR SAM CARRINGTON

'Expertly written … with plentiful twists and unforgettable characters. An insightful and unnerving read.'
Caroline Mitchell, no.1 bestselling author of *Silent Victim*

'A kick-ass page turner … I was knocked senseless by the awesome twist.'
John Marrs, no.1 bestselling author of *The One*

'Psychologist Connie Summers is a fascinatingly flesh-and-blood guide through this twisty thriller.'
Louise Candlish, *Sunday Times* bestselling author of *Our House*

'Keeps you guessing right to the end.'
Sue Fortin, no.1 bestselling author of *Sister Sister*

'This book is not only gripping, but it explores the mother/daughter relationship perfectly, and ends with a gasp-out-loud twist.'
Closer

'I devoured this story in one sitting!'
Louise Jensen, no.1 bestselling author of *The Sister*

'Sam Carrington has done it again. *One Little Lie* is a twisty, gripping read. I loved it.'
Cass Green, bestselling author of *In a Cottage In a Wood*

'I LOVED *Bad Sister*. Tense, convincing and complex, it kept me guessing (wrongly!)'
Caz Frear, bestselling author of *Sweet Little Lies*

'I read *One Little Lie* in one greedy gulp. A compelling thriller about the dark side of maternal instinct and love.'
Isabel Ashdown, bestselling author of *Beautiful Liars*

'A gripping read which moved at a head-spinning pace ... I simply couldn't put this book down until I reached the dramatic and devastating conclusion.'
Claire Allan, *USA Today* bestselling author of
Her Name Was Rose

'Utterly original and thought provoking ... This cries out to be made into a TV series.'
Amanda Robson, *Sunday Times* bestselling author of *Guilt*

'Engrossing psychological suspense about the effect of a murder on the mother of a teenage killer. Sam Carrington had me hooked!'
Emma Curtis, bestselling author of *One Little Mistake*

Sam Carrington lives in Devon with her husband and three children. She worked for the NHS for fifteen years, during which time she qualified as a nurse. Following the completion of a psychology degree she went to work for the prison service as an Offending Behaviour Programme Facilitator. Her experiences within this field inspired her writing. She left the service to spend time with her family and to follow her dream of being a novelist.

Readers can find out more at http://www.samcarrington.blogspot. co.uk and can follow Sam on Twitter @sam_carrington1

THE MISSING WIFE

SAM CARRINGTON

avon.

Published by AVON
A division of HarperCollins*Publishers* Ltd
1 London Bridge Street
London SE1 9GF

www.harpercollins.co.uk

A Paperback Original 2019

First published in Great Britain by HarperCollins*Publishers* 2019

Copyright © Sam Carrington 2019

Sam Carrington asserts the moral right to
be identified as the author of this work.

A catalogue copy of this book is available from the British Library.

ISBN: 978-0-00-831295-4

Typeset in Minion by Palimpsest Book Production Limited, Falkirk, Stirlingshire
Printed and bound in UK by CPI Group (UK) Ltd, Croydon CR0 4YY

MIX
Paper from
responsible sources
FSC
www.fsc.org
FSC™ C007454

This book is produced from independently certified FSC™ paper
to ensure responsible forest management.

For m

For Danika –
my daughter, my friend, my inspiration.

1

THE BURIAL

I can still feel the mud embedded deep under my fingernails, taste the dirt on my lips. I can still see the eyes: shining like glass, open and staring, deep in their sockets. Dead.

In my mind I watch the earth piling onto the body, slowly blotting out what's been done. Finally covering those eyes, so they can't judge anymore.

I'm confident no trace can lead back to me.

Part of me feels regret; a sadness that it came to such a drastic act.

For the moment, my conscience is telling me I'm guilty.

But that can be buried too.

2

THE SIGNS

The quiet murmurings that stopped as Louisa walked in the room, the closely guarded messages on his iPhone, the way he flitted about when Tiff was around – those were the little things that gave him away. He'd never been able to keep secrets. It'd been something Louisa had found endearing when she'd first met him on Millennium Eve at the party she shouldn't have been at. But nineteen years later, his inability to hide anything despite believing he could – and that he was good at it – had lost its appeal.

Noah screamed in her left ear. She shifted the small bundle from one shoulder to the other, dragging the damp, sickly-smelling muslin square along with him, and bounced him in a vain attempt to console his colicky cries. He'd been howling for three days straight, Louisa was certain. As certain as she could be in her 'new mum' catatonic state, where each day rolled into the next with no real context, no definition or concept of time. Instead of faffing about secretively on his phone, Brian would be better served taking Noah and giving her five minutes to herself. Even going to the loo was a luxury these days.

3

She wondered if Emily had been like this, but Emily's early years were a blur now. The teenage issues had long replaced any other bad memories of her infancy. Louisa shouldn't be dealing with a baby. In just over two weeks she was going to be forty. As far as she'd been concerned, Emily was their one and only. Becoming pregnant was neither planned, nor particularly welcomed.

Ultimately, Noah was a mistake. Perhaps that explained why she was struggling.

Louisa lowered her chin and nestled against Noah's soft, creamy skin, breathing in the distinct smell of baby, blocking his cries from her tired mind. Even contemplating him as a mistake sent a stabbing pain through her womb. Of *course* she shouldn't think that way. He was perfect, beautiful – there were women who'd kill to have what she did.

It was because she was almost forty. The thought of reaching the milestone was an overwhelming one. Her mind flooded with anxiety. She was too old to be doing all this again. Sleepless nights, endless days. Nursery, pre-school, junior school, comprehensive, college.

College.

For a moment, Louisa's memory displayed a vision – but it was lost as quickly as it appeared. She didn't like to think about the period of her life when she was seventeen and studying for her A levels. There were too many gaps during her second year, and mostly her mind refused to fill them – apart from the odd occasion when an image burst into her head. Random images; unrecognisable faces. Ones she knew she didn't want to, or need to, grasp hold of. There was little point in trying to piece together a past that wanted to be forgotten.

Noah's screams finally penetrated her thoughts again – her ability to block them only temporary. All the things she was going to have to experience again. All those 'stages' she'd assumed were long gone. But here she was beginning the journey all over again, and with such a big age gap. It petrified her.

Not only that, but she had the other end of the scale to deal with at the same time. Teenage angst, moodiness, rudeness, the pushing of boundaries. It was becoming too much. Even Brian: safe, dependable Brian, who'd been the doting dad when Emily was a baby, had shown less of an interest in Noah. He often came home from his shifts at the prison exhausted and irritable. Sometimes it was as though she had three children to look after, but no one to look after her.

Louisa strode up to him, thrusting Noah out towards his chest.

'Hang on, Lou. Can't you see I'm busy?' he said as he whipped the phone screen away from her so she couldn't see the display, his body turning away from their son.

'Funnily enough, so am I. And I've had this constant screaming pounding my ears for eight hours. Give me a bloody break and take him! I assume you do want to eat tonight?'

'Mum!' Emily's voice, loud to compete with her baby brother, burst into the lounge. 'What's for tea?'

Louisa closed her eyes, taking a moment before she offered an answer. Too soon and her response would come across brusque, unreasonable. Aggressiveness was not a quality she wished to show to her daughter.

'When I get five minutes to look in the fridge, I'll be able to tell you.'

'Oh,' Brian piped up, his phone finally in his pocket. 'You don't even know what we're having?'

'No, *love*. Why don't you rustle something up? Or take Noah. Like I've been trying to get you to do.' A pain shot through her jaw as she clenched it forcefully. She gave a tight smile, then held Noah out at arm's length for a second attempt.

'No problem,' he said, taking the noisy creature from her outstretched arms as though he was contaminated. He squinted his eyes as the noise came in close contact with his ears.

See how he likes it.

Louisa turned away from them and quickly slipped into the kitchen to make the most of her reprieve, closing the door to block out as much of the noise as possible. She hunched over the granite worktop, hanging her head and closing her eyes tight. God, her head ached. It was like having a hangover twenty-four hours a day, every day. Louisa reluctantly opened her eyes again. She stared at her lank, brown hair, which had splayed on the dark granite – split ends upon split ends, like branches on a tree, reminding her she hadn't been to the hairdresser for almost a year. Straightening, Louisa contemplated what she could rustle an evening meal out of. It would have to be something with chips. Until Brian took her shopping, there was very little in the fridge, and mainly bags of breast milk in the freezer.

That reminded her.

She pressed a hand to each breast. When had Noah last fed? Both breasts felt relatively soft, yet she couldn't remember feeding him; that could account for his screaming. But if it had been too long ago, her breasts would've become engorged and she'd be desperate to empty them. She tried to think back over the day: she usually fed Noah while sitting in the armchair in the corner of the lounge – what was once her favourite reading chair, before it became the feeding chair – and she always put the TV on while he suckled because it helped take her mind off the stinging sensation of her cracked nipples. What had she been watching the last time she fed him?

Worryingly, nothing came to her. The night-time feeds were always hazy, but not usually the daytime ones. The pounding pain in her head worsened the more she forced herself to remember, the pressure threatening to rupture her brain. Yanking open the bottom drawer of the kitchen cupboard unit, Louisa reached in, pulling forward the tea towels to reveal the rectangular packet she stored at the back. She turned it over and over in her hands before popping two pills from the foil pack. She stared at the capsules as the fear gripped her insides. A fear she hadn't experienced in a long time.

Was it happening again?

3

THE TEXT

Wednesday a.m.

'What are you doing?' Brian asked, his words slurred from tiredness. He threw the duvet off and sat on the edge of the bed, his head resting in his hands. The room was dark bar the illumination of the digital alarm clock's blue glow.

'Getting dressed.' Louisa zipped her jeans and, using her phone light to see, pulled at the soft-pink jumper under the mountain of discarded clothes on the tub chair in the corner of their bedroom, sending the rest tumbling.

'But it's five past five, Louisa?'

'Oh, is it? It feels later. I've been up half the night with Noah.' She tutted as she absently piled the clothes back up on the chair. She banged her hip against the dressing table as she stumbled towards the door. 'Sorry, I'm a bit on the clumsy side this morning, didn't mean to disturb you. You've got another hour yet, so go back to sleep.'

'You're clumsy every morning lately,' Brian mumbled as he sank back into the pillow.

Despite the strong urge to tell him he would be too if he'd been the one up every night for the last three months, Louisa said nothing and just closed the door quietly behind her.

Noah was sleeping now. Louisa crept past his nursery, barely daring to breathe in case she woke him. Emily's room, with a poster of P!NK adorning the door, was silent too. She seemed to sleep through Noah's cries. Just as well – she was moody enough without lack of sleep impacting on her. Her schoolwork was suffering. It had been prior to Noah's arrival but Louisa didn't want her daughter, who was as bright as a button, to go downhill further because an unexpected baby had disrupted the equilibrium. Louisa trod carefully on each stair, avoiding the edge of the squeaky middle one.

In the kitchen, she took her handbag from where it hung on the inside of the larder door and retrieved the packet of Marlboro and a disposable lighter. Standing at the open back door, Louisa dragged on the cigarette. Her head swam for a moment, a light airiness consuming it. After a few more puffs, she relaxed.

She had limited opportunities to smoke without being noticed. Early mornings were the best. As far as Brian was concerned, she gave up long ago. She *had* given up for four years. But yesterday triggered something. The compulsion to start again overtook her and she was relieved to find her secret packet was still in its original hiding place in the bottom drawer of her mother's old sideboard in the garage. When Brian was otherwise engaged on his mobile, she'd got them and popped them in her handbag. It wasn't as if Brian would ever go looking in that. He wasn't nosy, didn't check up on her; he'd never think to search through any of her things. He wasn't like that.

Louisa reached around to the outside and scraped the cigarette along the wall to extinguish it; then she hid the butt in one of Emily's discarded Coke cans. That girl was drinking far too much fizzy rubbish. She washed her hands in the kitchen sink, spread a liberal spray of Oust around and then closed and locked the back door.

Brian's mobile was charging on the worktop near the bread bin. He never took it to bed, always fearing he'd get a late-night call from his sister Alison, who lived in Yorkshire with his mother, taking care of her following the death of Brian's dad. She'd phoned several times in the middle of the night, worrying about their mother's behaviour and her health. It's not that Brian didn't care – he did. He was a good son on the whole. But his sister was needy and felt it was her responsibility to tell Brian every little detail of what was going on up there, while he 'lived life' at the opposite end of the country. She'd been bitter ever since Brian chose to move to Devon, where Louisa had always lived. And when they'd married, her bitterness intensified. For some reason, Brian felt Alison had always wanted to punish him for that choice.

Louisa took the phone, pressing the button to bring up the home screen. It was password-protected, but she could see the first part of each of the last few notifications and texts. Her breath caught. Tiff's message was the last one. She could only see the first line.

All good for meeting Friday still? I assume you've managed to keep it from

Louisa's face grew hot. She tapped the screen even though she knew she wouldn't be able to access the full message. She placed it back on the worktop in the same position she'd found it in. Her heart beat wildly; she could feel pressure in her chest. Friday was when he was supposedly going out with the lads; Louisa distinctly remembered him arranging it. To her knowledge, Brian had never lied to her.

She wondered why he would start now.

4

THE FRIEND

Wednesday a.m.

Noah enjoyed being pushed in his pram, as long as Louisa kept it moving. If she could spend every hour of each day treading the pavements of Little Penchurch, he'd be a quiet baby. Tiff only lived a few minutes from her house, so rather than take the direct route, she went the long way around, circumnavigating the village in the hope Noah may stay asleep once she stopped at her destination. It was unlikely, but nevertheless she had to try something – and she was determined that nothing would stop her seeing Tiff this morning.

Tiff's house was stunning, like her. It was detached – which again, some would say was one of her traits – standing in its own grounds set back from the road. Inside it was modern, spotless – like a show home. No husband or children to mess it up. Louisa opened the heavy wooden gate, manoeuvred Noah's pram through and closed it behind her before walking down the side of the house to the back entrance. It was easier to get the pram through the patio doors at the rear. She hadn't called ahead, so she hoped Tiff hadn't left yet – she couldn't remember if it was her yoga day.

'Well, this a lovely surprise,' Tiff said as she slid the patio doors fully open. 'A bit early for you.' She smiled, her wide grin revealing perfectly whitened, straight teeth.

'Yeah, hope you don't mind. I just had to get out of the house for a bit, and walking seems to be the only thing that keeps Noah quiet.'

Tiff crouched down to peek inside the pram. 'Aw, he's getting bigger. It's all that good milk he's getting.'

'Not sure he is getting enough milk, actually.' Now Louisa was inside her best friend's house, she let her guard down. Without even realising she felt sad, tears began to trickle down her face.

'Oh, lovely. Come here.' Tiff enveloped Louisa in a tight hug, rocking her gently. This only added to Louisa's unexpected outpouring of tears and suddenly she was sobbing.

'I don't know what's happening to me.' Her voice was muffled in Tiff's white T-shirt.

'Baby blues, love. They'll pass. Come on, let's get you a coffee.'

Louisa left Noah, who was thankfully still asleep despite the movement of the pram ceasing, and followed Tiff into her huge kitchen, wiping her tears with her jumper sleeve as she walked.

'Here.' Tiff handed Louisa a small cube of coloured tissues. Louisa took a few sheets and swiped them across her nose, annoyed with herself for crying the second she'd walked in. She watched through tingling eyes as her friend of eight years filled the see-through kettle with bottled water – she didn't trust tap water, convinced she'd get cancer from drinking it – and stared at the blue light radiating through the liquid.

'So—' Tiff turned to look at her '—I take it you're not sleeping, looking at *those* bags.'

Louisa couldn't help but laugh. 'Hah! Thanks, I feel better already!'

'Sorry. I'd be a total mess if I were you. If I don't get at least eight hours a night I'm a total bitch and I'd look like something from a horror movie.'

'I doubt that, Tiff.' She looked down at the scrunched ball of soggy tissue in her hand.

'It's a good job it doesn't happen often, I can tell you.'

The kettle clicked off, and Tiff busied herself making the two coffees. Louisa glanced around the kitchen. Her whole downstairs would fit in this space. Her thoughts turned to the text message, and how she could bring it up without making herself sound distrustful of her friend. Her only friend. Well, the only one that counted, anyway – she knew lots of people: colleagues from the accountancy firm she worked for, other mums of kids Emily's age, and now some mums from her antenatal and baby groups. But she didn't socialise with them. She wasn't like Tiff, who had dozens of close friends and revelled in moving in different social circles. That would only stress Louisa. Keeping a single friend was difficult enough for her, always had been.

'Any goss?' Louisa asked. It was the best way of getting Tiff chatting, so that she could find an opportunity to slip in her question.

'Ooh, well, yes, actually!' Tiff planted the mugs on two glass coasters and flounced away, disappearing through the double doors that led to the lounge. She returned, laptop in her hands. 'Did you see this?' Tiff twisted the screen to face Louisa. Sarah Weaver's Facebook profile was displayed.

'Oh, what's going on with her?' Louisa squinted at the page as Tiff reached around the laptop and scrolled down to Sarah's latest status update.

'Life is too short to be with people who hold you back. Embrace change. Don't be afraid to turn the page of your own story or you'll never reach the next chapter.'

'Okay, it's a bit deep – but I don't understand, what's wrong with it? It's just some motivational quote.'

'Haven't you been keeping up? Don't you realise what this means?'

Louisa sighed. Keeping up with Facebook wasn't something that had occurred to her during the last three months of sleep-deprived baby tasks. She hadn't been that great with social media prior to Noah's birth, but the most she used the internet for at the moment was searching for 'how to prevent colic' or 'tricks to make him sleep like a baby'. As well as the chat rooms on Mumsnet – they were her current lifeline. Not the goings-on with friends-who-weren't-even-real-friends on bloody Facebook. If it wasn't for Tiff having set up her Facebook profile in the first place, she'd never have bothered with it. Fake lives and fake friends were not her thing.

'It's not something I've been compelled to do, no. I've been a little preoccupied . . .'

'Well, yes, I guess. You are useless at posting anyway, and you *never* respond to my posts, even if I tag you.'

'Sorry.' It was quicker and easier to apologise rather than get into a debate about the negative aspects of splashing your life online.

'Not to worry. Anyway, I digress. Back to Sarah. After being "found out" last month, she's been keeping a low profile. But then, this. It has to mean she's still seeing Mark, doesn't it? We're all going to the school fundraiser on Wednesday evening, so no doubt I will find out more then.' Tiff looked pleased with herself. She and Sarah had history and it was no secret they'd clashed over who was better at organising village events – whether it was for the primary school, the cottage garden society show or the church fund, Tiff liked doing it all. Without much help. And certainly not from Sarah Weaver, who she viewed as a nuisance and someone who put barriers up where there shouldn't be any (even if she was right). Tiff liked to think of herself as THE fundraising organiser of the village – the best and only 'go-to' person there was. Anything that put Sarah, her main competition to this title, in a poor light was a good outcome as far as she was concerned. So, if there were rumours, Tiff wasn't likely to do anything other than fan the flames.

Despite Tiff not having any children, let alone at the school, she'd managed to get in with the head teacher by volunteering to read with some of the younger pupils. Louisa suspected that Tiff's stated motive for doing it – so she could organise events – was only part of the reason. From some of the conversations they'd had over the years, Louisa deduced that Tiff regretted her decision not to have a family and now believed this was her way of being a part of something she felt she was missing out on. The fact she could be so pushy, and even hoity about it, always came as a surprise to Louisa.

She often wondered how they'd become such good friends. They'd met at a mutual friend's wedding eight years ago and somehow just clicked. As unlikely a friendship as it was, and a total surprise to Brian, they'd remained close ever since. Maybe it was because Louisa posed no threat to Tiff's aspirations: Louisa was never going to want to be an organiser of anything because she didn't even like events or parties. If she was coerced into going to one, she'd be the person keeping quiet in the corner of the room, drinking an orange juice and looking lost. Tiff was welcome to the attention.

Louisa was suddenly aware she was meant to be offering an answer – responding to Tiff's assumptions about Sarah's extra-marital affair in the way her friend wanted her to. As this finally sank in, Louisa realised it gave her an opportunity to bring up the real reason she'd visited today.

'Let me get this right,' Louisa said. 'You think Sarah has been having an affair with Mark – her best friend's husband?'

'Er . . . yes! I know you've been off the scene for a bit, but how come you've missed all of that? It's not like we live in a big village – it's tiny, and everyone knows everyone. I don't know, Louisa – sometimes you disappoint me.' She shook her head. 'And anyway, I thought we talked about this last time we had coffee?'

'I don't remember . . .'

'Baby brain,' Tiff mocked. 'Anyway, how evil is that?'

This was Louisa's chance to mention the text. But with Tiff's obvious distaste for what Sarah had done, why then would she be doing the same to Louisa? Although, it *was* always easier to judge someone else's actions rather than your own. And she may only be reacting to this because it was Sarah, not because she actually felt it was evil.

Louisa took a deep breath. 'Yeah, that's awful. Who would cheat with their best friend's husband?' She stared into Tiff's deep-blue eyes, expecting to see a hint of guilt.

'A bitch, Louisa. A total bitch, that's who,' Tiff said vehemently.

'You'd never do that to me, would you?'

The burst of laughter made Louisa jump. For a moment she was puzzled – she hadn't realised she'd said the words out loud, only thought them.

'What? God, of course not. And, you know, it's not as if Brian is my type.' She threw her head back and carried on laughing.

'What's that supposed to mean?' Louisa put her mug down hard on the coaster. She'd managed to go from mistrust to indignation in a beat.

'You're serious,' Tiff said. The laughter stopped, her smile disappearing. 'I'm confused, Lou. What's up with you?'

'I'm sorry, I'm just hormonal. It's nothing.'

'No, go on. It's obviously something or you wouldn't be reacting in this way.'

'I feel bad now. I – I shouldn't have looked . . .'

'Looked at what?' A mask of concern darkened Tiff's face. Louisa regretted saying anything, but now she'd come this far she may as well continue.

'A text. On Brian's phone. He's been weird lately, acting suspiciously, on the bloody mobile all the time. All hush-hush stuff. I thought he must be having an affair . . .' Louisa looked up at Tiff, her face stony. 'Maybe it's with Sarah.' Louisa gave a nervous laugh. But it was too late to make jokes – Tiff knew what she was getting at.

'No. Not Sarah. But not me either. Not anyone, Lou. He only loves you.' Her voice was cool.

Louisa swallowed hard. 'Why are you arranging to meet then? Friday, you said in the text.'

Tiff got up and walked around the kitchen island to Louisa.

'Look, Lou,' Tiff said, putting an arm around her shoulders. 'Even *if* Brian was my type, I'd never cross that line. I'm a lot of things, but I'm not a husband-snatcher. And I would *never* go after my best friend's husband. I'm going to put this down to your sleep-deprived state – and your loopy hormones, like you said – and try not to be deeply hurt that you'd even think such a thing. Now, how about another coffee?' Her hand slipped from Louisa's shoulder as she straightened and moved away.

Louisa frowned. Tiff hadn't denied the text, although she'd put up a convincing argument about how she wouldn't have an affair with Brian. Because of her reaction Louisa didn't feel she could carry on the conversation or ask anything more about Friday – not without alienating her further.

There was something more, though, she could sense it.

Louisa realised she only half-believed her best friend. And that didn't sit well at all.

5

THE REQUEST

Thursday p.m.

Louisa awoke with her head and torso slumped over her lap. She straightened, taking a deep breath as she looked round the room. She was in Noah's nursery, in the chair.

Her heart gave a jolt. She'd been feeding Noah.

She looked down. He was quiet. Still. Cradled in her arms. She'd fallen asleep over him.

Louisa shook him gently.

Nothing.

She jumped up, holding Noah upright.

A sharp cry.

For a moment she was relieved. But the cry was her own.

'What is it? What's the matter?' Brian crashed through the door, hair ruffled, his face ashen.

'No – ah . . .' Louisa gasped for air, holding the limp baby up towards her husband.

'What? What about him. He's quiet, Lou, leave him to sleep.' Brian's brow was furrowed.

'I – I was feeding him, I fell asleep – he's – he's not breathing, Brian!'

Brian hit the light switch. A soft yellow illumination filled the small room.

'Louisa.' He reached out and took her arms. 'Louisa, he's just asleep—'

'No. I squashed him, look . . .' Louisa was afraid to gaze down again, fearful of seeing the damage she'd done. But suddenly her arms felt light.

She looked down.

Noah wasn't in them.

'You must've been asleep and dreamt it, Lou. He's fine. He's in his cot, and he's breathing. I promise.' Brian pulled Louisa gently towards the cot and placed her shaking hand on Noah's chest. 'See?'

Louisa's breathing slowed as she felt the steady rise and fall.

Tears of relief slipped down her cheeks. It hadn't felt like a dream. She'd been certain he was in her arms.

'Come to bed.' Brian's voice – soft, coaxing – relaxed her.

Louisa could only nod as Brian took her hand and gently guided her to their room. She climbed into bed. But she didn't fall asleep again. A coil of fear remained – an ache, a pain she couldn't rid herself of – the question of whether she'd hallucinated purely because of sleep deprivation lay heavy in her exhausted mind.

She waited for Brian's deep guttural snoring to start, then she crept out of bed.

Her online search yielded a long list of hits. Louisa's anxiety at what had happened – her belief she'd suffocated Noah when he wasn't even in her arms despite her eyes telling her otherwise – lessened slightly. It seemed hallucinations were one of the most common effects of lack of sleep. One article mentioned that the effects of sleep deprivation could mimic mental illness.

Louisa began to panic that having Noah, and the lack of

sleep that came with him, might have triggered her old problem. Or was the article right – was she merely experiencing the effects of not sleeping? She didn't want to think about it. Louisa closed Google and was about to log into Mumsnet, but then decided Facebook might take her mind off things more. Thinking about what Tiff had said about Sarah, and the fact Louisa had never responded to being tagged, she thought now was as good a time as any to catch up. She may even find evidence of something going on between Tiff and Brian. They were both aware she didn't really use Facebook and therefore would be unlikely to spot anything untoward – they may have taken advantage of that.

After a few failed attempts at logging in, Louisa finally recalled her 'easy-to-remember' password that Tiff had set for her and the homepage popped up. She immediately searched Tiff's and Brian's profiles. There were a few 'likes' – and Brian had commented on Tiff's last profile picture she uploaded – simply saying 'lovely' – but surely that was nothing to worry about. She scrolled through the last two weeks of status updates, new photos and every comment on Tiff's account, checking to see if Brian had said anything inappropriate. Then she did the same on Brian's. Even though she was analysing everything as if under a microscope, she couldn't find anything that looked suspicious in terms of them having an affair.

She then clicked on to Sarah's profile. At first glance, her life looked perfect. Every photo Sarah posted showed smiling faces; happy families – on outings, all sitting around the table having a family meal, the kids all behaving. The picture of perfection – then she did the dirty? Facebook is a lie, Louisa concluded. In fact, she would go as far as saying it was evil. The fakeness appalled her. It was why she kept off it, although, deep down she knew that wasn't the only reason.

As she moved the cursor to close it down, vowing to herself

never to go back on the site, Louisa's attention was caught by the number beside the miniature world icon on the top right of her page. Thirty notifications.

Ignore them.

It's not like she had tons of friends – real or otherwise – so despite a long absence she hadn't expected to see so many notifications.

Louisa relinquished and clicked on them.

Her breath ceased for a few seconds. Every one of them was from a single source, and it was not Tiff, as she'd expected. And all but one of them was the same.

Oliver Dunmore invited you to join the group *Exeter College Leavers 1997*

The newest notification was the only one that was different.

You joined the group *Exeter College Leavers 1997*

How had she joined? She hadn't accepted the invitation.

Oliver was not a person she wished to remember, and neither was her time at Exeter College. Louisa's head swam.

She slammed the laptop lid closed.

6

THE OFFER

Friday a.m.

'You look dreadful. You can't go on with this little sleep, Lou.' Brian's opening line as he walked into the kitchen holding Noah was an unnecessary statement.

'I know that. I'm really feeling it. Last night scared me.'

'Me too. You were so utterly convinced you'd killed him.' Brian passed Noah to her, then gave her shoulders a squeeze before sitting down at the table opposite her. 'Your eyes . . . they were manic, Lou. You didn't look like you.'

'I'm so sorry for freaking you out.' Louisa dropped her gaze, not wanting Brian to see the fear in her eyes. She smiled at Noah's scrunched-up face as he yawned.

'I'm having Noah tonight. There's enough milk in the freezer and he'll be okay with me bottle-feeding him for one night. I'm going to take you to Court Farm this afternoon. I've booked you a room there – you need to get some sleep.'

'What? No, Brian. It's a lovely thought but I can't leave Noah. I won't sleep if I'm away from him, I'll just worry all the time.'

'He'll be absolutely fine with me. Don't you trust me?'

Four words. Ones that had huge weight attached to them. Louisa couldn't even answer immediately.

'I know I've not been pulling my weight.' Brian reached across, running his fingertips gently across Louisa's cheek. 'I'm sorry I've been selfish. But let me do this now. For you.' He looked at her with pleading eyes. 'Please?'

The text to Tiff was fresh in her mind. He wanted her out of the way so he could meet up with her.

'I don't feel confident. Not with how I've been feeling . . .'

'Tiff will be with you.'

'What?'

'Tiff is going to stay too. Separate room, don't worry – you need solid sleep, not to be chatting all night.'

'I don't understand.' Louisa frowned. This was an unexpected turn.

'I could see how badly this lack of sleep was affecting you. I've been talking to Tiff, asking her advice really, and together we thought this would at least give you a bit of a break . . .'

Louisa sank back in the chair. Had their messaging and the hushed conversations all been about arranging one night away from her baby? Louisa's face flushed. Shit. She'd practically accused Tiff of having an affair with her husband. As well as hallucinations, she could now tick paranoia off the sleep deprivation checklist.

'But it's a pub, Brian. I won't sleep with all the noise.'

'The rooms are in a converted barn adjacent to the pub so it should be fine. Even if you don't get to sleep until midnight, you could still get seven, eight hours of uninterrupted sleep. It'll be far better than what you've been getting.'

Louisa contemplated it. It wasn't as if her parents could take Noah, like they used to Emily. They were too old now: her mother too fragile, her dad clueless – plus, she hadn't even spoken to them for weeks, their relationship remaining strained. Even when they'd looked after Emily, Louisa had always felt it'd been something they'd done out of duty rather than love.

Each time her mum agreed to take Emily it was a decision edged with bitterness.

Louisa's rocky relationship with them, her mother in particular, was a hangover from her teenage years – she'd often been told how she'd been challenging, that her erratic behaviour when she was at college had caused no end of worry. Louisa had spent a long time wishing she could've gone away to a college further afield, rather than to the closest one. But commuting daily to Exeter was simpler and it wasn't as though she had much choice anyway. It wasn't like going off to uni, where it was expected you live away from home. She was only doing A levels and none of her friends had their own digs; all of them lived at home too, so she couldn't even crash at anyone else's. Things might have been very different if that had been a possibility.

Considering her lack of options, Brian's offer may well be her only opportunity to have some time out. One night couldn't hurt. And she really needed sleep if the last few days, and particularly last night, were anything to go by.

'Thank you.' She gave a grateful smile.

'Good. That's settled then.' Brian got up and moved to the worktop where his mobile was. He unplugged it from its charger and was immediately immersed in texting. Tiff, she presumed.

'We got any Coco Pops?' Emily breezed into the kitchen. No 'good morning', no eye contact.

'Unless you've eaten them all, then yes – in the larder.'

Emily huffed and sloped over to the larder, pulling the yellow box from the top shelf. Louisa watched as her handbag banged back against the door as Emily went to close it. She must remember to take the bag with her secret stash of cigarettes inside to Court Farm later. She'd also take her tablets from the drawer. While one night away from Noah might be beneficial, she had a feeling she'd need more help than that to sleep well.

7

THE DECOY

Friday p.m.

Tiff's car – a volcano-red Audi A8, so she'd informed Louisa when she'd bought it brand new – drew up outside at smack on five. Louisa watched from the window as Tiff got out, perfectly dressed as usual, her Ray-Ban sunglasses on, despite the March weather being quite dull. Louisa looked down at her own ensemble: the same jeans she'd been wearing all week and a plain black baggy T-shirt. She should've made more effort, but then again, it was meant to be a relaxing night away so it didn't really matter what she wore.

Brian had come home from work early and taken Noah out for a walk – Emily begrudgingly went with them. Louisa had said her goodbyes. In her head, she repeated, *It's only one night.* She knew it could only do her good.

She'd made sure her cigarettes and tablets were in her bag – she'd already taken two tablets that morning as a precaution, knowing her anxiety levels would be increasing. Checking the freezer, she noted there was a good stack of frozen milk, even more than she'd thought. How had she pumped off that much? As far as she could tell, her milk production had slowed to the degree she was considering supplementing Noah with formula.

At least she didn't have to worry about him going hungry. The bottles were freshly sterilised. All was taken care of. She popped two more tablets out of the aluminium pack, swallowed them without water, and threw the packet back into her handbag as she thrust it over her shoulder and walked towards the front door.

'Hi, hun! You not ready yet?' Tiff said as she embraced Louisa, then stood back to take in her appearance.

'Er . . . yes. I didn't see the point in dressing up,' Louisa said.

'No, no I guess not. Have you packed anything else?' Tiff's frown said it all.

'I've got another T-shirt.' Louisa held up the small overnight bag she'd found in the back of the wardrobe and that she'd stuffed with minimal supplies.

'Why don't you pop upstairs and grab something nice for later – a dress or something.'

'For later? I was planning on *sleeping* later, Tiff.'

'Yes, yes. Of course. I thought I'd treat you to a nice dinner though, before you bed down for the night. You're looking pasty lately, like you're in need of a good meal. And you know, a drink or two, which I'm sure will help you settle quicker.' She smiled.

Louisa knew it was futile to argue so she bounded up the stairs, pulled her old faithful off the hanger – a flower-print jersey dress – and shoved it inside her bag. She grabbed her make-up bag too. *Pasty*. She would make a small effort, just to get Tiff off her back.

'Right, let's go!' Tiff was out of the door before Louisa could say anything.

The room was small but adequate. Louisa had often been to the restaurant and bar at Court Farm but living so close meant there'd never been a need to stay. It felt weird to be sleeping away from home when it was only two miles away. She really hoped she felt better after tonight; Brian would be so disappointed if his plan didn't work, but Louisa knew that she'd need far more than one night for a difference to be made.

A knock interrupted her thoughts. Louisa opened the door to Tiff.

'My plan is that you shower now, dress up, slap on some war paint and we hit the bar in an hour. Sound good?'

'Well, I guess.' Anxiety coursed through her body like a rapidly spreading virus. It seemed a lot to do in an hour, and the double bed with its fluffy pillows and crisp, clean bed linen looked really inviting.

'I'll go and get some wine. It'll be like old times, getting ready to go out.' Tiff's enthusiasm made Louisa smile in spite of her misgivings. When they'd first been friends, Tiff regularly dragged Louisa out on a Friday night – not clubbing, those times were long gone – but they'd go into Newton, traipse from one pub to another, Tiff drinking more than was sensible, and they'd have a good laugh. It was the time getting ready at Tiff's house that used to make Louisa's night. She always went to Tiff's because there, Louisa had no one making any demands on her: she could avoid Emily's bedtime and leave the calming-down period and story-telling to Brian, so it was more fun. She'd have been fine with just that, not even bothering to go out. Louisa wasn't much of a drinker, not since her college days. She'd allow Tiff to get her a drink now, though. One wouldn't hurt, and it wasn't as though she had to feed Noah.

'Okay. I'd better jump in the shower then.'

'Excellent,' Tiff said as she did a dramatic twirl and left the room. Louisa took out the dress she'd squashed into her bag, brushing it down and hoping the creases wouldn't be too visible once it was on her. This could be just what she needed – a shower in complete peace, a few hours of being 'normal', a nice meal, a good natter and an entire night of undisturbed sleep. Just in case though, she would take a couple more of the pills. She didn't want to waste the opportunity of getting rest by lying awake all night worrying. Her mind always came alive the second her head hit the pillow, so it was worth having a back-up. She swallowed the capsules with water from the tap and went into the bathroom.

Tiff had convinced Louisa to have two glasses of wine while they were getting ready, and her head now felt woozy. She should've waited to eat before having the second. They made their way out of the accommodation building, which, just as Brian had told her, was adjacent to the pub. Tiff had her head down, busy texting. Louisa prickled, irritated that Tiff couldn't stay off her mobile for even a few hours. Louisa shook her head. She hoped tonight wasn't a mistake. Shuffling along behind Tiff, who was now quite forcibly pushing through some people standing at the bar, Louisa kept her head lowered. An uncomfortable sensation rippled through her; she didn't want to make eye contact with anyone, suddenly feeling exposed – everyone staring at her.

'We've got a table in the upstairs room,' Tiff said, finally turning to face Louisa and ushering her up the stairs first. Louisa was glad to be escaping the busy, noisy bar area to the more subdued upstairs. She stumbled on the steps, grabbing the rail to regain her balance. Two wines mixed with the tablets was clearly not the best of ideas.

Nearing the top of the stairs, Louisa's chest tightened. Tied to the bannister, floating ominously, were a couple of *Happy 40th Birthday* balloons. Her feet refused to move forward, but Tiff nudged her on.

'Go on, it's all right,' she coaxed.

The room, which a moment ago was quiet, erupted into a frenzied noise of singing.

Oh, God no.

Her eyes darted around, her brain attempting to put it all together. What the hell? Her birthday wasn't for another two weeks so this must be for someone else. As the out-of-tune rendition of 'Happy Birthday' continued, Louisa noticed that balloons displaying the big 4-0 adorned every table. The room was filled with people she didn't recognise, who all appeared to be clapping and cheering for her. The dizziness returned, threatening to cause her legs to give. Her eyes settled on Brian, who was smiling, standing with Noah in his arms at the front of the gathering. Noah wasn't crying. Even Emily, standing at Brian's side, was smiling.

'Surprised? I wanted to make sure you did something special for your fortieth.' Brian grinned. Louisa's mouth opened, but no words would form. She couldn't fathom why he would have thought this was a good idea in her current state. She had a strong urge to turn around and run back down the stairs, but more people came up behind her, blocking her route. Fleeing didn't appear to be an option.

This was the worst thing that could've happened. What about her relaxing night, the one where she was meant to *sleep*? A hot ball of irritation burned in the pit of her stomach. This was not a happy surprise but now that she'd been forced into the situation, and quite clearly couldn't get out of it, Louisa lifted her chin, put her shoulders back and made her way properly into the guest-filled room. After a few hellos and polite *thank you for coming* statements, Louisa sat at the table nearest the window. If she didn't sit, she'd collapse. The throng of voices blurred into the background as Louisa stared outside. More people were coming. Surely not for her? How many people did Brian invite? She didn't even *know* this many people.

She felt a hand on her knee.

'I know I tricked you into this, but I really thought . . . well, *we* really thought it would do you good. I'm still taking Noah home with Emily after the meal.' He bounced Noah gently in one arm, but it appeared as though there was no need – the baby was content and settled. 'So you'll still have time to yourself.' His eyes sought hers for approval. She attempted a smile, hoping it looked grateful rather than stabby, which was how she was really feeling.

'How did you arrange this?'

'With Tiff's help, of course. The night away with Tiff was the perfect decoy. It got you here, ready for the surprise to be sprung on you.' He sounded so chuffed with himself – and granted, he'd actually done a good job keeping it from her. It seemed he was better at keeping secrets than she'd given him credit for. Part of her was relieved that the party was the reason for his constant texting, his sneaky behaviour. Another part, though, couldn't shake the foreboding sensation deep in her gut.

'Tiff helped? What's she done – invited all *her* friends?' Louisa gave a quick sweeping glance of the room trying to pinpoint some people she actually knew.

'No, silly.' He gave her a hug, kissing the top of her head. Thank God Tiff had convinced her to shower and wash her hair. 'She went through your friends list.'

'My what?' Louisa's jaw slackened.

'Your Facebook friends – she said she knew your password as she'd set your profile up and you'd never changed it. Sorry – I thought it would be okay if she did it. She even managed to track down your old college buddies thanks to an invite you'd had to join the alumni. Took her ages – she's pretty amazing at all this organising stuff, isn't she?' He beamed.

The blood in Louisa's veins cooled, an icy sensation creeping underneath her skin.

She shook her head, unable to formulate the right words. She wanted to scream but, instead, a numbness took over.

'It wasn't easy – you've never talked about any of them despite me digging over the years – but we thought it would be the ideal time to do some catching up. A reunion of sorts. What better time than this milestone?'

Her breathing shallowed; the room closed in on her. There would never have been a good time for that.

She had to escape this room full of strangers. Because that's what they were, in effect. None of them really *knew* her. She silently prayed that none of those on the Exeter College list would turn up. Surely after twenty-two years none of them would even remember who she was? She'd left after her A levels while the majority of her friends had gone on to university, scattering far and wide across the country. Louisa hadn't kept in contact with anyone. They wouldn't bother to come to her fortieth when they'd not set eyes on her for all that time. The thought of it even being a possibility, though, set her nerves on edge. Grabbing her handbag, and without looking at Brian, she got up.

As Louisa pushed through the people, she heard multiple 'happy birthdays' and her name being spoken, arms reaching out and hands touching her. Muttering her thanks, she quickly moved on, her eyes focused on the stairs. As she reached them she bumped into someone coming the other way.

'Long time, no see,' the smooth, deep voice said. A voice that caused tiny electric shocks to spread inside her body. Her prayer hadn't been answered.

Louisa was paralysed to the spot.

She hadn't seen him since 1997, but his face was instantly familiar.

Oliver.

8

THE GUEST

Friday p.m.

After what felt like five minutes of silently staring, Louisa's brain kicked in, her feet finally moving. Without being able to speak, she pushed past Oliver and the unknown woman by his side and, with as much composure as she could muster, descended the stairs. Tiff's blonde hair was visible above the group of punters congregating at the bar, and as Louisa struggled to get to the exit, she heard Tiff shout to her.

'Where are you off to?'

Louisa shoved through more people, anger propelling her towards Tiff. Without daring to speak, she snatched one of the glasses of wine off the round tray Tiff held in her hands and knocked back the bitter-tasting liquid in one, before continuing towards the door leading out to the beer garden.

Whatever good intentions Tiff believed she had in going through her Facebook friends list, she shouldn't have done it. Going one step further than that and accepting the group invitation to join Exeter College leavers on her behalf was just wrong. It wasn't Tiff's place to decide what group of friends she should be involved with. And inviting Oliver? *Jesus.*

Finding a quiet corner of the garden, away from prying eyes,

Louisa unzipped her bag and took out the pack of cigarettes. Her head swam, as it usually did with the first few draws. It was worse now though – she had too much alcohol in her system, as well as the tablets. Likely a dangerous mix, but no more dangerous than the mix of people in that room.

'Are you mad at me?'

She turned sharply at the sound of the voice. Tiff approached Louisa with another glass of wine in her outstretched hand. 'Here,' she said. 'This might take the edge off the shock.'

'I doubt it.' The words carried more venom than she'd realised she possessed. She took the drink anyway, not making eye contact with Tiff.

'I'm sorry. I really thought we were doing something positive, and that it would give you a lift. Organising a small party—'

'Small? Call that small, Tiff?' She waved her arm towards the pub. 'Shit. Small would be my little family and you. And that would've been fine. I'd have coped with that. But not *this*.' She dragged on her cigarette. Her eyes stung. From the smoke, or from tears, she was unable to distinguish.

Tiff was silent, her eyes downcast. She didn't even mention the fact that Louisa was smoking – it was Tiff who'd helped her give up four years ago, but she'd obviously decided now wasn't the time to give a lecture.

'I realise you were trying to do something nice. But why invite all the people from my Facebook? And – for God's sake – why did you accept that stupid invitation to the Exeter College group and then invite Oliver Dunmore here?'

'Shit. Because you didn't talk about other friends – you never have! But, you know, I *assumed* those on your Facebook were friends, so didn't see the harm—'

'Tiffany. Really?' Louisa shot her a disdainful look. 'You were the one who added half of them when you set up the account in the first place, remember?'

'Well, yes, but they are still your *friends*.'

'So, you're friends with everyone on *your* Facebook are you? Should I invite Sarah to our next girly night? You'd be good with that, would you?'

'I – no.' Tiff sighed loudly. 'Sorry. Okay, okay. Fair point. But *chill*. So you don't actually like some people I invited, no biggie – you don't have to speak to them all. Everyone will be eating soon, and drinking loads – they won't notice if you're not being particularly sociable. And Oliver said only good things; he made it sound like you were great friends.'

Tiff telling her to 'chill' was bad enough, but her last line was the one requiring Louisa's response.

'How exactly did you contact Oliver, Tiff? There were no messages on my Facebook.'

'There'd been one. I deleted it as soon as I read and replied to it, giving him my mobile instead. I immediately fessed up, Lou. Told him I wasn't you, and that I was arranging this surprise party for your fortieth. He jumped at the chance to come.'

'I bet he did,' Louisa said, her teeth clenched.

'Weren't you good friends then?' Tiff's eyebrows knitted, a brief look of panic fleeting across her perfectly made-up face.

'We were more than that, Tiff.' Louisa put her cigarette out in the ashtray on the closest wooden table. 'He was my first love. He broke my heart. Broke me, in fact, and when he left he took a part of me with him. A part of my memory at least.'

Louisa didn't want to explain more. Couldn't explain more even if she'd wanted to.

'Oh. I've screwed up then, haven't I?' Tiff's face paled.

'Quite possibly, Tiff. Yes,' Louisa said as she drained the glass of wine and turned to walk back inside.

9

THE PARTY

'Mum, where've you been? Come on, the food is out. It's the most food I've seen in ages.' Emily's eyes were wide as she took Louisa's arm, dragging her towards a long table to the side of the room filled with a buffet-style feast.

'Oh, sorry, love. Just had to get some fresh air, it's all been a bit overwhelming.' Her tongue felt funny: tingly and enlarged. She worried she was slurring her words.

'I bet. I did tell Dad it wasn't a great idea – that you were dreading being forty so a bloody party drawing attention to the fact would only make matters worse.'

'Language, Emily. But thanks.' Louisa put her arm around her daughter and pulled her in close. She realised it was the first moment of real closeness they'd had since Noah's birth. Louisa had always felt lucky to have such a good relationship with Emily; they shared a closer bond than she'd ever had with her own mother. There'd been times when Brian had commented they were more like sisters: chatting about the latest films and TV programmes, gossiping and going clothes shopping together most weekends. Louisa hoped those moments would return once she'd got through the awkward early months with a new baby.

She turned her face towards Emily and bent to kiss her cheek. 'You were right,' Louisa whispered in her ear. As she lifted her head again, her balance faltered, and she had to hold on to Emily to keep herself upright.

'What's the matter?'

'Lack . . .' Louisa took a slow, deep breath in and out. 'Lack of food. Blood sugar's low I think.'

'Dad!' Emily's voice was shrill in Louisa's ear. Damn. Now everyone was looking over at her. But it wasn't Brian who came to her side.

'Are you okay?' Oliver had obviously been right behind her the whole time.

'I'm fine. Emily's just making a fuss. I'll take these roasties and sit down for a bit. I'll be all right.'

'I'm not fussing, Mum. You looked as though you were about to faint.'

'Don't worry, Emily. I'll take her, you go find your dad.' Oliver's dark eyes found Louisa's – the intensity in them was one thing she hadn't forgotten about the past, but the strong arm she felt around her waist was something new. He'd always been fit, but the thickness in his arms now was clearly the result of regular weights. Her heart picked up speed. She hated herself for it.

Oliver sat her down, placing the plate of food in front of her before sitting down himself.

'How have you been?'

'For the past twenty-two years? How long have you got?'

He gave a quick, nasal laugh. 'I guess it's been a long time. How about you tell me over lunch one day?'

'God, Oliver,' Louisa said, shaking her head in disbelief. The same slick Oliver who'd been the centre of her world for two years before he left her in their small town while he escaped to the University of York – the opposite end of the country – to do something with his life and 'be something; someone import-ant'. She wondered what, or who, he'd become, but she wasn't going to ask.

'Why are you at my surprise party?'

'You mean apart from the opportunity to meet up with old friends?' He cast his eyes around the room, but clearly not spotting any of those said friends, returned his attention to her. 'I've just moved back here, temporarily at least, to oversee a new business project.'

'Right.' Louisa didn't want to get into a conversation about what precisely this business was; she didn't want *any* conversation really.

'And, well, if I'm honest, I've never stopped thinking about you, Lou-Lou.'

She straightened, her muscles tensing, her lips pursed. 'Don't call me that.'

'Sorry, old habits.' He grinned. Louisa looked at his face properly for the first time. The square jawline, once smooth, was now dotted with stubble. It suited him. He still had black hair, but the hairline was higher up and less defined at the crown and temples than it'd been when he was eighteen. There were crinkles at the corners of his eyes, but they weren't deep like Brian's crow's feet – somehow, Oliver's made him appear distinguished. Rugged. He'd practically been a boy when he left. Now Louisa was sitting opposite a man. She didn't know him anymore, but the spark that had drawn her to him at college alighted again now. Despite her mixed feelings, she was still attracted to Oliver Dunmore's charm and good looks.

Louisa knew she had to bring herself back to reality. She thought about the woman standing beside Oliver on the stairs. 'So, you're married?'

'Yes, but not for long,' he said, matter-of-factly.

'Oh, I'm sorry . . .'

He tilted his head back laughing. 'No, we're not separating. I meant she's not been my wife for long. Married last year.'

Louisa's stomach dropped. She urged herself to get a grip. It didn't matter if he was married, so was she.

Louisa's gaze bounced from person to person around the room, searching for Emily and Brian. She needed them to interrupt this encounter, give her an excuse to get away. The food on the plate Oliver had put in front of her looked unappetising. It would be physically impossible to consume solids right now; she'd choke on every mouthful. Her pleasant, relaxing night away had rapidly turned into a nightmare.

'Look, I'd best do the rounds, you know – mingle a bit seeing as all these people are apparently here for me.' If Brian wasn't coming to save the day, then Louisa had to excuse herself. 'Thanks for coming. It was . . . well, good to see you,' she managed. On trembling legs, Louisa got up and walked across to the nearest table, a fake smile in place to meet and greet her non-friends.

'You're doing great,' Tiff said as she handed Louisa a bottle.

'Bloody hell, Tiff – what's this now? Lager? I've had far too much already.'

'Nonsense. We used to put away loads more than this.'

'But I haven't—'

'You haven't got to worry about Noah,' she cut in, 'and I'm reliably informed you've expressed enough milk to feed all the babies in Devon. Let your hair down, woman!'

Louisa conceded. She had no strength to argue and couldn't be bothered to correct Tiff's memory of them drinking loads. It was always Tiff, not Louisa, who had got drunk. But if having more drink now helped get her through the rest of the party and then sleep solidly for eight hours, she'd take it.

An hour passed with Louisa managing to mingle with a few

people, passing the time with basic-level chat, mainly consisting of telling stories about the exploits of their respective children. She'd lost count of how many drinks she'd consumed but she guessed it'd been too many judging by her blurring vision and the reduction in her ability to balance – even while sitting. Her swaying body was beginning to make her feel motion sick.

'I'll be back in a bit.' Her mouth had begun to water as a wave of sickness rocked her. Louisa made her excuses and left the table.

The grass felt tickly and cool under her feet as she walked.

Where was she?

And where were her shoes?

Her handbag was over her shoulder, though. Good, she hadn't lost that.

She stopped walking and pulled at it, trying to find the zip. Her fingers finally found the little metal pull. She reached inside. The bag dropped to the ground. Louisa's eyes couldn't focus well enough, her right hand swooping several times but failing to pick it up. She'd get it in a minute. She had the packet, at least.

A voice came from behind her.

'Can I blag one of them off you?'

Louisa turned unsteadily to face the person who'd asked but she was still staring down at the cigarettes as she blinked several times in a vain attempt to clear her vision. She shook the packet, not trusting her eyes. Damn. Only one. She thought she'd only smoked five. She didn't want to give her last one to a stranger.

As she looked up and her eyes finally focused, an image flashed in front of her. It wasn't like the other ones she'd experienced; this one made each of the tiny hairs on her body tingle and stand erect. She lowered her head again, avoiding eye contact.

'Yeah, go ahead.' A fear consumed Louisa as she held out the packet containing the single cigarette. This was no stranger; she was sure it was someone she used to know.

10

THE HANGOVER

Saturday a.m. – Day 1 post-party

It took a few moments for Louisa to remember where she was. It was daytime – the light easily penetrating the pale cream curtains. She didn't move; she couldn't. Any movement might make her sick. Had she already thrown up? The taste in her mouth suggested she had. Slowly, she slid her mobile from the bedside table and tried to focus on the display.

10.23 a.m.

She stared in disbelief at the time. She couldn't recall the last time she'd slept in that late, and she had no memory of waking during the night. That had obviously been Tiff's plan all along – get her blotto knowing she'd pass out and be guaranteed to get solid sleep.

She didn't feel all that rested though, just hungover. And that was a feeling she hadn't had for a very long time. Her head screamed for water so, reluctantly, she eased herself out from under the covers.

Louisa winced as her feet made contact with the floor. *Shit.* They felt sore. Bruised. God, please say she hadn't been dancing barefoot, making a fool of herself in front of her family. Her fake friends.

Oliver.

She shivered. It was as if her alcohol-soaked brain had only just remembered he'd been there – and it was reliving the shock of seeing him all over again. Louisa tried to recall if she'd spoken to him again after their first brief conversation. She screwed up her eyes. No. No memory of talking to him. But there was something – some elusive image teasing her, coming to the edges of her memory but no further. She couldn't capture it. Tiff would more than likely fill her in on the night's events, though she was probably feeling as rough as Louisa was.

Like an old woman – hunched and slow – Louisa walked to the table-top fridge in the corner of the room and retrieved a small bottle of sparkling water. The liquid she expected to be flavourless was sour in her dry, foul-tasting mouth, but it refreshed her. As she was about to place it back inside the fridge, a sharp pain, almost like an electric shock, pulsed through her head. She dropped the bottle. Water spread and puddled on the grey carpet.

Blood.

Louisa stumbled backwards.

With her next blink, the vision of the dark red pool had shot away and she was left staring at the water-soaked carpet.

There was a sharp knock on her door. Louisa took a hand towel from the bathroom, placing it over the spilled water, before opening the door.

'Thank God for that.' Tiff, her face serious and completely free of make-up, stepped inside the room and closed the door behind her.

'What are we thanking God for?'

'For you being in here.'

'Where else would I be?' A knot of worry began to tighten in her already painful tummy.

'I lost track of you last night—'

'What do you mean, you *lost track* of me? Didn't we just get back here together?'

'You don't remember?'

Louisa's initial worry-knot grew in size and intensity, the sensation increasing the sick feeling. No, she didn't remember.

'I'd had a lot to drink . . . I think I have you to thank for that.'

'Sorry, you know what I get like after I've had one too many – I'm pushy.' Tiff smiled apologetically and sat down on the bed beside Louisa.

For most people, having a lapse in memory after a heavy drinking session was funny – an expected side effect that gave rise to mickey-taking from others who had witnessed the drunken antics. But for Louisa, any gaps in memory only added to the dread that it was happening again. A period of her life during her last year of college was a complete blur to her – not just a day or two, but a huge chunk. For a long time afterwards, Louisa had experienced regular panic attacks, often for no apparent reason. The distress of *why* she couldn't remember often overwhelmed her.

Her mum had pushed for her to see a doctor, saying it wasn't right for a healthy teenager to have such debilitating attacks of anxiety. Louisa had only agreed on the premise that she could go on her own – not wanting her mother to know what might be causing them. Deep down she'd known that something bad had happened to cause them; there'd been a trigger – but she'd pushed it to the back of her mind until her mum had forced the situation.

The doctor had said stress was a factor for the panic attacks, but in relation to the missing chunks of memory, he'd mentioned something called dissociative amnesia. This in itself had caused more stress than if she'd not gone to the doctor at all. He'd talked about how someone could block out certain information because they'd suffered a traumatic event. Louisa had obsessed about this, gaining as much information about it as she could through library books and journals at the time, then looking up everything about it online years later. The memory loss associated with the disorder included gaps in memory for long periods of time, or of any memories that involved the traumatic event.

What that event might have been had plagued her. But the more she'd tried to remember, the worse it got. She'd continued to see a specialist for six months after she left college and, in addition to being prescribed medication, she'd learned techniques on how to manage her episodes of anxiety. The sessions had also aimed to help her recall what had triggered her attacks, but when none of the missing memories resurfaced despite the therapy, she stopped going. Once she'd met Brian she'd pushed her fears, along with the desire to find out and to recapture those memories, to the back of her mind. It was only recently, after Noah, that the old issues had come creeping back.

Louisa took a steadying breath and tried to consider it rationally. Last night she'd been really drunk – that mixed with no sleep and anxiety pills had more than likely caused her lack of recall.

But the vision of blood had come from somewhere, and the question of whether it was from the supposed traumatic experience in her past or from something that had happened last night filled Louisa with a sense of foreboding.

'Earth to Louisa!'

Louisa started. She'd been so caught up in her thoughts she'd forgotten Tiff was even there. 'Sorry.' Louisa grabbed her bag from beside her on the bed and jumped up. 'Let's get out of here.' She ushered Tiff out the door first, then turned and closed it behind her. The resounding *click* was satisfying. Louisa hoped the events of the night, whatever they were, remained locked inside that room. She just wanted to go home and forget all about it.

11

THE RETURN

Tiff had booked them a taxi home – she'd quite rightly assumed she'd still be over the limit to drive. It was an uncomfortable journey and Louisa was grateful it was only a short distance. She didn't want to puke in the taxi.

'Are you coming in?' Louisa asked as the driver stopped in front of her house.

'Looking like this?' Tiff made a circular motion around her face with her finger. 'Er, no. I'll ring you later.'

Louisa could've done with the back-up. What if she'd behaved badly last night? Brian might be mad at her. And if Tiff hadn't 'kept track' of her, that must mean she hadn't been in the main room with the others. She hesitated on the doorstep, a sense of dread debilitating any progress. Noah's crying breached the door. One night away really hadn't been enough. She could turn around now, leave and never return.

The naivety of her own thoughts irritated her. She couldn't run away. Aside from not wanting to hurt her family, she didn't even know what she'd be running *from*.

She pushed the front door open and walked through the

hallway to find Brian pacing the lounge, Noah wailing uncontrollably in his arms.

'Oh, good!' he shouted above the noise. 'I wasn't sure what else I could do.'

The screaming was already splitting her head.

'Has he had the whole bottle?' She moved gingerly forwards.

'Yes, two, actually.'

'Oh. Well I expect it's wind then if he's had *that* much.'

'It is two o'clock, Lou – he would've usually had two feeds by now, wouldn't he?'

Yes. Of course he would've. Louisa had forgotten the time.

'Pass him to me.' Louisa took Noah from Brian and placed him over her shoulder and began jiggling him about. She looked into Brian's eyes, trying to gauge his mood.

'Are you still mad at me?' he said.

'I didn't realise I was mad at you to start with.' She frowned.

Brian lowered his head. 'Tiff reckons you were just overwhelmed by it all but I saw something else in your eyes when you shouted at me – that I'd made a huge mistake throwing a party.'

Louisa swallowed hard. Another part of the night she didn't remember. She was scared to ask what exactly he thought he'd seen in her eyes. Noah had quietened down despite his awkward position – his top half slumped over her shoulder so all she could see was his bottom and legs – and she swayed gently to keep him that way.

'I was overwhelmed, yes. If it'd been people I knew well, I might've coped. But all those, well, *strangers*. It was a little much. Sorry if I came across as ungrateful, though. I know you and Tiff had the best intentions. And I certainly slept well.'

'Yeah, I guess that was the goal really. That's why I tried not to take it to heart.'

'Take what to heart?' The pulse in her neck was no doubt perceptible; what else had she said and done?

'When you left early. One minute you were saying all you needed was fresh air, then you disappeared without even saying anything to the guests. Or us. Emily was pretty put out. But I explained that you were exhausted, and the party had taken it out of you. That you needed undisturbed sleep more than a surprise fortieth. Which, of course, was what Emily had said to start with. Sorry, I should've listened to our daughter.'

'I'm sorry. Everyone must've thought me so rude.' Her mind was dazed, confused at this new information. 'Did you come by my room? Check up on me?'

'No. I thought it best to leave you alone. And anyway, Oliver said he'd seen you going into the accommodation entrance, so I knew you were all right.'

'Oliver saw me? Did he speak to you then?'

'Yeah. Nice guy actually. We chatted for ages after you'd gone.'

Great, her ex-boyfriend and her husband getting buddy-buddy. That wasn't what Louisa needed to hear.

'Really? I take it he didn't happen to mention we dated back in college then.' Louisa thought that would produce shock from Brian – even though it was years ago, she imagined he'd feel curious about an ex showing up, maybe even a bit jealous – but his expression didn't waver.

'Yeah, he did say, but he brushed over it really – it was more in passing than anything. I don't remember you ever mentioning him, so I guess you didn't date for long, that it wasn't anything serious?'

It was a loaded question. If she said, 'no, not long, not serious,' Brian would wonder why Oliver had been bothered enough to attend her party. On the other hand, if she said, 'two years, and quite serious,' he'd probe further – want to know more details about their relationship. Oliver's motive for turning up to her fortieth birthday would also be more thoroughly scrutinised.

53

Louisa decided it was best to do what Oliver had obviously done – brush over it.

'We were teenagers, having a wild time at college – you know what it was like back then. How long or serious was any relationship? It was so long ago I can barely remember.' Louisa wiped the beads of sweat from her top lip then quickly repositioned Noah, lowering him from her shoulder and nestling her face into his.

'True,' Brian said, not appearing to notice her discomfort, 'and he didn't seem the type to hold on to the past or be someone who'd never got over his first love.' Brian laughed. Louisa almost asked what he *did* consider Oliver's 'type' to be, and how he could tell from one conversation. She thought better of it, instead shining the spotlight elsewhere.

'What about his wife – what was she like?'

Brian shrugged. 'Wife? He didn't mention a wife.'

'Well, she was *with* him. At the party.'

'Didn't see him with anyone. Well, not in a couple-type way. He was talking to lots of people. Seemed to take a shine to Tiff . . .'

Who didn't, Louisa thought. In her hungover state, the complexities of the evening were too much to decipher. As Noah was quiet, Louisa thought she'd take the opportunity to lie down with him. If she had a nap, things would be clearer afterwards. For the moment, Louisa had no idea what on earth had happened at her party.

But something felt off.

12

THE MESSAGE

Lovely to celebrate your milestone birthday with you last night. Being with you brought back so many memories. Can we meet? I need to see you. Something happened. Oliver xx

Louisa was sitting on the double bed, her back against the headboard and Noah asleep on a pillow on her lap. She stared at her phone in her hand. She'd reread the Facebook message several times since opening it an hour ago, each time attaching a different meaning to it.

The worst of those meanings was that she *had* gone back to her room, as Brian had told her, and Oliver had followed her in and they'd slept together.

Louisa prayed that was the worst-case scenario – and the wrong one. But what other meaning could '*something happened*' possibly have?

Why the hell had Brian taken her ex-boyfriend's word that she'd made it safely into the accommodation building? Granted it was only yards from the pub, but still. She was clearly drunk; she'd have expected Brian to check up on her himself, not to take some bloke's word for it. Someone he'd only just met. This was his fault.

But whosever fault it was, Oliver's words now glared at her accusingly.

Delete it. Don't respond.

She didn't delete it, closing the Facebook app on her phone instead. She'd block him later, so he couldn't contact her again. She never should've bothered logging into Facebook; she knew full well it was a bad idea the first time, and why was she looking again now? She should delete her entire account and be done with it. But she'd read his message, and now she couldn't unsee it. Whatever may have happened last night, it would've been a mistake. She'd been under the influence. Not only of drink, but of medication too. Unprescribed at that. Louisa tutted at her own stupidity. She'd only wanted to sleep, though. Who could blame her for that?

Louisa wrote out a text to Tiff. She went around the houses a bit – first off asking how her head was, then moving on to mention the party before finally asking if she'd had any recollection of seeing where she went after going out for 'fresh air' and not returning. It seemed odd to Louisa that she would say that and then not bother returning to the party. Unless she'd felt so ill she decided she'd be better off in her room.

Yes, that had to be it. She was worrying over nothing. Having not set eyes on her for over twenty years, Oliver had no reason to lie about having seen her stumble into the entrance to the rooms. His message must be to do with something else.

Either way, she knew she shouldn't contact him. She was in a vulnerable position – an exhausted new mum, trying to cope with a baby as well as a teenager, hormones all over the shop. She feared it wouldn't take much to fall under Oliver's spell once more, and she had to avoid that at all costs.

Remember, he left you. Left you alone to face the consequences.

This thought, which appeared in her mind out of nowhere, made her legs go numb.

The ding of a text sounded. Tiff.

Feel like death. As far as my memory allows, though, it was a good party! That Oliver was a bit of a dish. Can't believe you never mentioned him before! And no, I really don't know where you disappeared to – last place I have a clear memory seeing you was the beer garden. But I only saw you from the window while I was chatting to some random, and you were with someone too, so I assumed you were OK. I'm sorry I was too far gone to come and find you. What a friend I am. ☹ Forgive me! xx

She wasn't any use then. If Tiff had said she'd been chatting to Oliver after Louisa had done a disappearing act, that might've put her mind at ease a bit; he couldn't have been in two places at once. But no – some 'random'. Louisa cursed Tiff again for going through her Facebook friends. It could've been anyone.

Louisa carried the pillow with her sleeping baby on it to the nursery, placing it inside the cot. Carefully, she slipped Noah off and he gently rolled onto the mattress. Louisa let out her breath. He grumbled, wriggling a little, but then, thankfully, he settled. Transfer successful, she crept out of the room. Brian and Emily's voices drifted up as Louisa hesitated on the stairs. She couldn't make out what they were saying, but she caught the words 'worried' and 'acting weird'. She turned and headed back to her bedroom.

She couldn't face her family right now.

13

THE SHOCK

Monday – Day 3 post-party

There'd been little mention of the party, or its aftermath, on Sunday. Louisa had managed to cook a roast chicken lunch while Brian took care of Noah. If nothing else, he seemed to be making more of an effort. Perhaps now his secret party organising was over, he'd be more attentive.

Thankfully, now it was Monday, everything was back to normal. Brian left for his shift at 7 a.m. and Emily bolted out of the door, late, with a piece of cold toast in her hand at 8.10 a.m. The school bus would already be at the stop, but she always cut it fine and had only missed it once. That one time was awkward enough, though. Brian was at work, Tiff was unavailable, and Louisa had ended up paying for a taxi to get her to school. There'd been very few occasions in the past that Louisa regretted her decision not to drive and because her mum had been so involved when Emily was a baby, often taking them out, she hadn't had reason to. Louisa had passed her test at seventeen but had only driven for just over a year – driving had never been something she'd felt confident doing.

Now, the feeling of being restricted with a newborn and being stuck inside the house, or only able to venture within walking distance unless she wanted to chance public transport with her screaming baby, made her think she should've been braver. Too late now.

The house was quiet and Louisa hoped she wasn't jinxing it when she thought to herself that Noah had become more settled in the last few days. He definitely wasn't crying as much. The break from her had done him good, clearly. She'd heard once that babies pick up on their mother's moods, so it was likely he'd been distressed because Louisa was, and not the other way around. It was an interesting thought.

Louisa downed her third coffee and stared out into the street from the lounge window. The caffeine content was the only reason she drank it; she didn't care for its bitter taste. She had to stay alert today. No more memory lapses, no more panic about whether she'd fed Noah. She had an idea. Placing her coffee on the table, she got a pen and pad of paper from the table drawer and put the day and date, then listed times from 7 a.m. to 6 p.m. in columns. Those were the times she'd be on her own today. Emily was going to her friend Evie's straight from school to work on her science project, and Evie's dad would drop her home after they'd eaten tea. Brian was due home between half five and six.

Louisa put a tick next to 7 a.m. Noah hadn't fed for very long – literally two minutes, which wasn't usual – but he'd seemed satisfied after. She recorded that too. Doing this meant she'd keep on top of things and if her memory blurred, she had this written proof she'd fed him.

All had gone well up until 2 p.m. Louisa cast her eyes down the paper at the ticks. Noah had fed three times. Each time for ten minutes from each breast. The length of time was definitely shortening; he either wasn't taking as much, or she didn't have as much to give and that's why he was feeding more quickly.

It had been such a long time since she'd fed Emily, she could no longer recall what her feeding patterns were like – maybe it was normal and she shouldn't worry. Just in case, Louisa made a note on the paper to call the health visitor to discuss it. Although Noah seemed more content, that might be a bad thing coupled with not feeding enough. He could have something wrong with him.

The ringing of the doorbell jolted her from her catastrophising. She stared down at her sleeping baby and considered ignoring the bell. Moving might disturb Noah, and as all good advice informed parents: *never wake a sleeping baby.* It rang again. She decided she'd answer in case it was a parcel, and shuffled to the edge of the sofa, slowly making her way to the door. If it was important, they'd wait.

Through the textured glass, Louisa could only make out a large dark figure standing on her doorstep. Not someone holding a parcel, she noted. With Noah cradled in one arm, she opened the door tentatively with the other.

A split second after seeing the person in front of her, Louisa's brain caught up with itself and she recoiled. Instinct told her to close the door and lock it. Her heart couldn't be so blunt.

'What are you doing here?' She shook her head slightly in disbelief that Oliver would be so bold. 'Who told you where I live?' If bloody Tiff had something to do with this, their friendship was going to come under some serious scrutiny. Regaining some composure, Louisa tilted her chin up as she waited for him to explain himself.

'You didn't reply to my message,' he said, clearly disregarding her second question.

'I don't reply to lots of messages, but the sender rarely shows up at my door because of it.' A surge of annoyance permeated her tone.

Her curiosity at what his message had meant outweighed

the warning signals. When it became clear he wasn't going to respond to her comment, she continued.

'I really shouldn't invite you in.' Louisa stuck her head outside, checking up and down the road. Oliver's eyes followed hers.

'I don't think anyone is watching. You're safe.' He smiled.

'Fine. Not for long though, you hear?' She turned, placing Noah in the pram in the hallway before facing Oliver again.

'Okay, Lou-Lou, anything you say.'

She was transported back – seventeen again – staring into those hypnotic deep-brown eyes, her whole body filled with admiration and love; naive and completely trusting the gorgeous boy who made her stomach shake, her hands tremble, her heart flutter furiously each time he said her name.

She must be careful now.

Louisa stood aside, letting Oliver slide past her into her house.

Into her life once more.

14

THE DISAPPEARANCE

Louisa didn't go back into the lounge; she didn't want Oliver making himself too comfortable. Instead she showed him into the kitchen, indicating he could sit at the table. On a hard, wooden chair. So much had been left unsaid since she'd last known him. Despite their proximity now, twenty-two years of nothing but absence separated them, and Louisa didn't have a clue where to begin. She didn't know what to say, how to behave. Did he expect her to be angry with him? Or pretend she didn't remember the fact he'd left her?

'I know it must be weird, me turning up out of the blue at your fortieth birthday party after all this time. Sorry for springing myself on you like that. I had tried to contact you before, you know.'

'Oh, the Facebook group invites? Hmmm . . . No, Oliver, that really isn't trying, is it? You only invited me recently, so what about the other twenty-odd years? Where were your efforts during that time?'

'You're angry with me. I can see that. But you know why I had to leave, Lou. I did it for you.' He reached across the table, laying his hands on hers. She snatched them away, hot rods shooting through her. The man was deluded if he thought that leaving the girl who he told he would love forever was for her own benefit. Louisa balled her fists.

'No, Oliver. I don't think so.'

Oliver's eyebrows raised, then knitted together, his brow creasing. 'Is that what you tell yourself?' He shrugged. 'If that's how you made it through, then I guess that's up to you.'

Louisa was enraged at his attempt to wriggle out of being to blame for leaving her, but she wanted to move this on and, specifically, uncover precisely what had happened the night of her party.

'Whatever. So anyway, what exactly is it that you want?'

She didn't expect his answer.

'Melissa is missing.' His eyes glistened with tears.

For a second, Louisa struggled to make sense of his statement. Then, perhaps sensing her confusion, he added, 'My wife, Melissa. I haven't seen her since the party.'

'Oh, my God, Oliver. Missing, like, need to call the police missing?'

'I've held off calling them – didn't want to create a fuss, not yet. We'd had, well . . . a bit of an argument. Melissa often gets emotional; angry too. She goes off on her own sometimes to sort her head out – doesn't contact me for days, then comes waltzing back as though nothing ever happened. I assumed this was one of those times. It might still be, I guess. It's only been just over forty-eight hours.'

'Assumed. You said *assumed*. What has changed now, to make you think it might not be one of those times?'

'You. You happened.'

'Ah, no . . . no.' Louisa put both hands up to her temples, her elbows resting on the table. 'Don't bring me into this. What have I got to do with it?' Louisa got up then, moving away from Oliver. She strode across the kitchen and opened the door leading to the hallway. 'On second thoughts, don't answer that. I'm not interested. You can't show up after twenty-two years and land this on me. I think you should leave now.' She swung her arm towards the door. 'Please,' she added.

'Louisa. I need you. Your help. I'm about to go to the police and report her as missing. They're going to ask me all sorts of questions – they'll blame me, I know they will.' He was beside her now, the warmth of his body perceptible. He laid a hand on her shoulder. 'It's always the husband, Lou. That's what they believe – the police, the general public. Always.' His eyes pleaded with Louisa's. 'You can help me. Like I once helped you.'

Louisa reeled back from him. 'I don't know what you think you did for me but I can assure you, I can't help you, Oliver. Go to the police, do what you have to do. I really hope Melissa is just having some time out and returns home quickly. Good luck.' She ushered him through the hall and out of the house.

Leaning against the closed front door, Louisa's breaths came in short bursts.

You can help me, like I once helped you.

She repeated the sentence in her head. Did his voice have an edge of desperation? It'd sounded almost menacing.

She screamed as a force banged against the door, propelling her back away from it.

'Please, Lou. At least come with me to the police? I can't do this on my own.' His voice sounded distorted through the glass.

'Why? Why should I? I'm sorry about Melissa, Oliver, I really am. But I'm not coming with you,' she shouted.

'But I think it might have been to do with your party. Something happened there, I'm sure of it. Please, Lou-Lou, they'll want to ask you about the party anyway, may as well come with me – it'll save you time later.'

His words created a wall of fear around her.

Something *had* happened that night.

She opened the door again.

'But I didn't see Melissa at the party,' she said coolly. Her voice belied her feelings.

'You must've.' His voice was almost a whisper. Worry, or concern – or maybe disbelief – etched itself on Oliver's face.

'I – I don't remember. I'd had so much to drink. The evening is pretty much one big blur.' Louisa regretted her words instantly. If she couldn't remember anything, she couldn't tell the police anything. But at the same time, it meant she couldn't confidently *deny* seeing Melissa, or knowing anything about her disappearance either.

Louisa's stomach twisted as she suddenly questioned whether Oliver could be lying. He did say Melissa had gone off for days at a time before – it was possible he knew this was just one of those times but was making it out to be more purely to make Louisa feel sorry for him.

She should call his bluff.

'Wait there, then. I'll get Noah's car seat.'

If it was a bluff, it was a convincing one, and Oliver had now taken it to the next level.

Louisa waited on a plastic chair in the reception of Newton police station, Noah in his car seat next to her. Oliver had been in there for over an hour, and Louisa's bum was now numb, her patience wearing thin. It crossed her mind that if Melissa really had gone missing, then some woman with a baby accompanying the missing person's husband to the police station might look a bit off. Particularly if they discovered she was Oliver's ex-girlfriend whose party he'd just so happened to be at when his wife was last seen.

Finally, a door opened along the left-hand corridor and Oliver sloped out, his head hung low. The impossibly tall man, who'd introduced himself as Detective Sergeant Mack, then called her name. She picked up Noah's seat and made her way to the room Oliver had just vacated. As she passed him, Oliver placed a hand on her arm, giving it a squeeze. He looked terrible – his usually tanned skin now looking pale and waxy.

Louisa was only in the small interview room for about twenty minutes. DS Mack asked her a list of questions relating to her party: the time it started and ended, how many guests, if she remembered when people left, if she remembered seeing Melissa. There was a lot about what she *remembered*. Louisa's head spun. She told him she didn't remember some of the details, like when it ended, because she'd gone to bed before the guests had all left. She stated she had not seen Melissa. Her memory couldn't exactly be classed as reliable, so it was best not to give information that might turn out to be misleading. After all, Louisa may well have been mistaken – her shock at the surprise party had meant she wasn't taking in everything right. The woman at Oliver's side when she'd first encountered him at the top of the stairs could've been another guest arriving at the same time as him.

The drive back to Louisa's was peppered with awkward silences. Oliver only spoke a few sentences – mainly repeating the same thing:

'You *know* I wouldn't harm anyone. You know that, Lou-Lou, don't you?'

From what little he'd said about how he'd been treated in the interview room after reporting Melissa as missing, Louisa had to conclude that Oliver had been right: the suspicion he was somehow involved in her disappearance was clear. He'd told the police of their argument and once he'd mentioned that, he said the atmosphere altered.

'They're assuming they'll find her under my floorboards,' he said. He appeared serious. Louisa suddenly felt sorry for him.

When they reached Louisa's road it was five-thirty. Brian's car wasn't parked outside, so Louisa allowed Oliver to drop her right to the gate so that she wouldn't have far to carry Noah's car seat.

'I hope she comes back, Oliver. She might already be at your place when you get there.'

The *humph* sound he made suggested he didn't believe that but something niggled inside Louisa. Did he know she wouldn't, *couldn't*, return?

Oliver cupped Louisa's chin with one hand, turning her face so she was looking directly at him. Their noses were almost touching. Oliver's eyes narrowed.

'I didn't have anything to do with it,' he said. His breath tickled Louisa's skin. She closed her eyes, trying not to think about how close their faces were – how easy it would be just to kiss him.

'I wasn't saying you had,' she said. But Oliver's expression was one of disbelief, like somehow he'd just read her thoughts.

'Really, Louisa. I've no idea what went on. I think it might've been something at the party that sparked her to disappear voluntarily. Or it wasn't voluntary and someone else from that night is responsible.'

Icy tendrils touched her spine.

Not only had she not wanted, or asked for, a party full of people she barely knew – but now this party was turning out to be a nightmare, one that clearly wasn't going to go away any time soon. Not if Oliver suspected something at her party had caused Melissa's disappearance. Not knowing how to respond, Louisa instead told Oliver to let her know if there were any developments and, breaking the strange bond that had held her in his gaze, she turned away from him and opened the car door.

Blood.
Blonde hair matted with blood.

A woman.

Louisa gasped and sat bolt upright, pulling the duvet off Brian. Despite this, he slept on, oblivious to her rapid breathing and distress. Sweat trickled down her back. She didn't know why she was seeing these images, but she was convinced that the woman in her dream was Melissa. In reality she'd never seen Melissa's face, but in her dream she *felt* it was Melissa; *knew* it was her. But now, just moments later, she could no longer recollect the woman's face. Scrunching her eyes tightly, she did manage to retrieve a vague memory, but only of the woman's body – her below-the-knee black dress, slim, tanned calves and her feet: pretty gold-painted toenails.

So, she *did* remember something about her.

Cold grass. Tickling her feet.

She didn't know where her shoes were.

She wanted a cigarette.

A voice behind her.

Louisa clutched her abdomen as a wave of nausea rippled through her as quickly as the memory had.

Something bad happened on Friday night. She could feel it. It was a feeling she'd known before.

15

THE CHAT

Tuesday – Day 4 post-party

'Hey, Tiff. Are you free for a coffee this afternoon?' Louisa fiddled with her dressing gown cord, twiddling it in one hand as she held her mobile to her ear.

'Um . . . I've got a meeting at school at lunchtime, so would be towards two-ish, will that do you?'

'I'm not going anywhere.' Louisa gave a dejected laugh. 'Pop around when you finish.'

'Is everything okay? You sound a bit down.' Louisa could sense Tiff's concerned frown.

'I could do with a chat, that's all.'

'Sure thing. I'll drop into the shop on my way, get some yummy pastries!'

'You know the way to my heart, Tiff.'

'Of course, darling. Right, must run. See you soon.' And the line went dead.

Louisa sighed. She'd felt numb ever since Oliver turned up at the house yesterday; she'd wandered around not really knowing what to do with herself. Being on her own most days, with only Noah for company, was beginning to make her stir-crazy. She should be going to every baby group running because being with other mothers and babies would make her feel as though everything she was experiencing was normal, but she couldn't shake the awkwardness she'd felt when she'd been to Bounce and Play last time. Forty wasn't the oldest age anyone had ever had children, but she *was* the oldest in that group. She was experiencing different things to most of the mums; she didn't quite fit in, couldn't relate to all the chat. It appeared the worst of their worries was getting their flat bellies back.

She could really do with returning to work more quickly than planned, to get back to adult interactions again – avoid baby talk completely. She'd told the accountancy firm that she was taking a full year, but now a few months had passed she was coming to realise that was unrealistic. Yes, she wanted to give Noah the start – the attention – she'd given to Emily when she'd had her, but it was different this time.

The boss was fine with her taking the full year. Louisa had worked there since leaving college; she was one of the longest-serving accountants at the firm. Whilst other people saw that as an achievement, Louisa knew deep down it was because she couldn't face changing jobs, learning something new. She could carry out her role there without much thought, running on autopilot, which would suit her just fine when she went back with what Tiff lovingly called 'baby brain'.

Louisa checked her phone for texts, then her Facebook, just in case Oliver had messaged, updating her on Melissa's missing status. Nothing. He'd been all for gaining her help yesterday, begging her to go with him to the police – and now he didn't have the decency to keep her in the loop. Perhaps she should text him. The thought played on her mind for a few minutes before she gave in to it.

Any news on Melissa?

She'd kept it simple to ensure there could be no misinterpretation. Then she paced the lounge, waiting for her phone to ping.

Twenty minutes went by and he still hadn't responded. Perhaps she should turn up at *his* door this time, but she had no clue where his rented flat was. His Facebook account still stated *Lives in York*. Presumably he hadn't updated his page since he'd got married either as his relationship status read 'single'. He'd told Brian that following his whirlwind romance with Melissa, he'd persuaded her to move to York to be with him. Apparently, she was a Devon girl too, although Oliver hadn't gone into detail about how they'd met and supposedly Brian hadn't been interested enough to ask. Louisa knew they'd only come back to Devon recently, and that it was temporary – to set up a new branch of Oliver's business.

Louisa wondered whether it was because he wasn't planning on staying long that he hadn't bothered updating any of his social media. Mind you, she couldn't deduce much from Oliver's Facebook page because she wasn't actually friends with him. She could only see the posts he'd made public – and his profile pictures, which for a reason she'd never fathomed, were always public on the site, regardless. But none of those depicted Melissa, or the two of them together, which was rather odd being that he was newly married. Louisa had thought he'd want to show Melissa off.

She wondered if she should send a friend request so she could see more information though it was possible, she mused, that he was like her and didn't use the social media platform much. It may have been something he used purely to get in contact with her.

The thought made her feel queasy. Why, after all this time, had Oliver Dunmore looked her up?

Louisa didn't settle, her muscles tense, jumpy. Pacing

seemed to be the only thing she could do. She'd put Noah down to sleep after she'd fed and changed him at one, and he'd gone out like a light. She made sure to put a tick next to the time on the sheet she'd created for today's feeds, then made use of the time by pottering around in the kitchen. She'd even managed to collect a dirty pile of washing from Emily's bedroom floor and put it in the machine. Now, at just after two o'clock, she noticed Tiff's car draw up outside. Louisa rushed to the door before Tiff could ring the bell and wake Noah up; she needed uninterrupted time with her friend.

'You're a sight for sore eyes.' Tiff gave Louisa a one-armed hug, her other hand holding a bag of pastries. She walked on through to the kitchen, and retrieved two plates from the cupboard. Tiff often made herself at home and knew where Louisa kept everything.

'I assume you have bottled water?' she asked, bending to check the fridge.

'Not cold, no – there's a bottle in the larder, though.' Louisa allowed Tiff to take over her kitchen. In a weird way, she enjoyed being mothered. Her own mum didn't visit anymore, and after their 'falling-out' episode, Louisa only made infrequent trips to her parents' home and even then it was only if one of them called, usually to say there was a problem that only Louisa could deal with.

The last time had been almost a month ago, and that was to change the hallway lightbulb. They'd barely set eyes on Noah – and for a reason Louisa couldn't understand, didn't seem all that bothered that they were missing out on his early months. She knew they were getting old now, but she had to admit, their lack of interest hurt her feelings. No matter what they'd fallen out about, their baby grandson should not be the one paying for it. Emily was in the midst of her teenage 'I don't want to visit them' stage anyway, so she wasn't worried about the lack of contact.

The argument had been so pathetic, too. Louisa remembered it had started when her mum had made a flippant remark about her anxiety attacks back in college – how Louisa had been poor at coping even back then. But as with most family arguments, she couldn't remember how it had progressed to this point; how it'd stretched on for years. It was as though now it had begun, one of them had to carry it on to the bitter end, neither wanting to be the first one to 'give in' and apologise.

'Here you go,' Tiff said, handing Louisa the *You're My Queen* mug Brian had bought her for Valentine's Day. Because they needed more mugs.

'I know you said you couldn't remember much about my party, but I need you to tell me everything you *do* remember. You said you'd met Oliver; did you meet his wife too?'

'Bits and pieces came back to me, you know how it is. Of course I remember the delightful Oliver. He's so gorgeous, Lou.' Tiff gave a coy smile.

'Yes, yes – he's certainly pleasant to look at . . .'

'I can't remember him even mentioning his wife though, let alone seeing her. Are you sure she was there?'

'Well, this is the thing, Tiff. I think I saw her standing alongside Oliver when I first saw him, but I was too shocked seeing him there to take her in. Brian doesn't remember seeing her, and now, neither do you. And I'm not sure enough to say either way.'

'What does it matter?'

'She's missing.'

'God, really?' Tiff gasped. Louisa observed an immediate spark of interest light up her face.

'Yes, and the last place Oliver saw her was at *my* party.'

'Did she just go home early?' She frowned. 'I mean, it wouldn't surprise me if she'd got the hump – Oliver was rather, let's say, *familiar*, with some of the female guests.'

'You, you mean.'

'We seemed to hit it off, yes.' A smile played at the edges of her mouth. She really could be incorrigible at times.

'He was smooth even when he was only eighteen. He's downright slippery now it seems.'

'I didn't get that kind of creepy, smarmy vibe though, Lou. And let's face it, my radar for those types is pretty good.'

'Yes, I know. But something isn't right about all this.'

'Like?'

'The timing for one. Why after all these years has he decided to make an effort to contact me – and just a year after getting married? And why make that first contact at my surprise birthday party of all places?'

'Opportunity? I gave him that by accepting his invite to join the Exeter College group, didn't I. So, he took it. I don't see anything malign in that.'

'No, I suppose. I'm obviously reading too much into it.' She almost conceded, then remembered what he'd said. 'But he said something that set my nerves on edge; the way he spoke it had an air of menace to it. A threat even.'

'Oh, Lou, I'm sure you must have read him wrong.' Her voice rose in pitch. 'What did he say exactly?'

Louisa tried to ignore the slightly condescending tone. Tiff obviously thought she was over-reacting. 'He was asking for my help – wanting me to go with him to the police to report Melissa missing, and when I said no, he said: *You can help me, like I once helped you.* And it was the way he said it. Like I owed him. And he had the gall to say he'd left *for me.* When I challenged him, he made out that I'd been lying to myself about the reasons he left me. He didn't make any sense. But I did go

76

to the police with him, and now I feel he manipulated me into it.'

Tiff looked thoughtful for a moment and Louisa was hoping she'd have to agree with her that Oliver's behaviour had been odd.

'What did the police say?' she finally said. Louisa's shoulders slumped. Tiff had chosen to only pick up on the last part.

'Oliver said they asked loads of questions, about the party, who Melissa'd been with, about her friends and family, places she might go to – she's apparently gone AWOL a few times in the past.'

'They aren't treating her as a vulnerable person, then, otherwise we would've heard more. Did they ask *you* about the party?'

'Yes! And I felt such a fool. Kept having to say I couldn't remember. I really wish I hadn't drunk so much.'

Tiff screwed her eyes up, giving Louisa what appeared to be a silent apology for her part in that. 'They might want a list of people who were there. We'd best go through your friends list, the one I used to invite everyone. If I'm honest though, I have no clue which of them were there, and which ones weren't. Obviously I knew some of our mutual friends, but not the other randoms.'

'Do you think it'll come to that? To the police asking for names?'

'If Melissa doesn't show, and the police can't find any evidence of her using her phone, her bank accounts or anything, then yes, they'll scale up the investigation.'

'How come you know so much?'

'I went through it once. A long time ago now, but it still sticks in my mind.'

'Oh? You never told me that. Who went missing?'

'My friend – someone I'd met through my charity work

when I was in my early twenties, so a *long* time before I met you. It was so sad – they never did find her.'

'How awful. I'm sorry, Tiff. God, I do hope Melissa is found quickly. And safe and well.'

Darkness.

Blood.

A body – crumpled and still, lying on the ground.

A figure looming above it.

The image popped into her head, the words *You can help me, like I once helped you* echoing in her ears.

Louisa wished these images would stop. They had been coming more frequently since her party.

Since Oliver.

She hoped he would hurry up and return her text message.

16

THE PAST

Tuesday p.m.

Tiff had left once Noah's screams reached an intensity she could no longer bear, and Louisa didn't blame her. She put a tick next to 3 p.m. – it'd only been two hours since his last feed, but she hoped that was a good sign, not one that meant her milk wasn't enough for him. At any rate, she was pleased the chart system was working well.

Sitting in the feeding chair, eyes fixed on the TV, Louisa tried to concentrate. But despite looking at the screen, it was the vision from earlier that she was seeing. She'd always assumed the flashes of images that came to her were from her past, tiny fragments of memory she was unable to piece together and didn't even try to, believing they'd do more harm than good. If her brain was preventing the memories from returning, there was a very good reason for it. Up until now she'd coped with the random images because they'd been far too quick, too blurry and nonsensical to take them seriously. Now though, they had a form to them. Although they were still quick, they were not blurry. They were not nonsensical.

They were scary.

They were of a figure standing over a body. A bloody body. And a figure that she knew was her.

Louisa's heavy eyelids closed. The pulling on her nipple had ceased and Noah was quiet.

She drifted.

'Get away from me!' Louisa's eyes flew open, her muscles primed to leap from her chair to confront her attacker.

'It's just me, sorry, love. It's okay.' Brian's hushed tones brought her rush of adrenaline back down again. It was only him taking Noah from her arms. Not a stranger; not someone wishing to harm him as her first thought had been. She'd been dreaming.

'What time is it?' Louisa rubbed her eyes with the palms of both hands. She felt as though she'd been shocked out of a long, deep sleep.

'Just after six. You were sound asleep and I was hoping I could lift Noah off without waking you.' Noah nuzzled in to Brian's neck, his mouth open and searching. 'Although, I think he's hungry, so . . .'

Louisa sighed. Because she'd slept, hardly any time seemed to have passed since she'd fed him at three. The thought of him pulling at her nipples again made her feel physically sick. 'Can you do it? Give him a bottle. Please? I can't face another feed right now.'

'Yeah, sure. Can you sort a bag of milk then?'

Louisa got up and headed for the freezer. It wouldn't take long to defrost one of the milk packets she'd made up for Noah. Letting Brian have some time with his son would be good for them anyway, she thought as she pushed aside a pang of guilt at not feeding him herself. She'd done well during the day – breastfeeding regularly, even if not for long – she shouldn't have anything to feel guilty for.

Her fingers stung with cold as she rummaged in the freezer drawers for one of the bags of milk.

'Brian,' she called from her bent position in front of the freezer, 'have you moved the milk?'

She pulled some boxes of potato waffles forward, checking behind, but no see-through bags with the blue strip were visible. 'Brian!'

'Stop shouting, Louisa.' Brian came into the kitchen, Noah doing his 'start-up' cry – the one that would continue to rise in pitch and decibel until his appetite was satiated. 'No, I haven't moved them. There were stacks in here last time I looked. Here, take him; I'll check.'

'I'm not missing them, Brian,' Louisa said as she straightened and took Noah from him. The second he landed in her arms his cries increased in severity. 'They are simply not there. You must've used up the supply when I was away on Friday.'

'I didn't.' Brian was shaking his head, but whether it was out of confusion, or annoyance with Louisa, she couldn't tell. 'Are you sure you haven't supplemented him today?'

'I'm sure. I've been keeping a log of each feed since yesterday. Look.' Louisa walked into the lounge, Noah still in one arm, and grabbed the paper with her list of ticks, then marched back to Brian, holding it out as proof she'd been breastfeeding all day.

Louisa watched his face as she waited for an apology. What she saw instead was his Adam's apple bobbing as he swallowed hard, his brow furrowing. He looked up from the paper at Louisa, his eyes intense.

'So?' she asked.

'How much have you slept today?'

Louisa's stomach knotted. 'Only that short time before you came home. Tiff was here before that. Why? What's that got to do with anything?'

'I just wondered if you'd been . . . dreaming, or if—'

'Christ's sake, Brian. No, why?'

He held out the paper towards her. 'I'm not sure what you've done,' he said.

Louisa snatched it from him. He flinched.

She stared at it. All the times were written down the side, as she'd marked them first thing this morning, just as she had yesterday. The tick for his first feed at 7 a.m. was there in pen.

Every other time since was blank.

No ticks.

'That doesn't . . . well, that's wrong. It doesn't make sense. I remember marking ticks alongside the times. I did. I *remember* doing it.' Her own voice now took on a higher pitch, the shrill-ness almost matching that of Noah's cries. She paced the kitchen, bouncing Noah vigorously as she strode back and forth.

'Louisa. Stop.' Brian stepped in front of her, preventing further movement. He pulled Noah from her arms. 'Go and sit down.'

Louisa was light-headed, from the pacing and from over-breathing. She did as instructed. She felt faint. With her head hung low between her legs, Louisa tried to regain control. What was going on? If she remembered ticking the sheet of paper each time she'd fed the baby, then why weren't they visible now? It was the same paper; no one else had touched it. She was losing her mind. That was the only conceivable explanation. The only thing Brian would believe too. And she couldn't blame him for that.

The cries had ceased in the kitchen.

'What are you doing?' she shouted, her voice muffled because of her position. Brian didn't answer. Then she heard a car start. Despite feeling woozy, Louisa leapt from the chair and ran to the window just in time to see the back of Brian's car disappear down the road. Louisa grabbed her mobile and dialled him. It rang six times before the voicemail cut in. She dialled again. And again. Each time, her anxiety level increased a notch. When he still didn't answer, Louisa rang Tiff.

'He's probably driving Noah around to stop him crying, Lou – you know he likes the movement.' Tiff's calm tone began to ease Louisa's anxiety.

'That's true, but why didn't he tell me he was leaving? He literally left without even saying anything. Surely he'd know that would panic me?'

'No doubt as soon as Noah stops crying, he'll call you. Try not to worry. What exactly went on? You sound really upset.'

Louisa reluctantly explained. Saying it out loud – telling Tiff about the lack of ticks – made her feel stupid.

'You're exhausted – we all know that. One night away, getting a single night of good sleep was nowhere near enough. Maybe you need some help, Lou? You know, like an au pair or something. That way, they can take care of Noah so you can catch up on sleep.'

Louisa immediately opened her mouth to dismiss that idea out of hand. But she couldn't. As much as she hated even the thought of someone else taking over the care of her baby, a niggling feeling deep in her gut was telling her there might well be a need for just that. For Noah's sake.

'I'll think about it.'

'Good. I really think it would help, Lou.'

The front door opened. 'He's here. Thanks, Tiff, gotta go.' And she hung up.

'Where the hell have you been and why did you do that?' She launched herself towards Brian, hot tears tracking down her face.

'Calm down, Louisa,' Brian said. 'I took him for a ride and I went and got this.' He handed Louisa a Mothercare carrier bag. There were two tins of formula milk inside. 'I checked with the woman which was the best. She said they were all similar. I remembered seeing SMA on the telly the other night though, so plumped for that.' He placed the car seat, with a sleeping Noah inside it, on the sofa in the lounge and then headed into the kitchen. 'Come on,' he called to Louisa, 'let's make up some bottles now. And when we're done, you're going to call the health visitor to make an appointment for her to come and visit.'

He didn't trust her to look after Noah properly – to feed him. Didn't believe she was nourishing their baby – that's why he'd got the formula. He thought she was forgetting to feed him, or was forgetting when she *had* fed him. She wanted to be mad at him, angry that he didn't trust her. But she couldn't be, not when she wasn't sure enough herself.

As much as Louisa wanted to blame her forgetfulness and confusion on sleep deprivation, there was something else too. A hidden reason – one that had lain dormant for a long time. The timing of the memories, or visions – whatever they were – and seeing Oliver again were no coincidence. The way she was reacting now was linked to all of it, she felt sure.

Louisa's party had set off a chain of events and now they were in motion, she felt powerless to prevent the direction they were heading in. With Oliver back in her life, however much uninvited, Louisa was going to have to face her past.

17

THE VISIT

Thanks to Brian bottle-feeding Noah during the night, Louisa had managed to sleep solidly for four hours. Annoyingly, the other hours she could've spent asleep were wasted because her mind wouldn't switch off – thoughts of Oliver, Melissa, the visions and half-formed memories all preventing it.

Emily had darted out the door this morning not long after Brian left for work, leaving in a state of annoyance because she didn't have a clean school shirt. It was Louisa's fault, of course. And the argument that ensued did nothing to allay Louisa's fear that she was 'losing it'. She *had* picked up Emily's dirty laundry yesterday, and she had a clear memory of putting it in the washing machine. But when Louisa stormed upstairs, shouting about the fact Emily didn't ever look properly – she found the pile in the same place on the bedroom floor where she'd first encountered it. Emily had rolled her eyes, hastily putting on yesterday's shirt and leaving before getting into a conversation about it.

It was the exasperation on Emily's face that'd hurt. Like she was fed up with having to put up with her mother's inability to remember things. It was more than that, though. Louisa felt

85

sure Emily was avoiding being left alone with her. She couldn't get away quick enough in the mornings and she'd come home later than she'd promised last night. Her assertion it was because the project took longer to complete didn't ring true. Louisa got the distinct impression Emily wanted to spend as much time out of the house as she possibly could. It was conceivable that was part of being a normal teenager, but it was equally possible it was because she thought her mum was going mad.

After she fed Noah and cradled him in her arms until his eyes fluttered closed, she placed him in his Moses basket. The guilt at giving him formula milk rather than her own was all-consuming. She was letting Noah down. Taking her mobile, Louisa scrolled through her list of numbers until she reached Sandy's. She pressed the button to make the call to her health visitor. The answer machine kicked in after only a few rings. In a forced upbeat tone, Louisa left a message requesting that Sandy give her a ring to arrange a home visit as soon as she was able. Hopefully Louisa hadn't come across as desperate. She didn't want Sandy coming over today; she had to clean the house first.

With that job done, Louisa checked her Messenger app to see if Oliver had bothered to reply yet. Nothing – even though a tick beside her message informed her that it'd been 'seen' at 13.45 on Tuesday. She paced the room, her mind frantically considering what reasons he'd have for not replying once he'd seen it. The resulting conclusion was that something else must've happened: like Melissa had been found and he simply didn't need Louisa anymore.

Louisa huffed and got up to make another coffee. So, if Melissa had been found and he no longer required Louisa's help and wasn't going to contact her again, why had he gone to such lengths to look her up in the first place? That had happened before Melissa went missing; he hadn't needed her then. Unless . . .

86

Louisa's mind raced. No one remembered seeing Melissa at the party. Or at least, no one she'd spoken to. That in itself was odd. But even the notion of Oliver concocting a story to make it *seem* like Melissa had been there when in fact she hadn't made Louisa uncomfortable.

You can help me, like I once helped you. Those words. How he'd spoken them. They turned her insides to liquid.

The ring of the doorbell pierced through the quiet house.

'Good morning, Mrs Cullen.' The uniformed police officer who spoke was standing back from the threshold of her door with a stern-looking woman by her side who didn't make eye contact – she was busy giving the house a once-over, her dark eyes travelling to the pathway that separated Louisa's house from her neighbour's and that led to the rear of the property.

'Morning. What can I help you with?' Louisa's insides quivered. There was only one reason they would be at her door.

'I'm DS Farley, and this is my colleague, DC Patel. We were hoping to have a chat with you today about the night of Friday, fifteenth of March. You informed us at the station on Monday it was your birthday party that evening?'

Her earlier assumption about Oliver not being in contact because Melissa had turned up was clearly misplaced. Louisa did not want to invite these officers into her house. Didn't want to be a part of this investigation. But she had little choice, and so she ushered them in.

'Did you know Melissa Dunmore well?' DS Farley asked. She'd seated herself opposite Louisa at the wooden dining table; her steel-grey eyes stared directly into Louisa's as she spoke. DC Patel was hovering near the table, having declined the offer of a seat.

Louisa swallowed before she replied, but her throat was so dry, she coughed.

'Sorry. Er . . . actually I didn't know her at all. I didn't even see her at the party.'

'But you knew her husband, Oliver. It *was* you who came to the station with him to report her missing.'

'Yes, that's right. He asked me to go with him. Moral support, I think.' Already Louisa felt as though she'd said things she shouldn't have. Having police in her house was an uncomfortable experience – one that put her on edge and made her feel guilty even though she had nothing to feel guilty for.

Or have you?

Her own thought shocked her, momentarily causing her to freeze.

Cool grass.

Bare feet.

Blood.

A woman's face.

Louisa scrunched her eyes up, attempting to force the images away. She took some slow, deep breaths, hopefully discreetly enough for the officers not to notice.

'How long have you known Oliver Dunmore?'

'I knew him when I was at college, so a long time ago. In fact, my party was the first time I'd set eyes on him since he left for university in, well, must've been 1997?'

DS Farley sucked air through her teeth. 'That's a long gap. Any reason for that?'

Louisa's face flushed. Yes, there was a reason. He left her.

'Look, I've just had a baby, I'm struggling to remember my own name at the moment, let alone the reasons I lost contact with people over twenty years ago.'

'How did Oliver come to be at your party then?' DS Farley continued without so much as a mention about Louisa's current post-baby state.

'Oh,' Louisa snorted. 'That would be thanks to my best

friend, Tiff. She decided it was a brilliant idea to go through my Facebook account and invite anyone and everyone who was on my friends list. While she was delving into my account, she accepted a request for me to join my old college group. And that's how she invited Oliver. And just about everyone else who was there on Friday night.'

'You don't seem too happy about that.'

'I'm not really in a great place right now – and I certainly was not in a partying mood when this was sprung on me. Tiff had the best intentions – she and my husband arranged it – but those she invited weren't exactly "friends". As I said to her, how many real friends are on *your* Facebook? I rarely see anyone other than Tiff, DS Farley. To me, most of those at my party were relative strangers.'

'Whoever they are, we're going to need the invitation list from you. It seems your party might be the last place Melissa was seen so we'd like to chat to your friends . . . sorry, *guests*. Can you put us in touch with your friend Tiff?'

Louisa gave them Tiff's details. Before they left, DS Farley told Louisa they'd need to speak with her again at some point. She may need to be interviewed at the station as the investigation was escalating now that it'd been five days since Melissa was last seen, and they'd been unable to find proof of life. The thought that this was going to go further horrified Louisa.

After she'd closed the door on the police, and with Noah still quiet, Louisa took the rare opportunity to have a nap on the sofa. Her eyelids were just dropping when the doorbell rang again.

'For God's sake, now what?' She swung her legs off the sofa and stormed to the door. The dark figure visible through the glass was unmistakable this time.

'Why were they here?' Oliver asked before Louisa had even opened the door fully. 'What were they saying, Lou? Did they ask about me?' Oliver's voice rasped. His face was drained of colour and he looked as though he'd had even less sleep than Louisa.

'Calm down, Oliver.' Louisa stepped forwards, putting her hand on his shoulder. 'How long have you been outside?'

'I was just walking up your path when I caught sight of a police car turning into your road, so I nipped around the side entrance of your house—'

'God, really?' Louisa hissed as she pulled Oliver inside. 'You were hiding around the back of my house the whole time the police were here?'

'I didn't have much choice.' His face took on a panicked expression. 'I didn't want them to catch me on your doorstep.'

'Why bloody not? You're not doing anything wrong.'

'It would look bad, wouldn't it – my wife missing and me visiting someone else's wife. An old girlfriend at that.'

'Have you told them that?' Louisa was suddenly worried. She hadn't mentioned to the police officers that she and Oliver had been going out at college. If they already knew, they'd have found it odd that Louisa didn't also tell them.

'No, I don't think so.'

'Good. So, I assume by their visit that Melissa is still missing?'

'Yes,' Oliver said, his eyes downcast. Louisa wrestled with what her head was telling her – to get Oliver out of the house as quickly as possible – and with what her heart was saying – to keep him there and offer comfort. Her heart won. She took him into the lounge and they sat side by side on the sofa.

'They want the names of everyone at the party. Like you said,' Louisa told him.

'Oh, I see. I just hope they find someone who saw her leave with another person or something.'

'That might be good for you, Oliver, but aren't you worried that if that's the case, then harm could have come to your wife?'

90

Louisa frowned at the broken man beside her. Broken because his wife was missing, or broken because he knew he'd be implicated if they didn't find out she left with someone else? It seemed selfish for him to think that way.

'Of course I don't want to think anything bad has happened to Melissa. But I don't want to be under suspicion! I know they are looking to find something, *anything* to pin this on me, Lou. I know it. They *want* it to be me.'

'Want what to be you? She's missing. Not dead. There's nothing to suggest she's dead, is there?'

'I don't know, Lou. But if she doesn't come back soon, that's the only possible conclusion, isn't it?'

'God, Oliver.' Louisa shuffled up even closer to him, placing her hand on his thigh. 'Don't think like that. You have to stay positive. You said she's disappeared for days at a time before. She'll come back.'

'I don't think she will, Lou-Lou.' His gaze found hers, and for a moment the sadness within them made her want to hug him. But something shifted behind those dark-brown eyes. Something that made Louisa's insides shaky.

It was the second time he'd made a comment like that. Like he knew something had happened to Melissa.

Louisa stared at the man beside her. She'd known him well once. She'd loved him. And apart from the fact that he'd deserted her, she'd trusted him. Twenty-two years was a long time, though. People could change.

18

THE FAVOUR

Wednesday p.m.

With the comings and goings from the police and Oliver, Louisa had forgotten to make up enough bottles for Noah. He'd awoken with hungry cries, demanding to be fed, and she couldn't make one quick enough. Powdered milk puffed up in the air as she scooped it too vigorously from the tin to the bottle, her fingers fumbling with the pressure of time. Tears of frustration bubbled at her lower lids.

Calm yourself.

Take your time.

It was times like this she became distraught. Overwhelmed by all of it, even the simple tasks. That's when she forgot things. She had to slow down. She didn't want to give Brian any more reason not to trust her capabilities. She hummed a tune to Noah as she continued to make up the bottle, louder and louder until her own voice expelled from her, drowning out Noah's cries – singing some lines from a song she didn't even realise she knew. She must have heard it recently and it'd stuck in her head. But the line about not caring what you did, as long as you still love me, resonated with her; it made her feel strange, like it meant something important.

As she thought about it, she remembered it was an old song by the Backstreet Boys from when she was at college. Well, it'd done the trick anyway – Noah had hushed.

'There we go,' she said as finally the bottle was ready and she lifted her baby from the basket and laid him on her lap. He sucked from the bottle eagerly, gulping quickly, milk dribbling from the sides of his mouth down into the folds of his neck.

Quiet.

Thank goodness. Louisa relaxed back in the chair. Noah's tiny hands gripped the bottle, his eyes gazing up at her, contentment on his face.

The lounge door swung open and Emily flounced in, dropping her bag before collapsing full-length on the sofa.

'Hi, love. Hard day?' Louisa wouldn't mention the dirty washing incident; it was best to move on from that.

Emily gave a grunt, but didn't offer an answer.

Louisa tried again: 'You had a tiring day too?'

'Mum. You have no idea,' Emily retorted without looking up. 'You get to sit there all day and don't have to use a single brain cell.'

Louisa was taken aback. 'Oh, so that's what you think, is it?' She tried to sound jokey, but her daughter's harsh words had cut her.

'Well, it *is* what you do. Although Dad said you weren't even doing that right.'

'Emily!' Noah stirred in her arms at her raised voice. 'Don't speak to me like that.'

'Well, sorry for repeating what he said.' She sat up then, and faced Louisa. 'I'm not being mean, Mum. Just stating facts.' She shrugged.

'I realise this has been a hard time for you; it's difficult having a new baby in your life when you're a teenager, I'm sure. It is for me too. It's not what I expected at forty.'

'You've heard of contraception, right?'

Louisa was too stunned by Emily's outburst to respond. She'd never spoken to her in such a way before, never been rude and nasty. This couldn't be as a result of Louisa forgetting to wash her uniform. There had to be something else bothering her daughter.

'Why are you being so unpleasant? Has something happened at school today?'

'No. And like I said, I'm not trying to be horrible. I heard Dad talking on the phone last night, saying you'd forgotten to even feed Noah. And it's not like you've anything else to do in your day – you haven't even been doing any laundry – so you shouldn't be forgetting something so important. There must be something wrong with you.'

'He said this? On the phone?' Louisa's jaw tightened. She couldn't imagine Brian speaking about her like that. 'Who was he talking to?'

'Tiff, obvs. She's the only person he speaks to lately isn't she?' She got up from the sofa, not making eye contact with Louisa. The door slammed closed as Emily left the room. Louisa heard her running up the stairs. She didn't know what to think. Emily's abrupt and hurtful manner was so unlike her. She was obviously worried, though whether her concern related to Louisa's own behaviour, or Brian's, Louisa didn't know.

'The police came today,' Louisa told Brian as soon as he walked through the front door just after 5.30 p.m. She wanted to ask him about the phone call Emily had overheard, but thought she should begin with a less direct approach. She didn't want to start an argument.

'What for?' He slipped his shoes from his feet and kicked them under the stairs, then took off his belt, the keychain clinking as he chucked that underneath the stairs too. It was his routine to discard half of his officer gear after coming home from the prison. Louisa watched him as she continued to tell him about her visit.

'Melissa's still missing, so they wanted a list of everyone who was at my fortieth party. I had to give them Tiff's name, obviously, seeing as she was the one who sorted it all through *my* Facebook.'

'Are you still mad at me for allowing her to do that?' Brian reached for Louisa's hands, taking them in his.

'Not mad, no. I wish she *hadn't*, but what's done is done.' Louisa drew him towards her and hugged him. She was afraid to see into his eyes when she asked the next question.

'Did you tell Tiff I was forgetting to feed Noah?'

'What? No, of course not.' He pulled out of the hug and stared at her. 'Why would you think that?'

'Something Emily said. She was in a really strange mood when she got home from school.' Louisa tried to make light of it now, not wanting to land Emily in it for eavesdropping.

'Well, I didn't say anything like that.' He dropped his gaze from hers now. Had she caught him out in a lie?

If Emily had also noted that he'd been spending increasingly more time talking to Tiff, maybe her own insecurities weren't as misplaced as she'd first thought. The fact that the party had been what they'd been discussing before didn't mean their frequent chats were over. And if Emily was right, they were still talking even after the surprise was done with. Brian wasn't saying he hadn't talked to Tiff, just that he hadn't said what she'd accused him of. Emily could be upset because of the other things they'd been chatting about. It must be disconcerting for a teenager to witness her mother's mental decline as well as hear her father talking to another woman. Perhaps she was scared her family was falling apart. Louisa could relate to that fear.

'How's my little man been today?' Brian changed the subject and walked away from her, making his way to the Moses basket.

'He's been all right, actually. Got a bit vocal earlier while he was waiting for me to make up a bottle, but then he took it really well and fell asleep straight after.'

'He's in his cot, is he?' Brian looked from the basket to Louisa. Her mind blanked as she approached the basket and saw it was empty.

'Um . . .' Louisa felt flustered. She'd put him in the Moses basket; she remembered doing it.

'Louisa? How can you forget where you put him?' Brian stormed past her and she heard him taking the stairs at speed. Her breaths came fast, a darkness clouding her vision. She was going to faint. Then she heard cries. Thank God. At least he was in the house. She turned to the door as Brian flung it open.

'Emily's got him. Didn't you know?'

A part of her felt relieved. She *knew* she'd left Noah in the Moses basket, so she hadn't forgotten. But why had Emily taken him without mentioning it? Her mind whirred. It was as if she wanted to make Louisa panic, wanted her to look bad – to confirm Brian's worries about her not being able to look after the baby.

The ding of a notification sounding on her mobile gave her an excuse to walk away from Brian. From his accusing question. He wouldn't believe whatever she said anyway.

Her pulse skipped as she read a message from Oliver.

The police want me to make a personal appeal for Melissa to come home. Tomorrow at lunchtime. Come with me? I can't face it alone. Please? I need you. O xxx

Louisa tried to breath through her panic. Going with Oliver to an appeal was the absolute last thing she was comfortable doing. She reread the message, its begging tone even more pronounced the second time. This neediness wasn't something she remembered from her time with Oliver; however, his tendency to exaggerate things was. It had always been a tactic of his to get her to do what he wanted. Maybe the 'I need you' part of the message was one such over-exaggeration. He didn't *need* her with him. He just *wanted* her there, for whatever reason.

'You okay? You've gone really pale.'

'It's Oliver,' she said. 'He wants me to go with him to make an appeal. I don't see how I can help.'

'Perhaps he wants moral support. It must be terrible going through something like that when you're away from your family.'

'How do you know where his family is?' Louisa's brow furrowed. As far as she remembered, Oliver's family lived locally.

'He told me. At the party. Said he'd left his family behind in York to come to Devon for a while to head up a new project to grow the business – and of course, then we got onto the conversation of all the old haunts we'd both frequented in York. I'm surprised I didn't ever bump into him, given that at one point we'd have been in the same area at the same time.'

The thought that they might've met years ago was a strange one, but she didn't dwell on that. 'Oh, I didn't realise they'd all moved there. I assumed it was just him, when he left for uni,' she said. It was still surprising to Louisa that her ex-boyfriend and husband had chatted so openly the first time they'd ever met. 'Did he also tell you how long he intends to stay here?'

Brian shrugged. It appeared that was all Louisa was going to glean for now.

'Are you going to go with him?' Brian asked.

'I don't know. I don't want to, if I'm honest.' Louisa stared down at her phone screen, a fluttering of nerves beginning to swirl inside her.

'I think you should.'

'Really?' Louisa's head snapped up with the shock of hearing Brian's statement. 'Why?'

'It would look bad if you didn't.'

'How on earth do you come to that conclusion?'

'It was your party, Lou. And it's the last place she was seen. If you don't show any interest in helping find her, won't the police question why?'

'No! Why would they? Christ, Brian, I'm just the person whose party it was – I didn't even invite her. And neither did Tiff, by the way. Oliver just showed up with her. Not that anyone even bloody saw her . . .'

'Still, I think it would look bad. Especially if they found out he was your ex, and that he was also the last person to see *you* before you disappeared from your own party.' The intensity of Brian's stare bore through Louisa's skull into her brain.

What the hell was he implying?

19

THE APPEAL

Thursday – Day 6 post-party

Louisa fidgeted – her fingers relentlessly twisting her gold wedding ring while her right leg bounced. Oliver placed a hand on her knee.

'You're making me nervous,' he said.

'I'm sorry. I can't stop it.' Even with his hand resting on her leg, it still bobbed beneath it. She gently pushed his hand away. What would people think if they saw that?

'Why are *you* so nervy?' he said, his eyes widening.

It was a good question. The bubbling noises her tummy was making, the sick feeling consuming her, were products of anxiety – she knew that. Taking some of her tablets to combat it might have helped, but since the party, and because of her continued forgetfulness, she'd been afraid they were making her worse, not better, so she'd decided not to take any more. The initial worrying she'd been doing prior to arriving at Newton police station had increased twofold the second she walked through the large glass doors and had been greeted with a curious look from DS Mack. He too was clearly questioning why she'd turned up with Oliver Dunmore.

Louisa reran the conversation with Brian in her mind. He'd

been adamant she should accompany Oliver to the appeal. When she'd said she couldn't go, couldn't possibly take a baby to it, Brian had called Tiff. Of course he had. She was his go-to for everything these days it seemed. Tiff was more than happy to oblige, saying she'd take Noah out for the entire day to give Louisa a break. Once she was back from the appeal, she could 'just sleep', Brian had stated.

Louisa had continued to argue about it, convinced that by going she was likely to open up Pandora's box. Brian didn't even question her about what she'd meant by that, which was just as well, as she wasn't altogether sure herself. Instead, he'd reaffirmed what he'd already said – that he was worried how it would look if she didn't go. Louisa didn't understand that thinking in the slightest. In her opinion, it looked worse that she was by his side. People would jump to conclusions about them – assume they were having an affair and that they'd 'got rid' of Melissa.

Maybe she was overthinking it.

Maybe not.

Judging by the way DS Mack had looked at her, she was inclined to believe the latter.

'I'm not sure,' she finally said in answer to Oliver's question.

'I really appreciate you coming with me. It means a lot to me that you're here.' Oliver's eyes shone. He seemed so vulnerable, Louisa felt her gut contract. What an awful situation for him to be in. If she was concerned about how things would look to others, how must he be feeling?

Louisa had watched an appeal similar to this a few years ago – when a young doctor had gone missing. Her boyfriend had tearfully spoken of his deep love for her, had put his head in his hands and wept when the police officer had talked about the circumstances in which she'd gone missing – and all the while, Louisa had sat in judgement. She'd vehemently stated,

'It's all fake. He already knows what happened to his girlfriend. He did it.' And a few months later, her assumption was proven to be correct when the news reported a body had been found and the boyfriend arrested after a 'shock confession'.

Oliver was right. No matter what he said today, people would automatically think he was behind Melissa's disappearance.

Did *she*?

Louisa kept her eyes forward once the appeal began, not daring to glance to her right, to Oliver, as he spoke about his new wife, how they had only just begun their lives together – how he loved her. All the things that other man had said in the appeal for information about his girlfriend. What else could he say, though? She'd be saying similar things too if she were talking about Brian.

The room wasn't big, so it appeared crammed. Flashes went off as journalists snapped away, capturing the distress, the desperation. The hope. Louisa blinked rapidly. She wanted to turn away from them, but she had to keep cyc contact. Had to make sure everyone could see that she had nothing to hide, nothing to feel guilty for. That she hadn't done anything wrong.

'The party she was last seen at, whose was that?' someone asked. Louisa's heart plummeted. Shit. She hadn't expected to be put on the spot like that. DS Mack spoke. She silently thanked him for taking over before her panic became obvious.

'It was a party held at a public house, Court Farm, in the village of Abbotsbury. It started at approximately 7.30 p.m. and the pub closed at 11.30 p.m. So we'd be interested to hear from anyone who thinks they saw Melissa between those times; even if they didn't talk to her, they may have information that could assist our inquiries.'

'Is there any CCTV footage of Melissa's last known movements?'

'I'm afraid not – the pub was not fitted with CCTV. As Mr Dunmore stated, he was with her until approximately 10.15 p.m. but after leaving her side to talk with some other guests, he lost sight of her.'

'Oliver,' a young woman called from the centre of the room; she stood up so she could be seen. 'Why didn't you report her missing that night? You left the party and went home without her. Why do that?'

Louisa turned her head involuntarily towards Oliver. That was exactly what had bothered her. She noted that neither Oliver, nor the police, had mentioned the argument they'd had at the party. But argument or not, what husband would leave and drive home without knowing where his wife was?

DS Mack cut in quickly, explaining how Melissa had previously gone off for days at a time when she'd lived with Oliver in York; therefore, this occasion was initially believed to be the same as the others – he hadn't immediately been worried. DS Mack added that because Melissa didn't have a job yet, or friends to occupy her time, her anxiety levels had increased, which ultimately led to a few disagreements, but none that he considered warranted her disappearing for days.

Louisa assumed all this information had come from Oliver, but she supposed it could well have come from Melissa's family too. She found it interesting that 'the argument' Oliver had mentioned to her had become 'a few disagreements', and that Melissa not having a job came up. Oliver had told both her and Brian his move here was temporary, so surely there'd be no need for Melissa to get a job anyway. Louisa again found herself wondering what the real reason for Oliver's return was. DS Mack deflected a number of other awkward questions before bringing the appeal back to its main focus. Then he held up an enlarged photograph of Melissa.

Long, auburn spiral-curls framed her pale, round face.

Freckles spattered her nose and cheeks. Her full lips were upturned in a smile that crinkled her blue-silver eyes. Those eyes made Louisa shudder. It was the first time she'd seen a photo of Melissa; she was certain she hadn't ever seen one prior to this moment.

The sound of the room was drowned out by the whooshing of her blood storming around her body. Her heartbeat pounded in her ears. She quickly turned away from the picture.

20

THE PHOTOS

Thursday p.m.

'How do you think that went?' Oliver asked the second they were alone.

'Yeah, okay. I mean, as far as I can tell about these things.' Louisa didn't want to sound too positive. They were sitting in Oliver's car in the police car park, each facing forwards, as if looking directly at each other would somehow cause their individual façades to crumble. DS Mack had seemed pleased with the appeal and hoped they would get people coming forward from Friday night saying they'd seen or spoken to Melissa there, or, more hopefully, afterwards. Sightings of her *since* the party was the outcome Louisa was pinning all her hopes on too. That way, not only would Oliver be in the clear, *she'd* be off the hook as well.

Grass, cold and tickly under my feet.

A body, bloody and broken lying on the ground.

Eyes staring.

Dead eyes.

Melissa's face.

'Hey, what's wrong? Are you okay, Lou-Lou?' A hand was on her arm, gently shaking her. She took a sharp intake of breath as she came back to the moment.

'Sorry, yes. Yes. I'm okay,' she said, her words breathy. 'Can you take me home now, please?'

The journey back passed in relative silence. She wasn't in the mood for talking. Especially not about Melissa. Seeing the photo at the appeal had unsettled her for some reason. Louisa supposed it was because she must have seen Melissa's face when she'd been standing next to Oliver on the stairs, but she couldn't shake the feeling that she looked more familiar than that, that she'd seen her somewhere before.

'Can I come in for a bit? I could really do with a debriefing session,' Oliver said. They'd come to a stop outside Louisa's house without her even realising they'd driven that far. She hesitated.

'Tiff has got Noah for me . . . so I can rest. I thought I'd sleep . . .' She hoped she didn't come across as insensitive – he'd just been through a harrowing few hours. But Louisa wasn't sure she could bear more time talking about this situation. More time alone with the man she'd once thought of as the love of her life.

'Oh.' He lowered his head. 'I understand. It must be hard being a new mum. You don't need some ex turning up with a missing wife creating even more stress, asking even more of you. I'm not being fair on you, am I?'

Louisa felt herself shrink a little in the seat. 'It's not that at all. I'm so tired, Oliver – and of course the added stress hasn't helped. I didn't even want a bloody party, let alone all this.' The irritation oozed through her words.

'I suppose I thought that one good turn deserved another, that's all.'

There it was again. The mention of her owing him a favour. She clenched her jaw. She should ignore his thinly veiled attempt at emotional blackmail – why should she feel bad about something he supposedly did for her over twenty years ago?

Something she didn't even remember? Whatever he may or may not have done for her in the past, it would never have been enough to mask the fact that he'd left her. He'd hurt her. She didn't owe him anything.

Louisa turned her body towards the car door and reached for the handle.

The lock snapped down.

For a moment she was confused, then she froze. 'What are you playing at?'

'Give me a moment of your time, please, Lou? You've got a few hours yet before Tiff brings Noah home, you could spare me just one of those hours, couldn't you?'

Her patience had worn thin, her sympathy for his predicament waning rapidly. 'I don't like the way you're going about it, Oliver. There's no need to make me feel bad, *coerce* me into letting you in my house. Unlock the door, please.'

'I'm sorry. I'm grasping, aren't I?' He gave a melodramatic sigh. 'It's like I'm hanging on by my fingernails for dear life, and they're tearing from the nail bed one by one. I'm not coercing you. I'm *asking* you.'

'You're making me uncomfortable.'

A snort made her snap her head around to look at him. He was smiling.

'And that's funny? That you're causing me to feel uncomfortable?' Her eyes widened in disbelief.

'It's just ironic,' he said. He looked out of the driver's side window, off into the distance. 'How the tables have turned.'

'What do you *mean*?' she asked. Although she didn't want to know the answer.

'You begged me for help, remember? And I didn't think twice. I'm not asking anything like what you asked of me, yet you act like you're too busy, too tired, too *whatever*.' He flicked his hand dismissively. 'It hurts, if I'm honest.'

Louisa was dumbfounded. She had absolutely no recollection of ever begging for his help, the thought was absurd. But the fact was, he could make anything up and she wouldn't be able to confidently deny or confirm it as it was clearly from the time when she had gaps in her memory. Although, to be fair to Oliver, he didn't know this about her. After he'd left, Louisa had gone downhill, isolating herself from family and friends. She knew this more from what her mum had told her than from actually remembering it herself. The chunks of time, the memories that had been forgotten, were not discussed. Ever. It was as though she'd been in a coma for months and awoken with amnesia. She remembered people, she remembered certain feelings, but she couldn't always piece them together. The time just prior, and just after Oliver leaving, were the worst affected. Probably because they held the most significance; the most emotional attachment.

If she said all of this now, she had the feeling Oliver wouldn't believe her. He would assume she was choosing her timing – possibly even faking memory impairment in order to get out of helping him, to avoid returning whatever favour he was constantly referring to. It would be easier to ask him outright: what exactly did you do for me, Oliver?

But Louisa's words wouldn't leave her mouth. She was too afraid of the answer.

Oliver might well know all about the traumatic experience she'd had at college. He could even have been the one who'd caused it. Now, even more than before, she wished she could remember something significant. When she'd pushed herself, during the time she'd spent with the specialist, she'd been able to recall her feelings of desperation, fear and panic – those that subsequently caused her panic attacks – but no images, no faces of the people who might have been involved ever came to her. It had been frustrating then, and now it was even more so.

But she'd never asked any of her friends what *they* remembered, if anything; she'd never confided fully in her parents or asked what their memories of that time were – it was as if there was a reason she didn't want to, like she was afraid of what she'd uncover. Somewhere deep in her subconscious she knew she mustn't ask, because whatever had happened must never be spoken of.

'Perhaps you should think about it. I'll leave you alone now seeing as you're so tired and I'll pop back tomorrow.' The door lock clicked up.

Louisa flung the car door open and ran up to her house without looking back.

The steam from the bath clogged Louisa's lungs. She'd only been in the hot, deep water for ten minutes before feeling closed in, claustrophobic. She was suffocating. Water sloshed up and over the edges as she stood up and stepped out of the bath, grabbing a towel and escaping the steam-filled room to the bedroom. She stood breathing the cooler air in deeply through her nose and out her mouth. So much for relaxing.

She'd paint her toenails – she couldn't remember the last time she'd pampered herself. After drying and dressing, Louisa opened the drawer on her side of the king-size divan and began rummaging for nail varnish. The rubbish she collected was ridiculous. The drawer was intended for make-up, toiletries and perfume. Those things were there, but there were also receipts, old birthday cards, odd bits of jewellery, purses she no longer used, diaries . . . all sorts. But no nail varnish. She tutted. Clearing the drawer was one of those jobs she always promised herself she'd do on a rainy afternoon, but there was never the time.

Well, she had time now. She yanked the entire drawer out

and emptied it onto her side of the bed. Now she *had* to sort it.

Louisa's hair had all but drip-dried an hour later. An hour after beginning the drawer cleanout, her bed was still strewn with crap because she'd been sidetracked. Cross-legged on the rug, Louisa sat with a box. Originally, it had contained perfume and body lotion. Now it contained photographs. Ones she'd forgotten she'd saved. One by one, Louisa picked up the photos and studied them. There were twenty-four in total. The amount that would've been on a roll of film. She'd been embarrassed about her Pentax camera at the time – a lot of people had digital cameras, but Louisa's parents didn't believe in buying into all the new technology and didn't see the point in changing their 35mm. *Don't fix what ain't broke,* her dad had often repeated. So she'd 'borrowed' the camera to take to college, take snaps of her college mates. To take pictures of Oliver really.

Louisa struggled to put names to those pictured. Apart from her and Oliver. They looked so young and naive. But what was troubling was how gaunt she appeared in many of the photos. It was then she realised the photos spanned a year, and it was the latter part of that year where she seemed the worst.

Louisa jumped as she heard a car door bang. Bundling the pictures back in the box, she got up to look out the window.

Tiff and Noah were back. A leaden sensation filled her stomach.

She hadn't even managed to have a nap.

21

THE LIST

'Hello, little one!' Louisa took Noah from his car seat and cuddled him in to her. 'Thanks for having him, Tiff.'

'No problem.' Tiff squished Noah's cheeks with one hand. 'He was an angel. Well, pretty much.'

'But you're glad to give him back?' Louisa raised her eyebrows. That's usually what people said about babies when they handed them back to their owners.

'No, actually. I really did enjoy having him – we've had fun. I can see how you don't get anything else done, like ever, though. A right little time-waster, isn't he?' Tiff walked on in to the lounge and sat on the edge of the sofa. She was obviously staying then. Louisa assumed she'd drop Noah and go. Louisa followed her in.

'What did you do all day?' she asked, laying Noah on his activity mat in the centre of the room, then kneeling beside him.

Tiff's initial cheery expression altered, became serious. 'We went to the health centre first thing . . .'

'Oh no, I'm sorry. You didn't say you had an appointment. I wouldn't have agreed to you having him if you'd said.'

'Well, no, it was fine. It wasn't for me. It was for Noah.'

Louisa's brow creased. 'He didn't have one either.'

'No. Not an appointment as such. More of a drop-in. For him to be weighed.' Tiff didn't make eye contact when she spoke the words, looking down at her lap instead. 'Brian said today was the weekly weigh-ins.' She carried on speaking before Louisa could interject. 'Hah – it's the first time I've ever been to a weigh-in where people didn't feel the need to eat Chinese and drink wine afterwards!' Tiff gave a forced laugh as she finally made eye contact. 'Don't be mad. Brian thought it would be one less thing for you to worry about. And you know, because of the mix-ups with feeds, he wanted to check Noah was gaining weight. And he is. Not much, but it isn't a loss. Sandy seemed happy enough anyway.' Tiff stopped talking, and began taking some slow, deep breaths. She knew she'd crossed a line.

Louisa fought to keep herself calm. Going behind her back, taking *her* baby to the clinic without telling her. Tiff and Brian in cahoots about it. Sandy hadn't bothered to return Louisa's call, yet she'd seen her baby? Why would she do that? Why would they *all* do this to her?

'I could've taken him myself, Tiff. I'm fully capable,' she said, her words measured.

'But you had the appeal today, so you had more important things—'

'Nothing is more important to me than my family.' Louisa glared at her friend, her cheeks hot with anger.

'I'm sorry. I thought I was doing you a favour.'

'You were doing Brian a favour more like.' Her words were edged with bitterness. And something else. Jealousy? Mistrust? Louisa didn't want to make it into an argument with Tiff, though. She'd save the reprimanding words, the hurt and annoyance, for Brian when he got home. 'I'm pleased Noah hasn't lost weight.' That was as good as a thank you as far as

Louisa was concerned, and was as far as she could stretch. Tiff shifted her position on the sofa arm – Louisa thought she was going to leave, but she slid down onto the sofa cushion instead.

'How did it go, then?' Tiff asked brightly, clearly keen to move the conversation on.

'I had some time for a bath, then—'

'No, no. I mean how did IT go? The appeal with Oliver.'

'Oh, um . . . difficult to say. I guess it went as expected.' Louisa shrugged.

'I hope something comes from it.'

'Me too. I want this to be over.' Louisa, her flare of anger passing for now, got up from the floor and plonked herself down in the feeding chair. It seemed so selfish of her to say that, and of course she wanted Melissa to be found safe and well, but she also wanted it over so that she could get Oliver back out of her life again.

'I'm sure Oliver wants that too. Poor bloke. You know, I'd only been back from walking around the Common with Noah for five minutes when the police came to my house.' Tiff raised her eyebrows, pausing for effect. 'I gave them "The List".'

Louisa's blood chilled. 'Oh, God. Do you think it'll be helpful?'

'Honestly, I don't know.' Tiff shook her head, her sleek hair swinging from side to side. 'I deleted all the messages after I sent them, so I went back through your Facebook assuming it would be easy to see who I'd invited, but I couldn't even be sure if I'd invited all the people who were on it. I should've done it as an event in hindsight; that would have made things so much simpler now, but at the time it felt too risky. There was a possibility that you *might* have logged onto Facebook and seen it, ruining the surprise.'

'I've literally no idea what you're talking about,' Louisa said, putting her fingers to her temples.

Tiff gave an exasperated huff, then waved her hand to acknowledge she was aware she was talking double Dutch as far as Louisa was concerned. 'My point is, there were only about a dozen of the people I'd listed that I could say with some certainty actually turned up. I duplicated the list for you,' Tiff said as she reached into her bag, then leant forward to hand a piece of paper to Louisa. 'You check it, see if you can remember any different ones to me. We need to give as full a picture as we can, try and help Oliver out. Find his wife. The longer this goes on, the more tragic the outcome's likely to be.'

Louisa almost laughed at Tiff's concern as she stared at the folded paper. Of course this kind of drama was right up her street, and having a part to play, however small, was going to give her a buzz. But her sympathy for Oliver bothered Louisa a bit. She'd only met the man once and she was acting like she knew him. After a long, hard day, which had been topped off with her best friend going behind her back with Brian, again, and now being presented with The List – Louisa just wanted Tiff gone.

As if Noah heard her silent wish, he gave a high-pitched squeal and began thrashing his legs.

'I'd best feed him.' She moved to pick him up, but opened the lounge door first. Tiff got the message and after trying to give a brief explanation of what the police had said as she was being steered out the door, left. For a few minutes after she'd gone, Louisa stood motionless in the hallway, her brain grappling to make sense of the last hour. She'd warm a bottle for Noah, then look at the list after she'd fed him.

According to Tiff, she'd written down everyone she could think of – everyone from Louisa's Facebook friends list she could remember. She said she hadn't done the 'invite all' option because she didn't want one hundred people turning up at the relatively small pub. But she had over-invited to take into account those who wouldn't bother responding, those who were too far away, those who said no and those who were bound to be 'last-minute failure-to-turn-ups'. Tiff had said that the police were going to go through it one by one. That much was obvious to Louisa. What wasn't so obvious was whether Melissa had even been at her party.

It was just before 6 p.m. when Noah finished his bottle and Louisa changed his nappy; the local news was just beginning on ITV. Emily hadn't come home, probably avoiding Louisa again by staying at her friend's until she absolutely had to come back. Even when she did return home, she'd no doubt disappear into her room without so much as a hint of conversation. Louisa needed to spend some time alone with her – like it used to be, before Noah. Show her that things weren't that different.

But they were. *Everything* was very different.

Noah's breathing became regular, little sighs of air escaping his puckered mouth. Louisa's insides fluttered. The deep ache in her stomach made it feel like something was in it, swelling, filling the cavity – as Noah had only three months prior. Even though she'd struggled so far with a new baby, the feeling of love was unmistakable. She smiled. She might have suffered sleep deprivation, mood swings, lapses in memory – but gazing at her beautiful boy now, she knew she'd get through okay. *They'd* get through.

Gently repositioning Noah to her right side, Louisa unfolded the paper and perused the list of names, looking at each one, trying to put a face to them. There were more names than she'd assumed would be on it. Thank God all of these people hadn't turned up. She'd have been horrified seeing all those faces. What had Tiff and Brian been thinking?

The best way would be to redo the list her way – putting them into categories: college friends, school-gate mums, mutual friends of hers and Tiff's, Brian's colleagues, their wives, Louisa's colleagues from the accountancy firm.

But none of them will be able to help find Melissa.

The thought came to her in an instant. She shook her head. She felt that something in an untapped part of her brain knew *something*, but the rest of it was fighting against her remembering. But then, Louisa wasn't the only one finding it difficult placing Melissa at her party. No one, as far as she knew, could remember seeing Oliver's wife. Apart from maybe her. But that was a big maybe. It was entirely possible Louisa had merely assumed it was his wife standing beside him at the top of the stairs. Oliver hadn't actually introduced her. All she could recall was him saying he'd only been married for a short time – but had he specifically referred to that woman as his wife? She really couldn't remember.

But if Oliver had said she was there – then surely, she must've been.

Why would he lie?

22

THE DREAM

'Louisa! Louisa!' Her name being shouted. Her body being rocked.

'Can't you hear him?' Brian's voice loud in her ear. 'Haven't you fed him?'

Louisa's bleary eyes took a moment to focus; her mind took even longer. Where was she? Why was Brian shouting at her?

'For fuck's sake, Lou.' Her body jiggled again, this time, more violently. She was in bed. Brian was making a meal of getting out of it – the mattress bouncing with each exaggerated movement.

'I'm sorry,' she said, her voice thick with sleep.

She wasn't sure what she was meant to be sorry for.

'When did he last have a bottle?' Brian's silhouette could just be made out as he sat on the edge of the bed, hastily pulling on what she presumed were his jogging bottoms.

'Erm . . .' She rubbed her fingertips against her temples, willing herself to remember. 'It feels like I've slept so solidly. What time is it?'

'Four. So, did you feed him at midnight?' His patience, what little he seemed to have for her lately, was wearing thinner with each passing second.

'I – I think, it was . . . no.' Louisa sat up, her disorientation beginning to pass. 'Ten. It was not long after Emily finally got home.'

'I'll heat up a bottle then, I guess.'

Louisa didn't have the energy to argue. Brian would need to be up for work in two hours; it wasn't fair to let him feed Noah. She collapsed back, her head hitting the pillow. She pulled the duvet up to her neck, turned to face the window and closed her eyes.

Screaming.

Blood.

A heap of clothes? Or a motionless body.

Silence.

Her heartbeat crashing against her ribcage; legs wobbly.

Cool grass, tickling her feet.

I don't care what you did.

The music loud in her ears.

As long as you still love me.

'Louisa. Lou. You're dreaming, sweetheart.'

Louisa came to with a start. Her head was groggy, as though she'd taken her tablets before bed, but she'd thrown them all in the bin days ago, so she had no idea why she felt so out of it.

'Sorry.'

'Don't be. It's becoming a regular thing for you lately.'

'Did you feed Noah and come back to bed? What time is it now?'

'I didn't feed Noah,' Brian said, his eyes squinting at Louisa.

'But you were shouting at me because he was crying . . . then you got up, said you'd give him a bottle.'

Louisa watched as a flicker of concern passed across his face.

'You must've dreamt it. Does that mean Noah hasn't been fed overnight?'

'It was too real to be a dream, Brian. Are you messing with me?' An overwhelming wave of anxiety hit her, making her breath catch.

'Shit, why would you even think that? I'm too tired and worried to be messing with you, Lou. Remember the awful dream you had when you thought you'd squashed Noah? That was real to you too. You've had another vivid dream. Or two. You must have something playing on your mind or something.'

'Or something,' Louisa muttered.

'What is it? What's getting you so worked up you're practically hallucinating?'

She hadn't broached the subject of him asking Tiff to take Noah to the clinic – she'd been too tired when he got back from work and didn't want to get into a heated discussion. She didn't want that now either, but as she'd opened the can of worms, she decided to let them spill.

'Well, let's see, might it be Melissa went missing from my party, I'm constantly having weird dreams . . . or could they be visions, me forgetting to feed my own baby, or you and Tiff going behind my back because you don't trust me . . . Will that list do you, Brian? Take your pick of those, but they're just for starters really.'

'Ah.' Brian wouldn't look at her.

'What – that's it? *Ah?*'

'I was worried. You needed some rest, so it made sense for Tiff to take him to the clinic.'

'I was *made* to go to the appeal with Oliver, actually. I don't call that rest.'

'But you had afterwards to chill—'

'That's not the point.' Louisa was totally awake now, adrenaline pumping around her body forcing her neurons to fire. 'You went behind my back, Brian. *That's* becoming a regular thing for *you.*'

'You're getting hysterical; I think it best we discuss this later. I'm going to get Noah. He will clearly need a feed. Can't believe he isn't screaming the house down if he hasn't had milk all night.'

Louisa was about to take her level of supposed hysteria up a notch to show Brian just how hysterical she *could* get, but his observation stopped her in her tracks. It *was* unbelievable that Noah wasn't screaming the house down. No feeds overnight, no nappy changes. That wasn't right.

She swallowed hard, tears bubbled – she stared, wide-eyed, at Brian.

His face mirrored hers. He was thinking the same.

Neither of them moved for a fraction of a second, then both leapt from the bed. Brian reached Noah's door first. Louisa hung back, her legs weak and shaking uncontrollably.

'Why hasn't he cried all night?'

'Could he have had his first night sleeping right through?' Brian said as his hand hovered above the handle. He was vocalising his hope. Their hope. Louisa watched helplessly as he leant his ear up to the door. Christ. He was afraid to go in. He was thinking the worst too, she could tell. His face was milky-white, his chest heaving with rapid breaths. Louisa wanted to scream, wanted to rush past him and get into the nursery. Lift Noah into her arms, hold him next to her, feel his warmth and his tiny puffs of breath against her cheek. She couldn't, though. Her feet were planted, her body paralysed.

Fuck. Fuck. Fuck.

She closed her eyes as she saw Brian pull down the handle. She heard the gentle whooshing of the door trailing along the plush nursery carpet as it opened. She held her breath, so she could hear the slightest noise coming from the room.

Please be okay.

Why wasn't Brian saying anything?

Louisa opened her eyes. Tears plummeted downwards, covering her cheeks, her chin, rolling underneath and down her neck. Sobs escaped her open mouth.

'He's not here.'

23

THE BABY-SITTER

'Emily,' Louisa said. Blood began to circulate to her legs again, enabling her to move. 'Emily must have him.' She flung Emily's bedroom door wide open, hitting it against the chest of drawers. Her room was empty too.

Brian was already halfway down the stairs.

'She's not here!' His shout seemed to hit the walls and reverberate around the house.

'Is the pram there?' Louisa steadied herself as she descended the stairs.

'Er . . . hang on. No. No, it's not.'

'Well, she's taken him for a walk then.' She took some deep breaths. It was fine. Nothing to worry about. Emily had obviously been woken by Noah's cries and taken him in his pram as she knew movement often comforted him.

'At six in the morning?' Brian moved past her. 'I'll get dressed and go and find them,' he said as he ran back up the stairs.

Was that the time? With her dreams still clouding her mind, Louisa had assumed it was earlier. Still, six was way earlier than Emily usually got out of bed. For her to have gone out for a walk was out of character. Louisa recalled how Emily had taken it upon herself to remove Noah from his Moses basket the other day without telling her. How she'd felt as though Emily had purposely done it to frighten her.

Brian, now fully clothed, rushed down the stairs and out of the front door, leaving Louisa standing in the hall. She should get dressed too, in case Brian couldn't find them.

Of course he'll find them, she whispered to herself over and over again as she climbed the stairs to throw on some clothes.

Ten minutes passed, and Louisa was about to walk out the front door when she saw movement outside. Three shapes approached the glass. She opened the door, her jaw gaping at what she saw.

Emily, Brian . . . and Oliver. *He* had the pram.

Brian raised his eyebrows at Louisa, but didn't offer up any explanation as he walked in, followed by a sheepish-looking Emily – then Oliver, who bumped the pram up and over the threshold.

'Sorry to worry you,' Oliver said, his hand on Louisa's shoulder. 'I saw Emily out on her own with the pram, thought it a little disconcerting at this time in the morning—'

'And why were *you* out at this time?' she said, glaring at him. He looked taken aback for a moment, then a mask slipped down, over his face – his expression serious.

'I haven't been sleeping, Lou. I've either been out driving or walking, trying to get my head around Melissa's disappearance. By this evening it'll have been a week. A whole week, and nothing.' He was doing the thing with his eyes again: head lowered, eyes upwards. Like a dog that thinks it's done something bad and wants to make itself appear cute and lovable so that the owner forgives it. Louisa didn't respond. She closed the front door.

Like a bizarre gathering, the four of them, plus Noah, stood in the kitchen, each leaning against a different part of the worktop. The kettle was boiling, and four mugs were lined up ready for coffee. Louisa could never have envisaged this scene in a lifetime. Brian turned his back while he made the drinks; the clinking of the spoon against the china was the only sound. Someone had to break the spell.

'How come you took Noah out, Emily?' Louisa asked, trying to keep her voice neutral. Calm.

'He was crying.' She shrugged.

'He cries every morning; you've never even taken him from his cot before. What made you do that today?'

'Thought it would give you some extra time in bed. You looked like you needed it. Dad and Tiff said—'

'Emily,' Brian cut in, his voice low; his tone a warning.

Brian and Tiff. Again. Louisa felt as though they were making some attempt to overthrow her. That they were mounting an intervention, or mutiny. Ganging up on her. She looked to Oliver, his eyes sorrowful. Because of Melissa, or because he could feel it too?

'Why are you even here, Oliver?' she said. Her words shocked her. Again, she'd had that thought, but didn't realise she'd voiced it.

Oliver smiled as he took the mug of coffee from Brian, then turned to face Louisa.

'Honestly?' He lowered his gaze again. 'I'm lost. I'm back in Devon, where everyone I once knew has long gone, apart from you. And my wife is missing.'

Louisa didn't say anything. It wasn't an answer to the question – not really. It was to secure sympathy.

'It must be terrible, the not knowing, and being away from your family, your support,' Brian said. 'If there's anything we can do, Oliver . . .'

Louisa spun her head to look at Brian, her mouth gaping.

'Thank you, Brian, that's really kind of you. I must say, it's a relief to have you guys on my side.'

127

'Sure thing,' Brian said.

Louisa saw him open his mouth in preparation to speak again. She had a feeling what he was about to utter wouldn't be good and every instinct screamed at her to say something to stop him. But she was too slow.

'How about a pint later? Say around eight?' Brian said, putting his mug down and giving Oliver a pally slap on his upper arm. There it was. Unbelievable. She wanted Oliver out of her life and her own husband was inviting him in. May as well have invited the head vampire into their home for the unwanted backlash it could have. Louisa willed Oliver to say no, but knew it was futile.

'Ah, mate – that'd be good. I could do with some time out. Cheers.' Oliver's grateful look to Brian made Louisa's stomach lurch.

'Settled then. Well, I've got to go to work. See you lot later.' Brian kissed Emily on the head and Louisa on the cheek. So, there wasn't going to be any discussion about Emily's behaviour – her taking Noah without telling either of them, not to mention then walking with Oliver, a man she'd met once and knew nothing about.

In fact, none of them knew much about Oliver.

Louisa had known him a long time ago. Even then, she was likely to have only scratched the surface.

She certainly didn't know the Oliver standing in her kitchen now.

Who he was, what he'd done.

'Emily – I'd like to talk about this with you after school,' Louisa said. She shot a look at Oliver and added, 'In private.'

'Fine. Nothing to talk about, but whatever. I'm getting ready for school then, see you later,' and she smiled at Oliver before breezing past Louisa without even looking at her.

'Teenagers, eh?' Oliver chuckled. 'You've got your work cut out there.'

'Thanks for the observation. Now, I need to get on, get Noah washed and fed. So . . .'

'Oh, right.' Oliver drained his coffee and placed the mug near the sink. 'Although, I haven't got anything to do, really. I'm at a loose end, as they say. I could hang around, help out. I'll be your baby-sitter if you like, so you can rest?'

'I don't think so. But thanks for the offer.'

'I'm not sure what you're afraid of, Lou-Lou.' He moved towards her, his eyes focused fully on hers. A shiver rippled down her back.

'Someone walk over your grave?' he said, smiling.

Louisa's eyes widened. She hadn't thought her shudder was visible. She tried to ignore the sensation that he was somehow inside her head, listening to her thoughts. 'Something like that.' Louisa made to move past him, but he put his arm out so it was level with her chest.

'I'm only trying to help. I think you could do with it, don't you? I'm sure Brian and Tiff would want to know you've got someone here to keep an eye on you.'

'What's that supposed to mean?'

'They've been worried about you. Being here on your own with Noah all day. It can get lonely, monotonous. If I stay, I can do all the feeds, look after Noah and you can catch up on your sleep. You may as well make the most of the opportunity. And it would help me so much, you know – take my mind off Melissa.'

Louisa had always found it difficult to resist Oliver's charm. It had been something he'd possessed even back then – always drawing people to him. All her college friends loved Oliver and she'd felt smug, as well as deliriously happy, that he'd chosen her.

'You can stay for the morning, if you must,' Louisa conceded, 'but that's it. You'd be better off going and looking for your wife, wouldn't you?'

'I've exhausted all the possibilities I had, Lou. It's in the hands of the police now.'

'Won't they be watching you, your movements? If they see you spending time here, with me, that won't look good, Oliver.'

'On the contrary, I think you and your family helping me puts me in a good light. No one would believe me guilty of anything if they could see that a good family, and one with a new baby, were willing to have me in their home to support me during this difficult time.'

Louisa wasn't so sure but maybe that was why he was there, why he'd been keen to have her help in the first place. She had such mixed feelings about him; even the way he spoke sometimes added to her apprehension – he could come across as manipulative and someone not to trust. But there was something else underlying his words. Louisa thought he was afraid. Genuinely worried about the outcome of his wife's disappearance. Was she being too harsh on him purely because she had a bad feeling about what had happened whilst they were at college? Or was it that she wanted to make him suffer now, like he'd made her suffer back then when he left her?

'Right, well, I'll get Noah sorted. You can make yourself some breakfast if you want. There's cereal, toast – maybe some bacon in the fridge. I'll see you in a minute.'

The smell of cooking bacon wafted upstairs. Then a shout came from the kitchen.

'Come and get it!'

Louisa reached the top of the stairs with Noah in her arms just as Emily disappeared down them and rounded into the kitchen.

'Wow, Mum,' Emily said with a stuffed mouth as Louisa walked in. 'Why don't you ever cook breakfasts like this for me?'

'I didn't know I had all this in the fridge,' Louisa said, ignoring Emily's question as she took in the three plates all holding a full-English breakfast. Damn him. She didn't want to be grateful, but she couldn't help herself. 'Thanks, Oliver, this is great.'

'I took a wild guess that you didn't get many breakfasts cooked for you, so I thought I'd knock this up.' Oliver grinned.

'Can you cook for us every day?' Emily said, tucking into the fried bread.

'I suspect you couldn't afford my services,' Oliver said.

Emily laughed. It was a rare sound, Louisa realised. She was even being nicer to Louisa, which was a refreshing change from her behaviour of late.

After Emily bolted out of the door for school, and Oliver had loaded the dishwasher, they sat in the lounge, a morning programme on TV playing quietly. Oliver had Noah in his arms. Louisa's tummy fluttered at the sight. She looked away.

'Why don't you close your eyes, Lou-Lou? Relax.'

The words felt strangely hypnotic, and with a giddiness that Louisa took to be tiredness, her eyes fell shut.

A door banged, and Louisa's eyes flew open. Brian was standing in the doorway, looking into the lounge.

'Oh, Brian,' she said, her hand on her breastbone to still her rapid heart rate. 'What are you doing home?' Louisa sat up. She'd fallen asleep in the feeding chair. She had no clue as to how long she'd been out. Her eyes travelled to the sofa. She froze.

Oliver was lying full length with Noah asleep on his chest. His bare chest.

She sucked in air as she tried to say something, but failed. Brian came into the room, and, without saying anything to Louisa, moved alongside Oliver and bent down.

'Hey, little man,' he said.

Louisa's held breath released itself. He didn't sound mad. Oliver moved, then, and shifted Noah. He'd obviously been asleep too.

'Sorry, Brian. Goodness, it's surprising how tiring looking after a baby can be.' He sat up, handing a floppy Noah to Brian.

'Why are you home so early?' Louisa tried to take Brian's focus off Oliver. Why didn't he have his shirt on?

'It's not early, it's six, the same as always,' Brian said.

'What? It can't be.' Louisa shot out of the chair. She was groggy from sleep, and for a moment wondered if she were having another dream. Another hallucination.

'I fed Noah two bottles; they're washed out and back in the steriliser,' Oliver said. 'Oh, and several awful nappies, urgh – how do you deal with those – I gagged for England and even managed to get it on my shirt.' He shot Louisa a glance before adding, 'Hence the bare-chested look. Sorry – I didn't want to disturb Lou's beauty sleep by asking for one of yours, Brian.' He smiled.

'Oh, mate, no problem, I'll get you one. I know just how lethal those nappies can be. I usually have to pull up my T-shirt to cover my nose!'

The two men almost fell about laughing.

Louisa felt a sense of unease watching the scene play out in front of her. Did Oliver have some kind of game plan? He seemed so intent on injecting himself into their lives.

'You may as well stay for tea, Oliver. Eh, Louisa? You could stretch the food for one extra, couldn't you?'

It was spiralling out of Louisa's control, fast. It annoyed her that Brian was even entertaining Oliver being there, especially given the fact he was her ex-boyfriend. She would certainly never allow one of his exes into the house and wouldn't dream of inviting her to the pub for a cosy drink.

What could she say, though? Thanks to her dismissive explanation about her and Oliver's past relationship, Brian didn't see an issue with him being around and would think her rude and ungrateful if she said no. And more to the point, he might question *why* she wasn't keen to have him stay for tea. Like she was trying to hide something going on between them now. Louisa tried to keep her eyes averted from Oliver's torso, but it was hard not to see; he was in her eyeline.

'Well, I suppose I could see what's in the fridge, but you still haven't taken me shopping, Brian, so it'll be slim pickings.'

'Oh, please, don't worry, Lou,' Oliver interjected. 'Why don't I order a takeaway? It's the least I can do to thank you for putting up with me.'

'Great idea – that's fine by me, can't remember the last time we had takeout. Then we can hit the pub – what do you say?' Brian's face seemed to illuminate at Oliver's suggestion.

'Perfect. And I can have Noah while you go shopping tomorrow; it's no problem.'

Louisa wanted it to stop. Wanted Oliver to quit the knight in shining armour routine.

'No, it's fine. Emily will look after him while we go,' she said, firmly, giving no room for interpretation.

'Okay, well if you change your mind.' Oliver's smile faded. Then his eyes narrowed as he looked to Brian. 'It must be hard only having the one car to share.'

'Ah, no – it's because Louisa doesn't drive. If she drove we'd get another car and she wouldn't have to wait for me to drive her around,' Brian said.

Louisa saw a frown appear on Oliver's face. 'You don't drive anymore, Lou?'

'No. Not for years, and I've lost the confidence now.'

Oliver nodded slowly, his expression giving the impression of understanding. Why was he looking at her like that? Oliver must've caught her confusion.

'It's understandable, given the circumstances,' he said, looking directly at her.

'Circumstances?' She had no idea what he was referring to.

'The accident. When you were at college – wasn't long after you passed your test, was it; so it was always bound to have a big effect.'

'You never said that was why you didn't drive, Louisa?' Brian turned towards her.

'That's because I didn't have an accident. You must be mistaken, Oliver.' Louisa was confused. She'd never been in an accident.

'Oh, okay. Memory playing tricks, I guess. Must've been someone else from college,' he said, giving her a strange look – one that made Louisa feel like he may as well have given her a nod and a wink. It was as though he was going along with whatever she said, like they were colluding in a lie.

'Right, come on, mate,' Brian said, turning his attention back to Oliver. 'Let's choose some food.' He got his phone out and opened an app. Oliver sidled in beside Brian, and they both began scrolling through the online menus.

The buddy approach from Brian was making Louisa's skin crawl, but she was glad to have moved on from the conversation being about her. She was going to have to tell Brian she didn't want Oliver hanging around. She didn't feel comfortable being around him, knowing how things stood with Melissa. More than that, she didn't want to be around him because she now felt sure that he knew more about what had happened to her back at college than she did.

24

THE DRUNK

Saturday a.m. – Day 8 post-party

Brian stumbled into the bedroom, knocking hard against the chest of drawers before finding the bed and falling onto it. Louisa tutted, though he hadn't actually woken her. She'd been struggling to drop off, probably due to her long daytime nap. That, and the fact her mind had been working overtime wondering what Brian and Oliver were talking about at the pub, meant she was far too wound up to sleep. Now, with him close to her, his uncoordinated movements, together with the overpowering smell of lager, made sleep impossible. She checked her phone. One-thirty-eight in the morning. Where the hell had he and Oliver been until this time?

'Pub have a lock-in, did it?' she said, her voice edged with annoyance.

'Yeah, good ole Marky-Mark was on good form tonight,' he slurred. 'Oliver made an excellent impression.' The bed bounced as he fell back onto it, his shoes banging against the bedroom wall as he propelled them from his feet.

'Could've taken them off in the bloody hallway, Brian.'

'Shhh. Don't be mad at me, Lou-Lou.'

Louisa tensed. Lou-Lou? He'd never called her that. She

yanked the duvet up, turning away from him. She'd ignore it for now, put it down to drunkenness. It wasn't often that Brian went out drinking, so she couldn't really complain. He deserved to have some downtime – she just wished it hadn't been with her ex-boyfriend, and husband to the missing woman. Oliver making a good impression suggested he was not playing the distraught, moping husband as people would surely expect in his situation. How was that going to do him any favours?

'Well, you can tell me all about it in the morning, once you've sobered up.'

Louisa felt clumsy hands groping for her beneath the duvet. She closed her eyes. *Not now*. Since having Noah they'd only had sex once; she was just too tired and too disinterested. She was certainly long past having drunk sex, especially when only one of them was inebriated.

'Go to sleep, love,' she said. 'We'll only get disturbed by Noah crying anyway.'

'Spoilsport. Oliver said you and him were at it like rabbits when you were together. But then, he is all manly and good-looking. You scraped the bottom of the barrel with me, didn't you?' His words, although slurred, clearly carried a hint of jealousy.

Louisa smarted. The thought of her husband and ex-boy-friend discussing their experiences of having sex with her was unbearable. She'd been seventeen when she'd first been with Oliver; it was all new and exciting. She couldn't keep her hands off him. It was incomparable to her relationship now with Brian. Hadn't *they* been at it like rabbits when they'd first got together though? Louisa reached back into her memory. Things had been very different with Brian, right from the start. Why had that been? She couldn't remember. Whatever the reason, she didn't want to be talking about it at almost two in the morning.

'Shut-up, Brian, before you say something you can't take back.'

He mimicked her words, childishly, before turning away from her. 'Oliver was right about you,' he mumbled into his pillow.

Louisa lay perfectly still, listening to her hammering heart – feeling the thud against her arm like a drumbeat. She wasn't going to humiliate herself by asking what that meant.

But it was going to be a long, sleepless night spent worrying about it.

Louisa sat feeding Noah in the chair in his nursery rather than downstairs watching television. She wanted the quiet – after the restless night, her head ached. Noah sucked hard at the teat, and before she realised, he'd drained the bottle. Great. That would mean a good hour of her trying to bash the wind out of him. She should've taken more notice, but her mind had drifted to Brian's drunken words. *Oliver was right about you.* In the cold light of day, Louisa didn't know which of them to be more angry with. She'd be having words with Brian when he surfaced; there was no way she was allowing him to socialise with Oliver again.

A gentle tapping on the nursery door disturbed her thoughts, and a moment later, Emily walked in and plonked herself on the floor in front of Louisa.

'You're up early again. *And* it's a Saturday. Everything okay?' Louisa gave her daughter, who was sitting cross-legged in her pyjamas, a concerned look.

Emily wrinkled her nose and shrugged. 'Can't sleep.'

'Sorry Noah is waking you. I'm hoping he'll settle into a better routine—'

'It's not Noah, Mum,' she cut in.

Louisa frowned. If it wasn't the baby, then what *was* bothering her teenager? There could be all manner of things, and in an instant, Louisa's mind had conjured some worst-case scenarios: she was taking drugs, she was pregnant, she'd been shoplifting.

'Oh, okay. Well, do you want to talk about what's on your mind?'

Emily lowered her head and began picking at the carpet pile. Louisa waited.

'You never told me about Oliver,' she said finally.

Louisa gave an internal sigh of relief, thankful it wasn't as serious as her imagined scenarios. If that was all that was worrying Emily, she could handle it. 'Well, there was never any reason to, really. I'd had a few boyfriends before your dad, as he had girlfriends before me. It's not usually something that ever gets discussed once you're married with children.'

Emily nodded gently, but then looked up – her eyes bright, her cheeks flushing. 'But Oliver said you and he would've got married if it hadn't been for something *you* did that meant he had to go away, and then you went and chose Dad.' Emily's words rushed out, as though she'd been holding them in her mouth for too long and the pressure of them had built to the point they were forced to burst out.

Shit. Why would Oliver have told her that pack of lies?

'Emily. That's not true. When did Oliver tell you that?'

'Yesterday. When he saw me walking the pram and joined me.'

'Yes, about that. Why did you take Noah and where did Oliver see you?'

Emily sighed loudly. 'I'm sorry. I don't know. I thought I was doing something good, to make up for being a total bitch to you lately. But I knew, deep down, it would make things worse if you woke up and he wasn't in his cot. I don't know what's wrong with me, Mum.'

'Oh, Emms.' Louisa inched forward in the chair, balancing

Noah as she stood. She placed him in the cot, hoping he'd be quiet for long enough to give her some time with Emily. 'Come here,' she said, her arms held out to Emily. Emily got up and went to her mum. Louisa embraced her, stroking Emily's hair. 'It's been a huge change, having Noah, for all of us. I know I'm the one whose behaviour has altered the most, and I'm so sorry, love.'

'No, don't blame yourself, Mum. Me and Dad could do more to help.'

Louisa gave a small laugh. 'Well, I wouldn't say no to that, obviously. But it's not for you to feel responsible – you've got enough going on just being a teenager.'

Emily laughed, but as she pulled out from Louisa's arms, tears were bubbling at her lower lids. 'I kinda like Oliver, Mum. He was nice to me yesterday, seemed really concerned I was out on my own with Noah.'

'Yeah? That's good,' Louisa said, although she wasn't comfortable with where this might be going. 'Where was he when he saw you?'

'Just at the end of our road, in the car. He was parked by the trees,' she said.

Louisa narrowed her eyes. Being parked within sight of their house that early in the morning was very odd. 'And he got out of the car when he saw you?'

'Yeah. I was walking the opposite way, but he caught up with me. Scared me half to death when he came running up behind me. But he was just worried, he said.'

'Worried about you being on your own?'

'Yeah, especially the fact I was out alone that early. He said the roads were practically empty, no one about. Said he wouldn't want anything bad to happen to me, like it had to Melissa.'

Louisa's breath caught in her throat. Maybe she was taking

a massive leap in the wrong direction – her head was telling her she was, but her instinct was on high alert. To her, that sounded more like a threat. To her, it sounded as though Oliver had done something bad to Melissa, and if Emily wasn't careful, the same fate would come to her.

'Did he say anything else?' Her voice shook. She hoped Emily wouldn't pick up on it.

'Oh, we chatted a lot as we walked. Went down past Tiff's and up near the common.'

'Jesus, Emily!'

'What?'

'Well, that's a long way, and the common? You don't know Oliver – you should've come straight home.'

Emily's eyes were suddenly wide. 'I'm sorry. You were talking to him at your party. I didn't think there was any reason to think he was a psycho or anything. I mean, he's not, is he? He's been lovely to you, to us.'

'Yes, I know, love. But you can't be that trusting. Not when Oliver hasn't been around for so long. We don't really know him.'

'He said you were the love of his life, Mum. Has he come back for you? Is that why he turned up at your party?'

'No. No, of course not.' Louisa's words carried no conviction. She couldn't be sure that Emily was wrong. She couldn't be sure of anything.

25

THE APOLOGY

Saturday p.m.

Louisa pulled at the cupboard doors and drawers in the kitchen, banging each shut again loudly. She needed to go shopping. Brian – still comatose following his heavy drinking session with Oliver – was not going to be able to drive even when he did eventually surface.

'Emily,' she said as she walked into the lounge, 'fancy helping me do an online shop?'

'Yeah, sure.' Emily put Noah down on his playmat. To give Louisa a break, she'd given him his feed, winded him, and had been playing with him for the last hour. All Louisa had done with that time was have a sneaky cigarette in the back garden and then crash around in the kitchen, all the while ruminating about what Oliver might have been telling Brian last night.

'Will they still deliver today, do you think?' Louisa put her laptop on the coffee table and got Tesco's groceries homepage up.

'It could be an issue leaving it this late on a weekend, but we can see what slots they have.'

'Great. Let's do this then.'

About ten minutes after they'd finished, Brian made a hesitant entrance into the lounge.

'You look like shit,' Louisa said.

'Good morning to you, too.'

'It's afternoon, actually.'

'God.' Brian gingerly moved to sit down on the sofa, lowering himself in what looked like slow motion, then held his head in his cupped hands. 'I feel really, really rough.'

'You deserve to.' Louisa was about to launch into an attack on his drunken behaviour but stopped herself. Last Saturday, she'd been the one hanging. She'd been the one making her way tentatively into the house in the hope Brian wasn't mad at her. She should cut him some slack.

'I'll make you some coffee,' she said instead.

Staring out the back window as she waited for the kettle to boil, Louisa contemplated how to proceed. As much as she'd like to bury her head and pretend Oliver Dunmore hadn't come back into her life, the fact was, that would be impossible now. Even if Melissa was found safe and well, his presence had already impacted on her little family. Whatever Oliver had been telling Brian last night now couldn't be untold, nor could him telling her daughter that he would've married Louisa. That if it wasn't for what Louisa did, he would've stayed.

Absentmindedly, Louisa made a coffee. Brian was hunched over the arm of the sofa when she walked in with it.

'Here you go,' she said, handing him the mug.

Brian straightened. His eyes were puffy and dark. 'Thanks. God, what a night.'

'Yes, so I heard.'

'What, Oliver's already given you the low-down?' He looked confused.

'No, Brian, *you* did that in the early hours of this morning.'

He groaned. 'Sorry, Lou. Was I a nightmare?'

'You don't even remember?'

142

'I remember leaving the pub. And waking up just now. That's pretty much it. No recollection of how I even got home.'

Emily, who'd been quietly sat on the floor with Noah, raised her eyebrows. 'Wow, Dad – what a role model!' She tutted as she shook her head.

'I know, I know. I'm old enough to know better. But Oliver kept them coming. No sooner did I finish one pint, than another was lined up. I don't think I've put that much away since I was twenty.'

'Emily, love,' Louisa said. 'Could you do me a huge favour and make up a few bottles for Noah?'

'You just want me out the room so you can tell Dad off, don't you?'

'Of course not,' Louisa said, winking at Emily.

'Sure.' She got up. 'Sorry, Dad. You're on your own.'

'Cheers, lovely daughter of mine,' Brian said.

'So,' Louisa waited until Emily was out of earshot, 'what did you and Oliver talk about all night?'

'We covered it all, Louisa – from when you two were together right up to the night of the party and Melissa's disappearance.'

'Oh, right. Well, no wonder you were so late then; that's quite a timespan.' Louisa hoped the apprehension she was feeling wasn't noticeable in her voice.

'It sure was. It was weird, hearing about your life with him.' His face seemed to darken. Louisa felt a tug of anxiety in her gut.

'Brian, I was seventeen when I met him. We were together for less than two years. We were kids.'

'Sounded more serious than that though, Lou. And it got me thinking. I met you at that Millennium party, and you'd been a mess that night. Emotionally, I mean. You'd even told me you shouldn't be at the party, that you were meant to be somewhere else. I don't think I ever asked you where that was.'

'I don't even remember, but it wouldn't have been to do with Oliver. He left me, Brian – moved away in ninety-seven, two years before I even met you.'

'I suppose.' He looked thoughtful for a moment before continuing. 'But, he told me that it was you who made him go. He said his hand was forced; he had no choice because of what you'd done—'

'Oh, for Christ's sake – *what*? What was I meant to have done? Did he bloody tell you? Because I'm fucked if I know what he's talking about!'

'Okay, calm down, Lou.' Brian's hands flew to his temples, as if to protect his aching head from the pitch of her voice.

'Sure you don't want to call me Lou-Lou, like you did last night?' She glared at him.

'Sorry,' he said, rubbing his hands over his face. 'I remember that now you've said it. I guess Oliver talking about how much in love you were, how you were always desperate for sex—'

'Really? That's the way he said it? Lovely.'

'Point is, I got jealous. He seems such a nice bloke, and good-looking. Fit, as you'd say – so I felt a bit aggrieved, and with drink involved, well, you know how it is. Paranoia is heightened.'

Louisa did know. And yes, paranoia was a terrible thing. She'd had a whole week of feeling that way and couldn't see the end in sight.

'Brian. Oliver is my past. You are my now, my future. But really, you don't even need to put yourself in that position – you don't have to be pals with Oliver. And you shouldn't be if it's going to affect our marriage.'

'I'm fine about it, really, just shocked me a bit. I know we're fine – just because I felt a bit jealous, doesn't mean I'm insecure, exactly. Anyway, it's clear to see how much he loves Melissa, so I don't think he's planning on stealing you from me.' He attempted a laugh. 'But seriously, the bloke's in bits about her. It's horrible to witness.'

Louisa was glad the conversation was steering away from her. 'Does he really have no idea where she might be, what happened to her? It seems strange to me.'

'I think Oliver's exhausted all the places she would usually go to. He has several theories, none of them resulting in Melissa being found dead. So, I think that's reassuring, don't you?'

'Maybe he's lying to himself.'

'To remain positive? Yeah, I guess he might be. I wouldn't like to think the worst either.'

It hadn't been what Louisa meant. She was angling at it being that Oliver was lying to himself because he knew Melissa *was* dead.

'Has he had any updates on the investigation?'

'Yeah, he said the police updated him yesterday.' Brian sipped at his coffee. His eyes were beginning to look less swollen now.

'But he was here all day yesterday, I didn't hear him take any phone calls.' Louisa frowned, wondering why Oliver would lie about that.

'Darling, you were asleep for most of the day, remember? He could have had people visit the house and you'd have been none the wiser.'

Louisa flinched. That thought hadn't crossed her mind. She'd slept so solidly the day had whizzed by.

'Right, of course. Okay, go on.' She didn't want to dwell on what might've gone on while she'd slept.

'He told me there'd been no new leads. That the police had been very apologetic when they informed him that no one they'd interviewed from the party remembered seeing Melissa.'

'They can't have interviewed everyone though. Tiff only gave them her list on Thursday. Someone must've remembered seeing her, Brian.'

'Don't know. From what Oliver said, they didn't sound optimistic.'

'Poor woman – to be unremarkable in people's minds – for them not to remember her being there, that's awful.'

It was possible that people were saying they hadn't seen Melissa because they didn't want to get dragged into the investigation. Louisa thought it was unlikely though. Most of the time people couldn't wait to be a part of something like that. A missing person would usually get people all bustling to tell their story – feel as though they were important. It was hard to believe that no one could remember seeing her that night. But then, if it hadn't been for Louisa's flashes of memory, she'd also be struggling to remember Melissa being there.

But had she actually seen Melissa's face that night? It was still bothering Louisa that the woman standing by Oliver on the stairs might not have been his wife. As was the fact she hadn't just asked Oliver outright whether it had been her. Like she was afraid the answer would cause more problems, or that he'd merely lie. Louisa's mind was going round in circles. She had to find someone who remembered seeing Melissa on the night of her party, and who could recognise her from the photo the police had shown.

Louisa waited until Emily was back in the room and for Brian to have sunk into a post-hangover slumber as the TV played in the background, then she went upstairs. Retrieving the list Tiff had given her, along with her own sub-lists, Louisa sat on the bed and searched through the names again. She should contact some of them. Thank them for coming to celebrate her fortieth with her, have a general chat, then drop into the conversation the terrible news about Melissa. You could always get people gossiping. And a hot topic like a disappearance must surely have got *some* chins wagging. Maybe being spoken to by the police was too scary, had prevented them

146

from remembering anything in detail. Speaking to a friend, however tenuous that friendship might be, would be more likely to draw out the memories.

Someone must know something. And if not one person on the list could remember Melissa Dunmore, then that raised questions Louisa didn't want to contemplate.

26

THE BRUSH-OFF

Monday a.m. – Day 10 post-party

'What are you doing, Lou?'

'I'm feeding Noah.'

'Come back to bed, love. It's still early.'

'When he's *finished*,' Louisa said. A bubble of impatience was steadily inflating in her belly.

'I think he has, Louisa. Look, he's asleep in his cot.' Brian encouraged her to look.

Louisa snapped her head up. Shook it. No, she'd been in the nursery chair, feeding him; she was certain. 'Oh.' She saw the little bundle, lying still, through the bars of the cot. 'I must've dreamt it.'

Why weren't the dreams, the hallucinations, stopping? Her sleep hadn't been as disturbed as before, not since Noah had begun bottle-feeding. They should've stopped now. Unless her hallucinations were linked with her mental health, like that article had stated. Had she been blaming her strange behaviour on Noah keeping her up all night when it had just been her all along?

As she walked across the landing behind Brian, a memory flashed across her vision.

Darkness. Trees.
Voices.
Her feet, cool in the grass.
'Can I blag one of them off you?'
The face.

Louisa swallowed hard. The images were gone but her fear remained. Whoever that had been in the beer garden at her party was someone who'd caused her to feel afraid.

Louisa got into bed, telling Brian she was fine, not to worry.

'Try and go back to sleep, Lou,' he said, kissing her on the cheek.

Sleep was impossible again now. Louisa lay on her back, staring up at the ceiling. Dark shadows from the trees outside danced along the edges like the lost memories dancing along the edges of her consciousness.

Tiff had said she'd seen her from the top window of the pub, and that she was talking to someone, but she couldn't tell if it had been a man or a woman. Louisa could see Melissa's face in her mind's eye. She remembered her hair – the long spiral curls. She tried to convince herself she was just remembering the photograph the police showed at the appeal, but deep down she knew there was something more. As soon as she'd set eyes on it she'd known it was a face she'd seen before.

Louisa wasn't looking forward to another day at home, waiting, hoping for news of Melissa. Waiting, dreading Oliver turning up. She'd take her mind off it by phoning the guests she'd marked as 'those of interest' on the list, at least get the ball rolling. For those she didn't have phone numbers for, she'd message on Facebook. Then she'd take Noah out in the pram for a walk – get some fresh air and pay Tiff a visit. She needed to get some of this weight off her chest.

'I haven't got time to chat, Lou. I'm off for a church meeting at ten,' Tiff said, keeping Louisa at the patio door.

'Oh, okay. Not a problem.' Louisa checked her watch. It was nine-fifteen. Plenty of time for a quick chat, plus Tiff looked ready: dressed in a powder-blue skirt with a white blouse, face fully made-up – it wasn't as though she was still in her pyjamas. She *did* appear flustered though.

'Maybe later – I'll pop over sometime this afternoon, yes? I'm assuming you've nothing else on?'

Tiff barely waited for an answer before she was sliding the patio door closed. Louisa stood there for a moment, stunned into inaction.

Her legs weakened as her mind jumped to conclusions. *Brian.* Tiff wanted to get rid of her quickly because her husband was inside.

She put her face up against the glass, cupping her hands either side of her head to get as good a view inside as she could. There wasn't a direct line of vision into the kitchen so she couldn't really see anything. She'd wait. Hang around outside, walk up and down the road a bit until she saw whoever it was make their exit.

Slowly pushing the pram back down the side of the house, Louisa made her way to the front. There was no point looking through the lounge window. Tiff rarely used the front room, and if Brian was in the house, that would be the last place they'd be – she wouldn't chance anyone spotting them so easily. Louisa shut the gate behind her and walked out and to the left, as if she were going back home.

She'd go as far as the church, then turn back.

Relief turned to anger as she spotted the figure emerging from Tiff's gate.

Not Brian.

Oliver.

Tiff had openly said how 'hot' she'd thought Oliver was after meeting and chatting to him at the party. But she hadn't expected her to do anything about it. Oliver was her ex. Oliver had a wife. A wife that was *missing*. What was Tiff thinking?

Her earlier thought of how Oliver's presence had impacted on her family now extended to the impact it was going to have on her friendship. Tiff had been keen to get rid of her when she'd knocked on the patio door; her abruptness clearly pointed to something untoward going on. Louisa remained partially hidden by one of Tiff's neighbour's privet hedges and watched as Oliver walked up the road a bit and then climbed into his car. That's why she hadn't seen it; he'd parked past Tiff's, further up the road. She ducked further into the driveway as Oliver's car drove by.

She waited a minute, then walked back out into the road. Back towards Tiff's house. She would have this out with her. There was no way she could ignore it.

As Louisa got within striking distance of Tiff's, she heard a car engine roar, and before she could reach the gate, Tiff's Audi sped out and passed Louisa in a blur of red. She wondered if Tiff had even registered it was her standing there.

27

THE LIE

Louisa took the longer route home to give her more thinking time, passing the Post Office and Co-op local, giving courteous 'good morning' greetings to the few villagers she saw, but moving on quickly so she didn't get caught up in mundane conversation. She took a right at the new children's play area – one of the many projects Tiff had been involved in fundraising for. It wouldn't be long until she'd be taking Noah there to play – another stage that she'd assumed was over before he came along. She had to give credit to Tiff though, she really had achieved a lot for the village, and given that Little Penchurch only had a population of about four hundred people, the villagers were keen to improve their local amenities; they were happy to help when Tiff asked them to dig into their pockets and give generously.

Tiff could be very persuasive.

Louisa walked towards her road from the opposite end to which she'd set off. As she pushed Noah up the steep incline, with the tree-lined street looming in front of her, she remembered Emily telling her that was where Oliver had been parked on Friday morning. She slowed down, and then crossed over to the opposite pavement. From that position, Louisa could see the front of her house clearly. This would have been the view Oliver had: far enough up the road to not be immediately noticed, but close enough to see any comings and goings.

Had he been waiting for everyone to leave so that he could visit her alone?

He couldn't have known that Emily would leave the house with Noah that early in the morning, but perhaps he'd been waiting for her to walk to school.

Louisa realised he'd probably been there *all night*, watching the house. Watching them.

She shivered.

'Morning, Louisa,' a voice came from her left.

'Oh, hi, Arthur.' She turned to face her neighbour. 'Lovely day, for a change.'

'Not bad, is it?' He deposited a bag of rubbish and banged the wheelie bin lid closed. 'How's the little 'un?' Arthur hobbled down his garden path towards Louisa and popped his head inside the pram.

'He's doing great, thank you. Better now, actually – we've had a bit of a rocky start.'

'Oh, I can still remember our lot. Noisy buggers they were, all of 'em. My poor Pearl, always up at night, had to sleep during the day whenever they did. We have the grandkids every now and then, but to be honest, it doesn't matter anymore – I don't sleep anyway.'

'No? How come?'

'Bloody back pain. For some reason I find it easier to sit than lie down, so I don't spend a lot of time in bed. I just stay in my armchair by the window and watch the world go by until the sun's up and I can get moving.'

Louisa looked to Arthur's window, then back at the street again. 'So, you see all the comings and goings then?'

'Yep, your local neighbourhood watch, me.' He smiled.

'Any cars parked along here lately that you don't recognise as being from this road?'

'Just the one. A dark grey Citroën. Noticed it parked by the trees a few nights on the trot. Gone by early morning, mostly. I reported it, like. Police non-emergency number, as you're meant to do these days, and they took details. I haven't seen it since Friday, so I assume they've had a word.'

'Yes, probably. Well, keep up the good work, Arthur. Nice to know you're keeping an eye on our road.'

'It's a good little village. People feel safe here. I want it to stay that way.'

So do I, she thought.

Back at home, Louisa bumped Noah's pram over the threshold and parked him in the hallway. After her eventful few hours, she needed a cuppa. She'd only filled the kettle and flicked the switch before the doorbell rang. Her heart sank. Not that long ago the sound of the bell would have elicited a positive reaction – it meant she had company, an enjoyable interaction with another adult to look forward to. But lately it evoked dread, causing her body to tense in nervous anticipation. *Please don't be Oliver.* She noted two figures through the glass: one reached the top of the door. She knew before she opened it who it was.

'Could we come in, please, Mrs Cullen.' DS Mack, his head skimming the top of the doorframe, flashed his badge, bent down and entered the hallway.

His colleague, a petite red-haired woman, who simply stated, 'DI Wade,' and nothing more, followed behind him.

Louisa guided them into the kitchen and offered them a drink. They declined. This set Louisa on edge. They sat down at the wooden table, the two of them unsmiling, solemn. Louisa's pulse galloped.

'Mrs Cullen, you said, when we first spoke with you, that you knew Oliver but not his wife. Is that correct?' DS Mack got straight to the point.

'Yes, that's right,' Louisa replied quickly.

'Mr Dunmore states that you were in a relationship with him. Although, you didn't mention that, so I wanted to hear it from you.'

Damn Oliver. She'd guessed it would come out, but she wished now she'd been the one to have told them. She looked from DS Mack to DI Wade and back again; both sets of eyes were squarely on hers.

'Gosh, that was years ago. I was only seventeen – it was when we were at college,' she said, keeping her voice light, breezy, like it had been something and nothing.

'R-i-i-ght,' DS Mack said, lengthening the word as though he'd seen through Louisa's attempt at being nonchalant. 'Exeter College, yes?' He thumbed through the pages of his notebook.

'Yes, I went there straight from Coombeshead Comprehensive. I was doing my A levels – Oliver was in the same Biology class. That's how we met. But he went on to university and I stayed here, got a job. That was it.'

'Okay. Well, anyway, we've spoken to almost everyone on the invite list now and, surprisingly, no one can remember seeing Melissa at your party. As you know, there is no CCTV footage available and although Oliver's car was picked up on several cameras on the way to the venue, we've been unsuccessful in being able to ascertain if a passenger was in the car with him. His car was not picked up after the party.'

'He probably went home through the lanes,' Louisa said absently.

'Yes, that's what he said.' DI Wade's tone made it sound as though she was bored, or had expected that response and didn't really believe it.

'So—' Louisa leant forward '—what you're thinking then is that you've no proof Melissa was even at my party?'

'Well, it's very odd that no one remembers seeing her, don't you think?'

Yes, she did think it odd. Should she tell them there was at least a possibility *she'd* seen her? She couldn't be sure enough, though. If she told them and caused the investigation to go in a different direction – the wrong one – she'd feel terrible.

'Mrs Cullen?' DS Mack coaxed.

'Sorry, I was thinking.' Louisa's mind was scrambled. She didn't know what to do for the best. The best for Oliver, the best for Melissa. The best for her.

'You seem quite anxious.' DS Mack was staring at Louisa's mouth. She realised she was chewing on her thumbnail, gnawing at it like it was a raw carrot. She pulled it away from her lips and sat up straighter.

'I am anxious. I don't know what to think right now.'

'About Oliver?' DI Wade cut in.

Shit. Her behaviour was making them think she didn't trust Oliver. She was going to land him in it in a minute. She had to pull herself together. Now, would telling these detectives that she *might've* seen Melissa be helpful to Oliver, or would it now look like she was trying to help cover something up? If she'd said immediately that she had a vague memory of seeing her, that would've been fine. But now, over a week later and after enough time had passed where she could've told them, it would look bad.

'About it all, really. There were a lot of people there, and a fair few people didn't know each other. They were busy with their own cliques, I suppose. You don't notice everyone in a packed room, do you? And you said you'd spoken to *almost* everyone on the list, not all of them yet. There's still a possibility one of those could help you. And Tiff could've missed people off the list.'

'Yes, that's true,' DS Mack said. 'But no one else came forward after the appeal. No one who wasn't on the list.'

'What about the bar workers? Didn't any of them remember seeing her?'

'We've interviewed all the staff. And no. Nothing.'

'DS Mack, are you pinning your hopes on someone from my party being able to remember something significant? Because if that's all there is to go on, I'm seriously worried for Melissa.'

'It's only one of our lines of inquiry, Mrs Cullen, don't worry.'

'Louisa. It's Louisa.'

'Okay. Look, Louisa.' DI Wade now sat forward, and offered the first smile since she'd walked through the front door. 'I know you said you'd consumed a lot of alcohol that evening, but we were really hoping something may have come back to you by now. Out of everyone at the party, you are the only person who knew Oliver. And you remember speaking to him, you told us that, so I find it difficult to believe that you didn't see Melissa too, at any point.'

'No. I really don't remember seeing her. Nothing has come back to me about that night, I'm afraid.' Louisa purposely made direct eye contact with DI Wade, and didn't waver. If she was going to tell a lie, she had to make sure she didn't display any of the 'tells'.

'And you have not met her previously?' DS Mack took over again. It was like a game of ping-pong between the two detectives. Louisa was reminded of the crime shows she'd watched over the years – the good cop, bad cop routine. At the moment, they were both being relatively 'good cop', but staring into the eyes of DI Wade gave her the uncomfortable feeling that it would be her who turned 'bad cop' if the circumstances called for it.

'No.' Louisa tore her eyes from the woman and turned to face him. 'Oliver left Devon over twenty years ago. My party was the first time I'd set eyes on him since then. I had no clue as to where he'd been, what he'd been doing. He told me at the party that he was newly married, and that was the first time I even knew about Melissa.'

'But he didn't introduce you to her?'

Louisa was beginning to feel agitated. She'd gone over this already. Twice. Why was he asking the same things again? It was like he was determined to catch her out.

'No. It was a brief conversation and then I got up and went to mingle with the other guests.'

'Weren't you the slightest bit intrigued? To see the woman who married your childhood sweetheart?' DI Wade raised her eyebrows.

'No. Why would I be? I've told you, I was seventeen when I was with him, eighteen when he left. It was my fortieth birthday party, so I think it's fair to say that I'd moved on with my life by that point. I'd forgotten all about him. Trust me, I'm really not bothered about Oliver Dunmore.' She instantly regretted her words. 'Bothered' was exactly how she'd sounded by saying that.

'Okay, I understand. Only sometimes, those we loved first are those we never quite let go of.' She stared intently into Louisa's eyes.

Her blush was impossible to control.

28

THE SECRET

Monday p.m.

'I have to speak with you, Lou-Lou. It's urgent.'

Oliver was standing on her doorstep red-faced and panting, his arm on the wall appearing to be the only thing holding him steady.

'Shit,' Louisa said.

It was bad news. They'd found Melissa and she was dead. That had to be it; the look on Oliver's face said it all. The questions she'd had clouding her head about why he'd been spying on their house, what he'd been doing at Tiff's, left her – sheer panic replacing them. 'Come in.' She stepped aside. It'd been her first reaction, despite telling herself she wouldn't let him in again. If the news was terrible, she couldn't very well leave him standing on the doorstep. He swept past her but stayed in the hallway, pacing it like a caged wild animal.

'Oliver, speak to me. What's happened?'

He pulled his fingers through his thick hair, and then stood with both hands interlocked on his head. Louisa's pulse banged. She tasted the tension. Her fear.

Blood.

A body on the ground.

161

Screaming.

Oliver pacing.

Louisa shook her head. That'd been the first time she'd seen Oliver in her visions. He'd been like he was right now, hands on his head, pacing.

She tried to clear her mind – concentrate on the here and now, not on something that may or may not have happened before. She reached for Oliver, putting her hands on his shoulders.

'Oliver, look at me. Have they found her?'

She wasn't sure she was ready for the answer.

'No. Not yet.'

Louisa's breath escaped in a rush. No news was good news. Or, at least, no news meant that she hadn't turned up dead at least.

'So, what then? Why are you so distraught?'

Oliver suddenly grabbed her, holding her tight against his torso. She felt his breath against her hair. The warmth from him radiated across her chest. She should pull away. But it felt comforting. Strangely, it felt right.

'They think I'm lying. They don't believe that I took Melissa with me to your party.' His voice was quiet, muffled in her neck. But she understood his words. Understood what the visit from DS Mack and DI Wade had been for this morning.

'Have they said this, specifically? Or is it an assumption?'

'They practically told me, just an hour ago. Said there's no evidence of Melissa being at Court Farm on that Friday evening. What else can I take from that?'

'But they haven't arrested you, so they have nothing to prove that she *wasn't* there either. They haven't caught you out in a lie.'

Oliver let his arms drop from around her and stepped back. 'That's because I'm not lying.' His voice was clipped, his face stern.

162

'I wasn't suggesting you were,' she said quietly.

'But we both know we're capable. Of lying, I mean.'

Louisa's mouth dried. 'I don't know that, actually. I've no idea what you're talking about.' She turned away from him and walked to Noah's pram, still parked in the hallway. His little chest rose and fell with quiet breaths. His eyes were closed; both tiny hands were curled into fists on each side of his head. She smiled. It was heart-warming to see him contented. 'Come and sit down in the lounge, Oliver. I think it's time we had this out.'

Louisa sat in the feeding chair, Oliver on the sofa opposite. The atmosphere had shifted in an instant, and now she didn't want to be next to him. Not too close.

'I don't know what you mean about *"having this out"*.' Oliver made quote marks with his fingers. 'I know it was a long time ago, but you don't forget something like that, Lou.' His eyes were narrowed in disbelief but she really *didn't* remember. How could she convince him of that? She'd have to give the full story – the only one she knew.

'I . . . well, I have huge chunks of time, from back when I was at college, that are lost – or full of gaps, anyway.' Louisa clasped her hands in front of her; her leg bounced.

'Really? That's convenient,' he said, looking away from her.

'No, Oliver, it's not convenient. It's anything but convenient. I've spent years of my adult life trying to find the reason why I blocked out some of those memories.'

He huffed. 'Well, don't worry – I can certainly help with filling in the bloody gaps.' He was red in the face again, his eyes wide.

'Why are you so angry with me? You've been harping on about how I should be helping you, like you once helped me, but now you're acting as though I've done something wrong!'

'You *did* do something wrong, Lou-Lou. You really don't remember?'

'No. Oliver. I really don't. Tell me. Tell me what it is that I'm supposed to have done.'

He got up from the sofa and knelt in front of her, then he took both of her hands in his. 'I'm not sure you're ready to hear this, in that case.'

'You're probably right. But I think it's something I *have* to hear. Go on.'

'Ah, my Lou-Lou, we swore to each other we'd keep the secret, no matter what. And I have, for all these years. I even left to make it easier for you. It's so hard now, to say it out loud,' Oliver said, squeezing her hands even tighter. Tears shone in his eyes as they looked into hers.

'Christ, Oliver. Don't stretch it out, it can't be that bad.'

'It is, I'm afraid,' he whispered.

Louisa's heart tumbled. 'For God's sake, just spit it out.'

Oliver took a deep breath. 'You killed someone, Lou-Lou.'

29

THE ACCIDENT

Louisa tilted her head back and laughed. That was one way to lessen the impact of what he was really going to tell her.

'No. Really. I'm not lying.' Oliver's expression was set. 'Do you seriously not remember anything about that night?' He leant in closer to Louisa's face, his eyes searching hers.

Blood.

A body on the ground.

Screaming.

Louisa's breaths were suddenly rapid, her lungs burning as she struggled to get enough air into them. Pins and needles spread down her arms. Her legs.

She'd killed someone.

Everything fell into place; her visions, the flashes of memory – they were from back then. Not from her party. Not Melissa. Louisa's mind wrestled with this new information, partly relieved it was nothing to do with Melissa, but horrified at the thought she'd been responsible for someone's death.

'How? Why?' She swallowed the rising bile.

'I'll get you some water, then we'll talk.' Oliver got up and disappeared into the kitchen. Louisa's world tipped on its axis.

A lightness filled her head, then darkness filtered in, slowly at first, then swooping.

'Are you okay?' Oliver's hands were back on her. 'You feeling faint?'

His words fragmented in her ears. She felt as though she were floating. Above herself. Above Oliver. Away from the reality of the situation. His hands, grasping hers, tethered her, kept her on the ground. The darkness passed.

'Take big, slow breaths. Come on, keep it together. Breathe.'

She did as he told her. She mirrored his breathing, and with his help, she calmed down.

It was several minutes before she could speak. She wished now that she hadn't pushed Oliver into telling her. Living with strange visions, the knowledge she had gaps in her memory, was far preferable than this. The truth.

She'd never be able to live with this.

'How did it happen?' As much as she wanted to put it back in the box she'd obviously been keeping it in all these years, Louisa knew she couldn't now. She needed to know all the details, however awful they were.

Oliver sat back on the sofa, fluffing the cushions and getting comfortable. Louisa slumped in her own chair. He was making it seem like it was going to be a long story.

'The secrets we bury have a way of clawing back to the surface, don't they?' He sighed; shook his head. Then he looked directly at Louisa. 'You'd been to a house party. I hadn't gone with you, mainly because I knew what kind of party it was likely to be. It was the end of term. You'd told me you deserved to let your hair down, seeing as you'd worked so hard and your parents were away for a long weekend in Brighton, so you wouldn't have to answer to anyone. You were mad at me for not going – it was one of our first arguments. I just wanted us to stay at yours, make the most of being able to spend time with you alone. Do you remember that?'

'No. Oliver, look – assume I know nothing, and just tell the whole story.' Her impatience for him to get to the point was overwhelming her.

'Fine. Sorry. So, you drove there. You didn't tell me you were going to drive. You'd not long passed your test and I knew there'd be drink, even drugs, readily available there. It was the Lakes' house. They were always smoking weed, drinking cider whenever I saw them out of college. Sometimes even in college.' He took a breath. 'Anyway, I got a call. It was two in the morning and immediately I knew something had happened. Something bad.'

Louisa placed her elbows on her lap, and cupped her chin in her hands, trying to steady the shakes.

'You didn't make any sense on the phone. You were half-crying, half-screaming. I panicked. Said I'd come over to you. I was there in ten minutes flat.' He smiled. 'I drove like a maniac, which is ironic, really, considering.'

'Considering what?'

'That the reason you were in such a state was because you'd been driving too fast – or erratically, anyway. Zipping through the lanes like you owned them. You'd felt more confident driving the narrow lanes than the main roads; loved the twistiness, how your little Mini seemed like it was doing eighty miles an hour, even though it struggled to hit fifty. But, fifty miles an hour in winding narrow lanes, well, that can be lethal if someone was to get in the way.'

'Stop. Stop a minute,' Louisa gasped. The blood. The body in the road. Her screaming. That had been because she'd hit someone. Speeding through the lanes. And Oliver was right, she did remember loving the feel of the twisting lanes, the fact they were always so quiet giving her the impression she was the only one ever to drive them. It made her feel as though she were free. But if she'd hit someone, why didn't either of them report it? Phone for an ambulance?

'I'm sorry. This must be an awful shock for you. If you've blocked these memories for so long, this must be like living it for the first time.'

It took a moment for Louisa to realise she was crying. 'Part of me is refusing to believe what you're saying. The part that thinks I'm a good person who would never intentionally hurt someone else and would never lie about it if I had. Not about something so huge. The other part of me knows you must be right. I did that. I ki—' Louisa couldn't say the word. She looked up at Oliver. She needed him close to her, wanted his arms around her, comforting her, making her feel safe. A small sob burst out of her. 'What happened, when you got to me, what happened next?'

'You were in pieces, so distraught that it took me an age to coax out of you what had happened. I thought it was something at the party, that someone had hurt you. I never imagined . . .' Oliver stopped, perhaps noticing that she'd lowered her head in shame, and he patted the sofa. 'Come and sit here, Lou-Lou.'

She got up and, her legs still numb, slowly moved to sit with him, thankful for his kindness. Glad that he still wanted to be near her. He put his arm around her and she rested her head on his shoulder. Tears immediately dampened his shirt.

'I was in shock when you told me about the accident. That your car had hit and knocked down a woman.'

'It was a woman?'

'A young woman, yes.'

'Oh my God.' She was going to be sick. She put her hand to her mouth, swallowing again and again in an attempt to keep her stomach contents in.

'You kept repeating over and over – *she's not moving, she's not moving*. After about ten minutes of your hysterics, the only thing I thought I could do to calm you down was to say I'd go and look. So I took my car and I drove the route you said you'd taken.'

Louisa prayed Oliver was about to say, 'But there was no one there when I got to where you said it'd happened.' But he didn't.

'She was dead, Lou-Lou. I checked for her pulse, but I could tell just looking at her, her staring eyes, her limbs at awkward angles. Her head split open like a melon—'

'Oliver! Please, no more.' She didn't need to know the gruesome bits. That wasn't going to help at all. 'What did you do?'

'All I could think of doing in that situation. I had to protect you, Lou. Like you knew I would. That's why you called me – to clear up your mess, help you.'

'No, surely I was just in shock. Distraught, like you said. I wanted you because you were my boyfriend. I wanted comfort.'

'No, Lou. You wanted me to make it go away. You'd been drinking. You'd been taking drugs. You were a mess. And you'd have been done for murder.'

A silence fell between them. Louisa contemplated what he'd said, wrestled with the notion of her wanting Oliver to help her cover up what she'd done. What kind of person did that make her? She swallowed hard to fight against the rising bile, dreading the answer to her next question.

'So you somehow got rid of the body?'

'Yes, that's all I could think of doing. It wasn't as if I had many options open to me. I'm not going to tell you where – I always swore I wouldn't. Just in case. You can always plead ignorance then, if it ever comes to it. Although it seems that's what you've been doing all this time anyway. It's been me who's been living with the truth all these years. The crushing guilt.'

'I'm so sorry, Oliver. I can't take this in. I don't know what to do.'

'You do nothing, Lou-Lou. No good can come to anyone if it comes out now.'

'I think her family would disagree, Oliver. How on earth did we get away with it, anyway?'

'Her body has never been found. I think the police had given up looking for her a long time ago.'

'You knew who it was?'

'Yes, I do now. I found the missing person stories in the newspaper a few years ago. Though it had all died out quite quickly at the time, I never stopped thinking about it. I had to find out more.'

'I don't understand – why did it die out so quickly?'

'Because the missing person reports had been for a year prior to the accident. She'd been a runaway. When you . . . when she'd been in the lane that night, I think it was because she was living rough in one of the disused barns along the back road to Torquay. No one knew where she was, her family had all but given up on finding her – no one missed her after I'd done the . . . the deed.'

'God. The poor woman, her family. They will still be wondering what happened to her, Oliver – still holding out hope that she's alive somewhere.'

'I know. Believe me, I know. I've suffered flashbacks, insomnia, huge guilt over covering it up – especially once I saw the aftermath: the articles and desperate pleas from her family members, all the while knowing their attempts to find her alive would prove futile. But I loved you.' He manoeuvred Louisa so that she was facing him. 'I still do.'

Louisa lowered her gaze from his. Doing something so terrible in the name of love was astounding, and she couldn't help but question if she would have done the same for him.

She had been besotted by Oliver; always thought of him as her one true love. Maybe she would've done. But now they were adults. Louisa had two beautiful children. If someone hit and killed Emily, if she disappeared and never returned, she knew she'd never cope. She owed it to this woman's family to tell them what happened to their daughter.

'We have to tell the police, Oliver.'

'What? No! Don't be stupid, Lou.' Oliver propelled himself off the sofa. 'You'd lose everything. I would too. And how would it look now, with Melissa missing?'

'What was her name? You said you knew who it was.'

'No.' Oliver shook his head fervently. 'It won't do you any good knowing. Really, trust me. It messes with your head and you'll never stop thinking about it, or her. I shouldn't have told you.'

Cries erupted from Noah's pram. Louisa stumbled from the lounge to get him.

'He needs a bottle,' she said, handing Noah to Oliver before going to the kitchen.

For the moment, she didn't want to look at Oliver – at the man who'd just destroyed her life in a matter of minutes.

This morning her main worry had been what Oliver was doing at Tiff's. The worst of her worries was what had happened to Melissa, and whether she herself had something to do with her disappearance.

This afternoon, she'd become a murderer and a liar.

30

THE SEARCH

Tuesday a.m. – Day 11 post-party

Louisa watched the screen of her mobile and silenced the alarm as soon as it began. She'd set it for 5.30 a.m. so she could be up half an hour before Brian, but she needn't have bothered. She hadn't slept at all. She'd lain awake, her head swimming with Oliver's words, his story about what she'd done. What he'd done. The secret they'd buried. How was she ever going to rectify it? There was only one way – she had to tell the police. Get Oliver to tell them where the poor woman's body was.

Although they'd carried on talking until Emily came home, Oliver had still not disclosed anything more about the victim. The woman Louisa had hit. The *young* woman Louisa had killed. She'd tried to act as usual when Emily had burst through the door, but she was sure it must be written all over her face. The horror. The shock. Guilt. All there, plain to see. But Emily had focused on Oliver. With a furrowed brow, she'd slumped down on the sofa, the opposite end to where Oliver was sitting, and stayed there, keeping an eye on him. Louisa had got the distinct impression that after their chat, Emily, despite liking Oliver, had come to mistrust why he was there. Louisa had similar concerns.

Oliver claimed he'd gone away *for* Louisa. He'd told her yesterday that after the accident, she'd shut down, become uncommunicative, withdrawn. At the time he was afraid that, with the constant reminder of what had happened, she would cave in and tell the police. It would ruin both their lives. He'd decided to leave. He wanted to go to uni anyway, so a move would've been inevitable, he'd said. Oliver told her that she'd broken down, begged him to stay with her. Said she'd never get through it without him. The part about Oliver leaving her was the one thing she'd held in her memory. Not for the reason she'd believed all these years, but because he thought it was the only way for them both to cope with the aftermath.

The constant references from Oliver about how Louisa owed him now made sense.

He'd done what he'd done for love. She'd done what she'd done for self-preservation.

The therapist had been right – Louisa had blocked the memories because, for her own survival, she'd had to. The accident had been the traumatic event Louisa had kept hidden from herself for the last twenty years.

And now she'd give anything to bury it again.

For hours during the night, she'd watched Brian as he slept. Turned on her side, tears soaking her pillow, she'd studied his sleeping face remembering how, when she'd first met him, she'd thought him to be quite boring. Now she recalled why she'd been drawn to him as he stood on the outskirts of a group of people at the Millennium party, looking lost. It was because he wasn't confident, wasn't drop-dead gorgeous. He was 'normal'. As different from Oliver as she could get. She'd felt uncomfortable being at the party – she hated them. And even though she hadn't been fully aware of why back then, now she knew.

Brian was safe.

Oliver was dangerous.

Or was he? Maybe she was the dangerous one in all this. After all, he'd saved her, prevented her from ruining her life. It appeared *she'd* been the dangerous one.

Oliver's words came to her: *Why ruin our lives too, Lou-Lou?* Louisa cringed at the thought she'd agreed to keep quiet. Selfish cow. Evil. That's the only explanation for covering something like that up.

She and Oliver were both evil.

Louisa threw back the duvet and swung her legs out of bed. A dizziness stopped her from standing; she stayed sitting on the edge of the mattress. She felt sick with tiredness. Typical – Noah had had the best night's sleep ever, and Louisa had just had the worst. All the years her mind had been protecting her, and now the truth had come out, it was going to make her suffer.

But that's what she deserved.

She turned to look at Brian. He deserved better than her. She wondered if he would stand by her if he found out, whether he'd still love her if he knew what kind of person she really was.

She also wondered if he would have made the same sacrifice as Oliver had for her.

Come on, Lou. Get up.

She took some steadying breaths, then slowly made her way into the nursery. A gentle cooing greeted her. Noah's legs pumped as she peered into his cot. Soon he'd be turning over and then the fun would start. Louisa had forgotten most of the developmental milestones and had to google almost everything now. She'd mostly had books back when Emily had been born, but was thankful for how different things were now with the internet so easily accessible on various devices. She lifted him from the cot and made her way downstairs. After feeding him, then getting Emily up and chivvying her along, Louisa was going to do some internet searches of a different kind.

Searching *Missing persons in Devon from 1995* on Google, Louisa felt nauseous. She closed her eyes as she hit the return button, bracing herself for the results.

The first article that came up was about the missing school-girl Genette Tate. That was back in 1978, nowhere near the time she'd put in the search bar. But nonetheless it made her shudder. She remembered her own parents, their friends, teachers, villagers – all talking about this case when she was growing up – it'd happened a year before Louisa's birth. Louisa recalled how she'd been out riding her bike with a few of her friends when she was ten, and her mum had given her the usual warning: *don't stop and talk to anyone you don't know, stick together with the other girls, don't cycle off ahead, or let them leave you behind. You know what happened to Genette Tate.* Yes, she did. It was ingrained in her mind. The girl had been thirteen years old, and had gone missing during her paper round. Scattered news-papers had been found alongside her abandoned bike in the quiet country lane near her village in East Devon.

Louisa's mind now conjured the image of the country lane she'd been driving down, of the body in the middle of it. Lying still, broken, bloodied. She wondered if something similar had happened to Genette. If someone like Louisa had hit her, killed her, then covered it up. Before yesterday Louisa would've never imagined any scenario where she could've done such a thing. But from one day to the next, she was realising that she wasn't the person she thought she was.

Clicking off the article, Louisa scrolled down the search results. UK Missing Persons Unit was at the bottom of the first page. Louisa tried searching, but the pages were mainly to do with unidentified case searches – for bodies of people who'd been found but were yet to be identified. She cursed herself for feeling relief when there were no unidentified females found in Devon that could relate to her woman in the lane.

Nevertheless, Louisa couldn't shake the uneasy feeling. It wasn't just that she'd found out what she'd done, what the traumatic experience that had clouded her adult life was, it was why. Why had she allowed Oliver to cover it up? And why was Oliver back?

He had a hidden agenda. He must have.

Louisa thought about his marriage to Melissa – it was new, but was it happy? Perhaps marrying her triggered something in him. Maybe Emily was right, and he'd come back to Devon for Louisa.

It was possible that the lie he'd lived with was too much to bear on his own, and it wasn't exactly something he could tell his new bride. Guilt could eat away at you. Destroy you. Keeping such a huge secret would certainly not be the basis of a good marriage.

Louisa had managed it, but that was before. There was no telling how this would affect her marriage now. Now she knew the devastating truth.

Being with the only other person who knew might be the answer.

Louisa filled the bottles with powdered milk, shaking them violently as she thought about Oliver and Melissa.

Cold grass under her feet.

'Can I blag one of them off you?'

A sense of dread.

Fear.

Running.

Falling.

Blood.

Louisa shook the vision away. While some of her flashes of memory could now be explained, this couldn't so easily be tagged to 'back then'. This felt recent. Something must have happened the night of her party to trigger the concealed memories to begin resurfacing. And Louisa now considered that her mind was mixing up the two separate things. Some flashes were from the night of the accident, but some, the cold grass, the person asking for a cigarette, they were from her fortieth party.

When Oliver had told her the secret, she'd assumed her visions had nothing to do with Melissa. But now she wasn't so sure. After all, if she'd successfully covered up something in the past, there was every chance she could be covering up something now. For the moment Louisa couldn't afford to worry that she'd done something else – she had to focus on the reason for her first episode of dissociative amnesia to begin with.

Oliver had been adamant he wouldn't tell Louisa who the victim was, where he'd disposed of her body. *How*. While she thought at the time he was protecting her by ensuring she didn't know the details, Louisa wondered now if there was an element of control. Oliver was controlling what she knew. That didn't sit well with her. Knowledge was power.

Having had no luck on the internet, Louisa refused to give up trying to find out who the victim was. She'd have to opt for something else – research the original missing persons case at the library, search out the archived newspapers for missing persons reports for herself. Oliver said that the woman had been missing for a year prior to the accident. This was Devon, surely there weren't that many missing people reported? She could at least narrow down a list and go from there.

The thought of taking Noah with her whilst she was researching struck a horrible chord in Louisa. She couldn't take him, *wouldn't*. Though she hadn't spoken to Tiff since the frosty reception she'd given Louisa at her house yesterday, she'd ask her to look after Noah while she went to the library. And when she got back, she could confront her about what was going on.

Not trusting herself to speak, Louisa tapped out a text.

Any chance you could have Noah for a few hours today? xx

She didn't give a reason, best not to complicate it. If Tiff returned the text asking what she was doing, she'd say she needed some time alone – wanted to get the bus into town without stressing about the pram and Noah screaming.

Her phone pinged.

I'm sorry, I can't today. So much on, lots of prep for the school end of term party. Hope all OK. xx

Louisa stared at the phone. Another brush-off. It could purely be that she was busy; organising stuff was her priority. But it was the tone of the message that wasn't right. Tiff was usually far more flouncy, her texts longer, gushier. And she'd usually give an alternative, like: *I can't do today, but what about tomorrow?* Something was going on.

Louisa started typing a message back but gave up. She didn't even know what she wanted to say. She'd go with Noah. She'd have to.

The baby-changing bag was fit to bursting. Louisa had filled it with everything she could think of to make the journey as stress-free as possible, but her muscles immediately tensed at the thought of catching the bus. It was never easy to get the pram folded with Noah in one arm, and her bag in the other. She'd done it once since Noah was born, and it'd been an experience she didn't want to repeat. She'd previously assumed that, living a small village, people would rush to help her. But no. Those already on the bus watched her in what appeared to be either amusement or pity as she struggled on board. They were elderly, mostly, so she guessed they could be forgiven. But the bus driver – well, he'd been plain rude, tutting at her as she dropped her bag, crashing the half-folded pram against the side of the bus. *Get out and fucking help me then!* She'd been close to screaming at him.

As she bumped the pram down the steps of the house onto the pavement, Louisa hoped today's journey would be better. The knot of anxiety grew as she walked to the bus stop. She was relieved to see some people standing waiting. At least one of them might help her.

The library at Newton was a short distance from the bus stop. The journey had in fact gone smoothly and, for once, Louisa had enjoyed the attention she and Noah had received on the bus. Lots of cooing over him and Elsie, an older woman from the village, had chatted incessantly on the journey, keeping Noah fully enthralled with her red glasses and cackly voice. With help from a teenage lad, she'd disembarked from the bus easily. All was going well on this outing to town. She silently prayed it would continue that way as she manoeuvred the pram through the entrance into the hushed interior of the building.

An hour later and Louisa was hot, bothered and disappointed. She'd found zero evidence of a young woman disappearing around the time of the accident, or the year prior to it. Noah squirmed in his pram next to her – she only had another five, maybe ten minutes before he turned from cute baby into screaming devil child. She needed to get to the library's café so she could warm his bottle. If he settled after, she might be able to come back and search through the archives for different years – perhaps Oliver had remembered it wrongly.

Or, perhaps Oliver had purposely given her false information. He'd said they'd agreed never to dig up the past, and now Louisa was trying to do just that. Oliver might've known she'd go looking. Maybe even now he knew more about her than she knew about herself.

31

THE PHOTO

Louisa had admitted defeat when she'd still failed to find evidence of a woman going missing in the Devon area during the years she'd searched – and time had run out, together with Noah's patience, which meant she'd been unable to check other dates. Deflated from a wasted afternoon, she'd made the trip home on the bus and was now sitting on the sofa, coffee in hand, scrolling through her Facebook feed, despite promising herself she wouldn't go on it again.

At first, she was horrified to find that she'd been tagged in a few photos from her fortieth birthday evening – inwardly cringing at the thought of what state she'd look – but then curiosity took over and she clicked on them. She studied each picture with an eye to finding Melissa in at least one of them. According to Oliver, the police said they'd looked at all the known photographs of that night and hadn't found any with Melissa in, but she felt compelled to check herself. Her calls to a few of the people on her friends list hadn't borne fruit – three of them saying they hadn't seen Oliver or Melissa, two saying that they'd assumed Oliver was alone as he was so flirty. Louisa's face had burned with what she thought was anger, but then burned further with the embarrassment that it was actually jealousy. The thought of Oliver openly chatting up her friends – or non-friends – had annoyed her.

Then there was Tiff.

Not only had Oliver been all over her *that* night, but she knew he'd also been to her house doing God knows what. Although she'd only seen him there yesterday, that didn't mean that was his first visit.

It was certainly a hell of a way for a newly married man to behave – let alone one whose wife was missing. It just didn't add up. Louisa typed out a Facebook message to Tiff:

Need to speak to you urgently.

No kisses. No fluff. Hopefully that would get her attention and elicit a response.

Noah stirred, then Louisa heard the revving up he did just prior to crying. She left the laptop open and went to his nursery to fetch him. He'd slept on the bus home from town, so she couldn't complain – he'd given her a few hours of peace.

As she walked back into the lounge with Noah's cries piercing her ears, Louisa glanced at the laptop. At the photo she'd clicked on before going upstairs.

She squinted. Now, standing further away, she noticed that what she'd thought was dark background was in fact a person behind the three women who were 'dancing' in the forefront of the picture.

'Shhh, Noah,' she said, bouncing him in her arms while she stepped closer.

The figure, a woman in a below-the-knee black dress, was blurred – caught as she was walking. Louisa blinked repeatedly, as if that would help focus the photo. It didn't. But what she could see was the woman's tanned legs.

Black dress. Tanned legs.

Noah's cries intensified. 'Okay, okay, baby. Milk's coming.'

As quickly as she could, Louisa warmed a bottle of milk. Rushing back in to the lounge she sat at the table and shoved the teat in Noah's mouth to stop the high-pitched scream. With one leg crossed over the other, Louisa balanced Noah so she could feed him and still have one hand free. Now she knew there was one photo, she had to search for others – hopefully there'd be one that was in better focus. Maybe even one of Melissa with Oliver.

There were no other pictures that Louisa had been tagged in, but there were likely to be more on others' Facebook pages from people she hardly knew and who wouldn't, despite having gone to her party, have thought to include Louisa in the tagging process.

She started with the obvious friends.

Tiff had loads of photos – mostly of her and random men from the bar it seemed, but there were several of people sitting at the upstairs tables eating the buffet food. Louisa smiled – there was actually a good one of Brian holding Noah, with Emily by his side. They'd been caught without their knowledge, and it was a beautiful shot of them deep in conversation. Louisa clicked on it and selected 'download'. After flicking through the rest of Tiff's photos, she realised Melissa wasn't in any of them.

On to the next 'friend'. Deana, one of the women Louisa had met at an antenatal clinic who'd been further on in her pregnancy than her, had only posted five photos. Louisa scrolled quickly through them not expecting anything. Lurching forwards to get a closer look, Louisa knocked the bottle from Noah's mouth. Milk leaked onto her jeans.

'Dammit.'

She rubbed it in, then repositioned Noah so he could carry on drinking. Her attention went back to the screen.

To the woman in the black dress. She was in clear focus.

The full-length photograph showed the woman and Deana standing together, drinks in hand. Tanned legs. Gold-painted toenails. Just as Louisa remembered. But that wasn't what caused her pulse to race.

Straight, shoulder-length blonde hair.

Deana had tagged the woman, and the Facebook comment that went alongside it read:

Me and Jo – first time out since having our babies – don't we look awesome!

Louisa read it, and reread it. Then she clicked on Jo's name. It took her to Jo's Facebook page, and although it was set as private, she could see her profile picture. Her and her baby girl.

The woman she'd seen on the stairs arriving at the same time as Oliver had not been his wife. Louisa now felt sure Melissa hadn't been at the party at all.

Oliver was lying.

32

THE GIFT

The realisation that the woman Oliver had been with wasn't Melissa put Louisa on edge. It threw up so many questions, none of which she could begin to answer. On the plus side, she felt better about not having informed the police that she'd seen Melissa at her party, but every other aspect of this discovery was negative. Why did Oliver tell the police Melissa went missing from Louisa's party? And if Louisa hadn't seen her, why had she recognised the photo the police had shown at the appeal?

Louisa ran upstairs and rummaged in the drawer of the bed, taking out the photos of her, Oliver, and her college friends she'd found the other day. She'd never asked Oliver how old Melissa was, but there was a chance she might have been at college with them if she recognised her face. The fact Louisa had blocked so much of that time from her conscious memory could explain why she didn't know Melissa, but as she skimmed back through the photographs, her hope diminished. She searched through all twenty-four again. Nothing. None of the people in the photos looked similar to how Melissa looked now.

Or how she had looked. She could look very different now: dead.

Louisa shivered.

It struck Louisa now that Oliver might have carefully orchestrated this entire thing. The thought that he'd purposely led her to believe that Melissa's disappearance had occurred on her party night, and then coerced her into going to the police with him about it, telling her she owed him, was in the forefront of her mind. The fact he'd then told her what she'd done when she was eighteen – the big secret – now seemed disingenuous. Manipulative. Louisa could just be a pawn in Oliver's game, his plan to get away with murder.

Louisa took a pen, and, turning over a photo depicting just her and Oliver, wrote:

Don't trust Oliver.

She didn't know where to go from here. It was as though she were on a speeding merry-go-round, turning one way then suddenly reversing. Currently she felt sick, she was whizzing around backwards, unable to make sense of any of the information she had. If only she wasn't missing large chunks of memory.

She knew one thing, though: she should back off. And from now on she shouldn't let Oliver in when he turned up at her door. He'd soon have to move on; he'd get the message that Louisa couldn't help him anymore. Which was true. She couldn't. She'd done what he'd asked, gone to the police, supported him. Now it was all in the hands of the detectives.

But why didn't this thought give her comfort?

She had a strong suspicion Oliver Dunmore was not finished with her yet.

The Facebook message from Tiff was as abrupt as her text message had been.

186

Louisa narrowed her eyes and huffed. Clearly something was going on. Without thinking through other options, Louisa unfolded the pram, bundled Noah in it and then grabbed the baby-changing bag and her house keys.

She'd walk over to Tiff's and find out what was going on with her. If she turned up at her house, she'd be less inclined to brush her off. Although, that hadn't stopped her yesterday. This time though, Louisa wasn't going to go quietly.

The pram wedged itself on the top step of the doorway.

'For God's sake!' Louisa pushed it, but the wheels were jammed. Carefully swinging the top part of the pram around and going out backwards, she was able to bypass the obstruction.

A large box, now slightly crushed, sat half on, half off the step. She didn't have time to open it – she wanted to get to Tiff's before she buggered off. Louisa unlocked the front door again and picked up the box, noting it wasn't for her anyway – it was addressed to Brian – and placed it just inside the hall. She hadn't received a gift from Brian other than her nightmare party, so she wondered if the box contained a present for her actual birthday on Friday.

Louisa took the direct route to Tiff's, no detours today. Approaching the driveway cautiously, she tilted her head to see over the hedge. The gate was open. For a moment, she slumped, disappointed that she'd obviously missed her. But then she saw the Audi in the driveway. A mixed feeling of relief and nerves consumed her. Whatever was going on with Tiff, Louisa had to consider the very real possibility that she wasn't going to like it.

But then, the last two days hadn't brought anything she *had* liked, so why should this be any different?

Louisa glanced up the road to where she'd seen Oliver parked before. No car. *Good.* In a swift movement, she entered the driveway and then marched up to the front door. She took a breath, then rang the bell. She wasn't going to risk going around the back as she usually did, in fear that Tiff would take the opportunity to make a quick getaway. No, this time she wasn't going to accept a brush-off; she was going to make sure Tiff invited her in.

Louisa pressed herself up against the door, listening for any movement from within.

She hesitated. Tiff might know she was on the doorstep and be keeping quiet, waiting for Louisa to leave. She rang the bell again. The little light blinked to show it was working. Nothing. Louisa backed up, her head tilted upwards, so she could take in the upstairs windows. The curtains in Tiff's room were closed.

Louisa's jaw slackened, her body becoming rigid.

Tiff was up in her bedroom with someone.

Walking back to the pram, Louisa pushed it up, positioning it sideways in front of the door. Taking her mobile from the changing bag, Louisa called Tiff's number. When that went to answerphone, she called the landline. The answer machine kicked in there, too.

Struggling to keep her rising temper under control, Louisa walked around the side of the house.

A voice reached her ears.

Tiff was in the back garden. Louisa knew she couldn't be speaking on the phone because she'd just called both numbers and neither had been engaged. With her back flat to the wall, she crept further to the rear of the house.

'I've literally no idea. She's been acting very strangely since having Noah. She has taken baby brain to a whole new level. It's difficult to trust anything she says or does.' Tiff's laughter floated in the air, carried along on the breeze around the corner, delivering it to Louisa in the form of a punch to the stomach.

The realisation struck her suddenly: it was possible Tiff always spoke about Louisa in that way. She wouldn't know seeing as she didn't socialise with the same groups of people. With any people. Tears burned her eyes. She was back at school – the unpopular spotty teenager who everyone talked about rather than talked to – hiding in the toilet block at break times, listening to the sniggering popular girls as they talked shit about her. It wasn't something she expected to be experiencing at forty.

Louisa inched forwards but stopped short of the end of the wall. What if Tiff saw her now? She'd be caught sneaking, and she'd know Louisa had heard her bad-mouthing her. As much as that should make Tiff look bad, Louisa had the feeling she'd be the one who'd come off worse. It was an awkward, embarrassing situation that she'd rather avoid.

But she desperately wanted to know who Tiff was talking to.

Sod it, she should purposely stride around the back, the way she always went into Tiff's so it wouldn't look out of place. *I want to see the look on her face when she sees me. Wriggle out of that one, Tiffany.*

Before Louisa could take a step in that direction, a whiny, nasal cry erupted to her right. Shit. Noah. Taking a few side steps, then turning and dashing to the front of the house, Louisa snatched him quickly from his pram and cuddled him, muffling the cries in her shirt.

'Sshh-sshh,' she soothed. Holding him tightly in one arm, she dragged the pram away from Tiff's front door and pulled it behind her out of the driveway. She waited until she was out of earshot, then popped Noah back into his pram and began walking. Her mind went over what she'd just heard. She wondered who Tiff could've been talking to. There were the usual suspects: Oliver and Brian. But it could well have been anyone. Louisa may not even know them, or they her.

In the last two weeks, Louisa had gone from having a great best friend, to having a friend she suspected of having an affair with her husband, to then having a fling with her ex-boyfriend. Was she going mad? Louisa had to admit, even if only to herself, she had been chaotic lately. The issues surrounding no sleep – the hallucinations, the forgetfulness – were bad, but if she was now becoming paranoid too, well that would add a whole new level of worry. And if it *was* paranoia, Tiff saying that her baby brain had reached a new level wasn't necessarily wrong. It was hurtful – but actually, Tiff was right.

But that didn't explain why Tiff herself was acting strangely – *she* didn't have baby brain. Louisa continued to pore over these thoughts as she pushed the pram towards home on automatic pilot.

A dull headache filled her skull, and it wasn't until she stumbled through her own front door that she realised she hadn't eaten all day. Something else she was forgetting lately – she either seemed to miss meals without even realising, or was craving chocolate biscuits and stuffing her face with them at odd hours.

'Hi, Mum.' Emily rushed past her and up the stairs, her feet making hollow thuds on each tread. Louisa hadn't even opened her mouth in greeting before she heard the bang of her bedroom door closing. She shook her head. At least she wasn't giving her any attitude. Louisa looked to the wall clock as she walked into the kitchen. She frowned, and put her fingertips to her throbbing temples. Five-thirty. She hadn't realised she'd left it so late to visit Tiff. She was sure she'd left the house at three, latest. She couldn't have been over two hours.

Lifting the clock from its hook on the wall, Louisa checked

the battery. Then she took her mobile and checked that. The clock was right. She must've been mistaken. So that meant Brian should be home any minute too.

Her breathing shallowed. If she'd been at Tiff's later than she'd assumed, it really could have been Brian who Tiff had been talking to in the back garden.

No. His car wasn't there – she'd have seen it.

Don't go jumping to conclusions again.

As if on cue, the door opened and Brian came in, his face grey, drained.

'Hi, everyone! Where are my favourite girls?'

Louisa heard him, but didn't move. Was the timing just coincidental?

'You've got a parcel,' she called from her position leaning against the worktop.

'Ah-ha! It's here.'

Louisa heard the tearing of tape and the box being ripped open. It wasn't a present for her then otherwise he'd have taken it somewhere out of Louisa's sight before opening it. She strolled out to the hallway. He didn't shout to go away, not to look. It was clearly not for her.

'What is it?' she asked, trying to keep the annoyance from her tone.

Brian didn't answer; he was too busy pulling out the internal packaging material. Then he stood back and held it up. 'How cool is this?' He sounded like a child who'd been given a new toy.

'What on earth did you order that for?' Louisa screwed her face up at the small, helicopter-like contraption Brian was proudly holding.

'Oh, I didn't order it. I'd never have thought of getting one . . .'

'It had your name on the label – has there been a mix-up?'

'Nope. No mix-up. It's a gift.'

'Riiiight. From who, exactly?'

'From Oliver.' And Brian brushed past her and walked through the kitchen to the back door. His new, shiny plaything in his hands. Louisa could think of no reason Oliver would give Brian a bloody gift at all. Let alone this.

Louisa followed Brian outside.

Five minutes later, the dark grey metal construction was airborne.

The drone buzzed above Louisa's head.

'Don't fly that thing near me, Brian. Or near the neighbours' garden. They'll be furious; it'll set their bloody dogs off. What the hell is the point in having it? Why has Oliver given that to you?'

'Calm down, love.' Brian didn't look at her while he spoke, his tongue poking out through his lips in concentration as he navigated the flying machine. 'It was just something we got talking about when we were looking at the aerial photos of the village at the pub on Friday. I guess he wanted to thank me for being supportive, so got me one.'

'I guess my present is still in the post then.' She mumbled as she went back inside, leaving the man she was feeling less and less like she knew, playing with his new toy.

33

THE QUESTIONS

Wednesday a.m. – Day 12 post-party

The weirdness of the situation weighed heavily on Louisa's mind. Sitting in the nursery chair she watched Noah as he drained the bottle of milk, but her head was swimming with questions and, she realised, worry. Oliver coming back into her life after twenty-two years was confusing enough – but to have somehow become best buds with her husband was bewildering. The fact that Brian was a willing party to this was even more concerning. He'd already suggested, albeit when he was drunk, that he was jealous of Oliver – of his good looks, charisma, confidence – and the fact he'd told Brian that Louisa had been a sex fanatic, which had been something that had clearly got his back up. Why then was he allowing Oliver to be a part of their lives like this?

Oliver had something on Louisa – a shared past, their secret. That's how he'd wormed his way into *her* life. But Oliver couldn't have something on Brian – he'd never met him before the night of the party.

Apart from his obvious jealousy, Brian hadn't treated Oliver in a way that would suggest he'd felt manipulated into being his mate. Quite the opposite. It was almost like Brian had latched on to Oliver, wanting to be in with the popular crowd for once in his life.

Poor Brian. His life would fall apart if he knew the truth.

The church bell rang out twice.

Two a.m. And even if Noah now settled well, Louisa knew sleep would not come for her.

Tiff. Brian. Oliver. Melissa. The unknown woman she'd killed. All scrambling together in her head.

She stretched her legs out, arching her back. Noah opened his eyes wide.

'Just shifting position, baby, no need to panic,' she whispered. Noah's fingers curled around Louisa's hand, then his eyes fell shut again.

So trusting.

'When is that innate sense of trust lost?' Louisa asked aloud.

She was certainly struggling with the concept right now. She couldn't even trust herself. Having resisted the urge to text or message Oliver on Facebook, Louisa now knew she would have to see him again. Her earlier thought about backing off, not letting him in the house, had been premature. There were things she needed to know first – things only Oliver could tell her. If she got answers to her questions, *then* she could begin the cooling-off period. Then she would shut Oliver out of their lives entirely. He didn't belong there.

As Louisa let her head fall back, her own eyes closing, she mulled over the questions she wanted to ask Oliver:

Why was he at Tiff's?

Why couldn't she find any record of the missing woman she'd hit in the lanes?

Why had he come back after all this time?

Where was Melissa the night of the party?

Louisa let her thoughts drift. If it wasn't for the police involvement, she would be questioning whether Melissa

194

Dunmore even existed, or whether she was merely a figment of Oliver's imagination. Louisa wished she knew more: what the police had discovered, what Melissa's family were saying about her disappearance, where they thought she might be. She was obviously a real person, and Oliver must have evidence of their marriage, but there were aspects of this whole thing that didn't add up. Like it was all a carefully planned ruse.

But to what end?

Usually, she considered, the people who duped others into thinking they'd disappeared and died were those trying to defraud their life insurance policies – like the man who'd staged his death during a canoeing trip, and despite his body not being found, his wife successfully claimed on his life insurance. He'd later turned up at a police station claiming memory loss, but it went on to be proven that he and his wife had obtained the pay-out by deception and they had both been jailed.

Could *that* be Oliver's plan? Melissa was actually safe and well somewhere awaiting her share of the insurance money? Louisa's tired mind was running through ridiculous scenarios now, but they kept coming – she seemed powerless to stop them. But, in the end, none of them held water. Apart from one.

The one where Oliver had killed Melissa, disposed of her body – possibly in the same place he'd got rid of the other woman's – and then tried to give himself an alibi by being at Louisa's party.

'Hey, Mum.'

Louisa's eyes flew open and she jerked upright. 'Oh, Emily. What time is it?'

'Just after six, sorry to wake you, but you don't look comfortable and Noah's slipping off your lap.'

She was astounded how she'd fallen asleep like that. Louisa

watched, her eyes cloudy and unfocused, as Emily took Noah from her.

'Sorry. Had been awake for hours, must've just drifted off.'

'Go and get a coffee. I'll play with Noah for a bit.' Emily sank to her knees and placed Noah under the baby gym on his playmat and began swiping at the brightly coloured hanging animals and mirrors, encouraging Noah to copy her. Noah's throaty giggle made Louisa smile. It was lovely to see her two children together. She hoped Emily wouldn't come to resent her baby brother – for the distraction, the attention he had inevitably taken from her. Not having siblings herself, she had no idea how it felt to no longer be the sole focus for her parents. At any age that must be hard, let alone when you were a teenager with hormones raging through your body. The age gap wasn't merely an issue for Louisa and Brian; it was for Emily too. And no doubt, as he grew up, it would be a problem for Noah as well, being the annoying younger brother whose sister would suddenly tire of him.

Thinking about her mum and dad, Louisa realised she'd had zero contact with them for over two weeks. Not even a hysterical call from her mum to tell her that her dad had mistakenly pressed the wrong button on the TV remote and made the entire thing go blank. That was his favourite thing to do – and Louisa's least favourite problem to sort. But nothing, no word from them.

Although their relationship had never fully recovered from the argument they'd had, Louisa would still frequently be called upon for help. The fact she hadn't heard anything meant they'd either been fine, or had asked their neighbours to assist them instead. If something serious had happened, one of the neighbours would've phoned her. Clearly, she just hadn't been needed; her services not required. Her dad may have finally got used to the buttons, or, as was more likely, her mum had confiscated the controls from him. Louisa would give them a ring in a while anyway. It would be a waste of time, but her guilty conscience demanded it.

As she got to the bottom of the stairs the smell of bacon wafted towards her, making her mouth water. Immediately her mind flashed back to Oliver, in her kitchen, cooking her and Emily breakfast. Louisa crept in, half afraid of finding him standing at the grill, apron on, grinning as he cooked. She let out her held breath as she set eyes on Brian.

'What's this in aid of?' she asked.

'Morning, oh gorgeous one, love of my life!' He smiled broadly and, brandishing silver tongs, gave a small dance as she entered. 'Just thought you deserved some breakfast in bed, or in the nursery at least, which is where you spent the night I assume.'

'Yeah, not a great night's sleep.' Louisa slid onto the stool at the breakfast bar and held her head in her cupped hands. 'But I'm not complaining about being cooked breakfast. This is a first. Have I missed our anniversary?'

'Cheeky.' Brian dangled the bacon up and away from the grill, fat globules dripping on the floor. Louisa closed her eyes, fearing words of criticism would fall out of her mouth if she continued to watch him. He was at least making an effort, which was more than she could say about herself. When she opened them again, Brian was directly in front of her, a solemn look on his face.

'What is it?'

'Nothing.' He placed the sandwich on the breakfast bar and turned back to the grill to get his own.

Louisa rubbed her hands over her face. Did she look terrible? Is that why he'd stared at her in that way?

'Do you have something you want to tell me, Brian?' It came to her, like a lightning strike. This moment, him making her breakfast, meant he was trying to make up for something. He had a guilty conscience – and that's why when he looked her in the eye his expression had altered, become serious. He couldn't hide it from her.

Oh God, what have you done?

Louisa's heart drummed against her ribs as Brian turned back to her and sighed.

'I'm really sorry.' His eyes slid away from hers.

This was it. What she had been dreading. Her paranoid thoughts about him and Tiff were not paranoid at all. They were founded.

'Is this about being with Tiff?' The words shook, her anxiety exposed.

'I have been spending some time with her, yes. Not in, you know, that way. She's just, well – different to you . . . She hasn't got any other things to worry about, so she can listen to me.'

The urge to butt in, to counter his words immediately, burned in her throat. But she held her tongue because there was little point in denying what he was saying. Yet. She had to allow him to continue, explain himself without her interrupting him. Let him get it all out before she prematurely exploded with anger. She raised her eyebrows: a sign for him to continue.

'She's been so supportive, you know that. I – we, couldn't have got through without her over the past few months. Don't you agree?'

Louisa, her lips tightly pursed, nodded slowly. She couldn't trust herself to open her mouth without spilling venomous comments. Brian's head dipped as he paced the small area between the kitchen sink and oven – one hand to his mouth, biting his thumb.

She stared at him. Waiting for the next instalment. This tactic was making him sweat, small beads of moisture appearing on his brow and nose. He pushed his glasses back up and chanced a glance in her direction.

'Nothing has happened between us, it never would. But I like being around her – she makes me feel, I don't know – better, somehow. Her bubbliness is contagious, isn't it?'

Finally, Louisa could take no more. 'What exactly are you telling me this for?'

'Because, well, although I like being around her, it feels wrong. Like I'm cheating on you.'

Louisa snorted. 'Have you had sex with her?'

'God, no!'

'Then why does it feel like cheating?'

'Because of the things we talk about, I guess. And you were so upset when you thought we'd both conspired against you taking Noah to the clinic to be weighed . . .'

'Yes, that hurt. It felt underhanded.'

'I'm so sorry. Tiff thinks the world of you, you know that. And obviously I do. We wanted to do the best thing.'

'Okay, well what's done is done. But this doesn't feel like you've told me the full story, Brian. You wouldn't be feeling this guilty about talking to Tiff. You never have been before. What else is there?'

'Nothing. There's nothing more.'

But, despite the fact Brian was looking her directly in the eye, Louisa did not believe those words.

34

THE MISTAKE

Wednesday p.m.

Following Brian's strange confessional at breakfast, Louisa stabbed out a text message to Tiff – one *demanding* her attention this time.

> **Either you come over here, or I'm coming to you in the next 30 mins. I'm not taking no for an answer.**

She had to confront the burning issues head-on, face-to-face. Whatever was going on with her and Brian, her and Oliver, their friendship – she had to know. Her phone pinged almost immediately.

> **On my way.**

Louisa lay the mobile down on the coffee table. Clearly, she should've tried that approach before, though Tiff's prompt response was more likely the result of Brian pre-warning her than Louisa's 'threat' itself. She could almost hear Brian's voice stating: *'Louisa's on the warpath, Tiff. Watch out,'* or something similar. She huffed and sank back into the leather sofa, waiting to hear the distinct roar of Tiff's car engine.

Less than five minutes later, the Audi's deep grumble came closer and halted outside the house. Louisa watched Tiff emerge from the car. Given she must've left in a rush, Tiff looked like she'd just stepped out from a salon – not a hair out of place, the long blonde strands neatly twizzled around in a loose, elegant bun. Leopard-print shoes and matching handbag completed Tiff's modelesque appearance.

Louisa had to suppress a pang of jealousy. She'd let herself go. Maybe that was one of the reasons Tiff was garnering so much attention from Brian and Oliver.

'What's the urgency, Lou? Someone died?' Tiff air-kissed her as she swept in through the front door.

'Not yet,' Lou said tersely as she closed the door. She took a moment to compose herself before following Tiff into the kitchen.

'No water?' Tiff said, bending down in front of the fridge.

'Garage.'

Tiff threw Louisa a blank look.

'The bottled water. It's in the garage,' Louisa said without moving. Tiff, finally realising she was going to have to fetch it herself, disappeared through the utility door. Louisa heard the fluorescent strip light in the garage pop several times before it illuminated, followed by Tiff's excited voice.

'Oh, wow, Lou! You never told me you had a *drone.*' Tiff reappeared in the kitchen, minus the bottled water, but with Brian's new plaything in her arms.

'It's new.' Louisa really couldn't muster the energy to explain further. All she wanted was to get to the point of why she'd asked Tiff over: to talk about Brian and Oliver, and find out what the hell was going on.

'Can I borrow it? Brian wouldn't mind.' Tiff fluttered her

eyelashes, and despite it being in a jokey way, Louisa flinched. Was that all she'd had to do with Brian? She turned her face away from Tiff, not able to look her in the eye. A knot of tension was forming in her stomach. One that would only increase in size unless she started asking Tiff the questions that were plaguing her. It seemed though, that first she'd have to get the flying thing off Tiff's agenda now she'd seen it.

'What would you want with that thing?'

'It'll be *perfect* for the church event! They're opening the tower tomorrow for villagers to climb up and see the view. Sarah is also involved—' Tiff rolled her eyes dramatically '—much to my annoyance. Reverend Forsey apparently asked her – but having this would be the best one-upwomanship ever!'

'How so?' Louisa was intrigued now, in spite of her underlying need to change the subject.

'Well . . .' Tiff held the drone up as she spoke, zooming it around like a child would a toy aeroplane. 'Don't you think it would be great if it recorded each person being at the top of the tower, while doing a three-sixty shot around the church? It would look awesome. *And* be a great permanent record of the celebrations. Does it take still shots as well as video?' Tiff twisted it around, concentration etched on her face.

Louisa shrugged. 'Yes, I guess so. And it's a better use for it than what Brian's likely to find.' Although it wasn't hers to lend, after that morning's conversation she assumed Brian would be fine with Tiff using it for one day. 'Do you know how to use it properly though?'

'Can't be that hard. It's got instructions, and I can read you know. I'm also a fantastic driver, so should be simples.' She smiled. 'Right. Water.' Tiff placed the drone on the worktop and went back into the garage. Louisa took some steadying breaths.

As soon as Tiff came back with the water, plus the box for the drone, Louisa dived in with her question.

'Why was Oliver at yours on Monday?'

Tiff's face blanched. She turned her back on Louisa, filling the kettle with the water from the bottle. She was buying time, Louisa assumed.

'It was nothing really, Lou,' she said, still facing away.

'If it was nothing, why did you push me away – telling me you were too busy?'

She gave a nervous giggle. 'I *was* busy. He popped in not long after you texted me, and I told him the same as I told you. But he was there, then, so I said I could give him five minutes.'

'What did he want? How did he know where you lived? Why cover up the fact he was with you when I turned up?' Louisa had so many questions they were almost tripping over themselves on her tongue.

'Hold on, hold on. There's no rush now, is there?' Tiff busied herself with pulling two mugs from the cupboard, then rummaging around for the coffee jar and a spoon.

'Stop stalling, and tell me what the hell is going on, will you?' Louisa strode across to Tiff, snatching the jar and spoon from her and quickly making the coffees to stop Tiff dragging it out any longer.

Tiff stood back, a look of shock on her face. 'I'm not stalling, Lou,' she said, indignation oozing from her tone.

'It seems that way to me. So, carry on. Tell me, why did Oliver show up at your house?'

'Just to talk, he said. He'd been out walking on the common, early, as he hasn't been able to sleep since Melissa went missing. He saw and recognised my car in the driveway as he passed by.'

'You don't think that's a bit stalkerish?'

'He's *your* friend—'

'No, Tiff. He's some guy I used to know a lifetime ago when I was at college.'

Some guy who covered up the terrible thing I did.

'Well, a lifetime ago or not, he seems to really want to help you.'

'Help me? What do you mean?'

'You know, help you with your lost memories.' Tiff took a sip of her coffee, but her eyes remained trained on Louisa's.

She'd never told Tiff about her dissociative amnesia. Not even hinted that she'd experienced a traumatic event during her college years. The fact Oliver had been talking about that with Tiff worried Louisa, and her mind raced as she jumped to conclusions about what else he might have disclosed.

'Has Brian been visiting you, too? Spilling his guts about how he's trying to help me as well? You really are the popular one, aren't you?' Louisa's neck burned, the heat creeping upwards like a plant seeking sunlight.

'Lou, don't.' Tiff shook her head gently.

'Why? Because you don't want people thinking the same about you as you do about Sarah?'

The words were out before she had thought through their implication.

'It was a mistake coming here.' Tiff tipped the contents of her mug down the sink and banged the mug down on the drainer. She grabbed her handbag and slung it over her shoulder. 'Perhaps we can talk again when you've come to your senses, Lou.'

'Don't be so *patronising*,' Louisa hissed.

'I'm just trying to be your friend. Lord knows you could do with one by all accounts.' She headed for the front door.

'Don't forget your fucking drone,' she shouted after her. 'It's important you look good in front of everyone.' Louisa folded her arms firmly across her chest.

Tiff turned back, her mouth in a tight line, air forcing its way through her nostrils.

'Thanks.' She lifted the drone and placed it back in its box, then carried it out the front door leaving Louisa, hot tears tracing down her cheeks, standing alone.

Regretting her words.

Regretting that she'd allowed her only friend to walk out the door without even confiding in her the real reason for her behaviour.

35

THE UPDATE

Friday a.m. – Day 14 post-party

Oliver stood on the top step, one arm reaching up, his hand pressed against the wall, the other hand brandishing a pink envelope. Louisa purposely kept him there. She didn't want him to assume he could just waltz right in like he belonged in her home.

'What do you want, Oliver?'

He frowned, then brought his arm down by his side. His posture appeared stiff, almost rigid. 'Wanted to wish you a happy birthday.' He smiled. 'Any chance you fancy a cuppa?' He lowered his head to make eye contact with Louisa.

'I was about to go out, actually. I need to see Tiff.' She watched for a reaction. His face didn't alter, but he was quiet for a moment, as if figuring out what to say.

'I wouldn't bother with Tiff.'

'Why do you say that?' She narrowed her eyes. Had she told him about their argument?

'I mean, there's no point going over there. I've just come from that way – her car's not in the drive.'

'Oh. Of *course*.' She tutted, her top lip curling in disgust. He'd probably been in her house again, doing whatever, talking about her, no doubt. She'd thought the unknown person in Tiff's back garden on Tuesday was Brian, but it could equally have been Oliver. Him and Tiff both slating her. That'd be about right. 'You two have become quite pally, haven't you?'

'Is that a hint of jealousy I hear, Lou-Lou?' he said, a smirk playing on his lips.

'No. Not at all. It's actually just bloody annoying.' Oliver looked taken aback, his ego clearly dented, but she carried on. 'Aren't you the slightest bit worried about your wife? Or have you moved on already?' Louisa bit her bottom lip – she hadn't meant to go that far. Now, seeing his face lose its colour, she wasn't sure if she'd made him angry, or whether he was merely upset by her harsh comment.

'Wow, Lou. That was cutting,' he said, his voice quiet, velvety. 'I'm going to put it down to the fact you're tired and you aren't feeling quite yourself after, well, you know. I don't think you really want to hurt me.'

He didn't take his eyes off hers. A prickly sensation crawled under her skin. She suddenly felt exposed and wanted to get back inside her house, close the door on Oliver.

'I just don't understand you, Oliver. I don't get why you're hanging around at Tiff's. I saw you and she said you'd been over there. Some crap about wanting to help me remember? I mean—' she snorted '—what's that all about? Why are you talking about me with her?'

'Calm down, Lou-Lou.' He took a step closer to her. 'I think you've got your wires crossed. Are you sure that's what Tiff told you? Because I'm wondering if you've misinterpreted—'

'No. There's been no misinterpretation. She was here on Wednesday and she told me that part at least. God knows what she *isn't* telling me.'

'But you have been mixing things up recently. I'm not saying that's the case here, but please think about it carefully first.

You don't want to be throwing accusations around now do you?'

It may be too late for that.

'I saw you, coming out from Tiff's house. I'm not throwing accusations about without having evidence, and I'm not mixing anything up. I saw what I saw, heard what I heard.'

'Oh, Lou. This is why we're all so worried for you, don't you see? Brian confided in me that you were suffering from hallucinations, strange visions that meant you were unsure of what was real and what was a dream. You have to accept this could be happening now, with all this nonsense about Tiff.' Oliver put a hand on her shoulder and gave it a squeeze. 'I feel responsible, in part at least – me telling you about the woman; well, that must've tipped you over the edge. I'm so sorry.' He smiled, and Louisa had an uncontrollable urge to slap his face. She clasped her hands together, taking a huge, ragged breath.

She knew what she'd seen and heard. It *had* been real. Tiff had been in her kitchen, had told her about Oliver visiting her and then she'd taken the drone. Had they talked about Brian and Oliver? She shook her head. Yes, yes – of course they had. She mustn't let Oliver put doubt in her mind. They had that conversation, they'd had that argument and Louisa had said things she regretted.

If only it weren't real, if only it had been a hallucination. But it wasn't.

'Let's stick to the here and now then, shall we? Come in.' She stepped aside to allow Oliver to pass her. She slipped her phone out of her jeans pocket and tapped the voice recorder icon before pocketing it again. This was one conversation she wanted to know for sure wouldn't be questioned later down the line.

'Here's your coffee,' Louisa said, handing Oliver the mug. She then sat at the wooden table in the seat opposite him. She repositioned herself so that her right side was closest to him, so her phone could pick up his voice clearly.

'Thank you. Here's your card,' he said, sliding the envelope across the table. She thanked him without taking it, leaving it unopened in the middle.

Oliver sighed. 'Right, let's start again, shall we? I hate feeling there's animosity, any mistrust, between us, Lou-Lou.'

'Me too.' She smiled. 'First though, I should apologise for being snappy with you and saying that about Melissa.'

Oliver flicked his hand in the air, brushing away her apology. 'No need. It's a really stressful time for both of us, bound to hit snags.'

'Yes, well. Have the police been in contact?'

'Only to say they've followed up all the information they'd received, which wasn't a lot anyway, and now they've hit another wall. No new leads, Lou.' He hung his head. 'It's only a matter of time isn't it, before they give up totally?'

'I think you should stay hopeful. Unless there's any reason you know of that you shouldn't.'

'What do you mean?'

'Well, you mentioned an argument, Oliver. You said it yourself – you've lied for a very long time about the . . . other thing . . . You're good at lying. Are you sure you're telling me everything about Melissa's disappearance?' She had to broach the topic, had to know why he'd have lied about Melissa being at the fortieth party now she knew it wasn't the case.

'Are you suggesting I had something to do with it?'

'Did you?'

'I'm not going to dignify that with an answer.'

'Says every guilty person ever.'

'What is *wrong* with you, Lou? I've never laid a finger on Melissa, never would. Yes, we had an argument; I told you that the very first day I came here – I never tried to hide that fact.

It was about you, like I said. But then she stormed off, away from me. Possibly away from the party, but no one seems to have witnessed that, so who knows where the hell she went and with who.'

'No one witnessed it because not a single person saw her, Oliver. Are you sure it's not you who's hallucinating?'

'Very funny. None of the guests knew her, did they, so all I can assume is they didn't take any notice of her and that's why they now can't recall seeing her.'

'Seems implausible to me.'

'So does killing a woman and then forgetting you've done it.'

Louisa's pulse jumped. He had a point. She fell silent.

'Stalemate,' he said.

Louisa pressed her hand to the mobile phone in her pocket. The recording would have to be deleted. She'd gained nothing apart from now having incriminating evidence against herself on there.

'What are you going to do now? Go back to York?'

'No. I thought I'd hang around for a while – I still have the business project to set up. And besides that, I can't face the thought of travelling back without Melissa. I need to be where she was last seen. She may come back to our rented flat. I would hate it if she returned to an empty place. She'd think I gave up on her.'

'I suppose. But, Oliver?'

'Yes?'

'I don't want you coming here again. I think it's best if we cut ties.'

'Really?' His voice rose an octave, panic fleeting across his face. 'But I need you, Lou-Lou. And Brian has been such a rock. Please don't take everything from me.'

'I haven't taken *anything* from you. Anyway – Tiff can be

211

your rock. That's a better option for you than me and Brian. You need to let us be. It's not right – your friendship with my husband, it's weird.' Louisa rose, making her way to the front door.

'But you are taking everything then. You took my heart a long time ago; now you're taking away my lifelines.'

'No, Oliver. You took mine. And all you've given me since you've been back is grief. I can't bear the thought of seeing you all the time. You're a reminder of what I did. What you did to cover it all up. I can't live with that on my conscience.'

'We'll see,' Oliver said. He got up from the table and left the house without a backward glance.

36

THE DRONE

Friday p.m.

She owed Tiff an apology. And the truth. She'd left it yesterday, deciding it would be best to let things cool down – she knew Tiff would be busy and preoccupied with the church event anyway. Today though, Louisa had to pay her a visit – explain why she'd been so stabby on Wednesday. After her awkward chat with Oliver this morning she needed to see her friend – to set things straight.

Louisa had run through it all in her mind. From the moment just over two weeks ago that she'd found the text message from Tiff on Brian's phone, she'd allowed her thoughts to go into overdrive. Conjuring all sorts from nothing, like a magician pulling rabbits from an empty hat. It was possible she was also doing the same with Oliver: blowing something up out of nothing. Oliver was right: she had received a shock, one that had rocked her very foundation. The fallout from that might be why she was now over-reacting to everything. Seeing things that weren't there.

The last two weeks *had* been hell. Today, her actual birthday, could go by without celebration as far as she was concerned. The card from Oliver was torn in half and placed in the bin, despite it having been the only evidence it was her birthday. She'd not even had a 'Happy Birthday' greeting from Brian when she'd awoken that morning. It didn't matter though; Louisa just wanted to forget all about it. She'd had the fuss, the cards, presents – the party – so there was no reason to mark the occasion now anyway. And if she was honest, hitting forty – which she'd been dreading already – had been the catalyst for everything bad that had happened since.

She wished she'd stayed thirty-nine. Wished Brian had never even considered throwing her a surprise party. Most of all, she wished Tiff hadn't hacked into her Facebook account and wreaked havoc. While she did regret her behaviour on Wednesday, she couldn't let her off the hook. In the end, this was all Tiff's fault.

She wasn't the one who killed someone, though, was she?

If *she* hadn't done *that*, then none of this would be happening now.

The fault was her own.

Louisa tapped out a long message.

Louisa had forced down a salad sandwich while feeding Noah. There'd been no response from Tiff since she sent the text two hours ago, which was hardly surprising given the way they'd left things. It would need more than a text to get their friendship back on track; it would have to be a face-to-face conversation. Louisa did want to apologise. She felt terrible about her accusations, but she also wanted to know the truth. She had to find out why Oliver had been visiting Tiff, because she was sure it was more than just friendly concern for her, and despite his assertion it was all in Louisa's mind – another hallucination – she knew it hadn't been.

And she wanted to know more about Brian's friendship with her. If it was more than that, an affair, or even the thought of one, Louisa needed to know. Straight from the horse's mouth. Oliver had said her car wasn't in her driveway so she could still be out and about, but he might well have been trying to put her off because *he* was going to Tiff's house himself and didn't want to be caught again. The thought made her cheeks burn.

'Come on, Noah – let's get some fresh air.' Louisa scooped him up out of his bouncy chair and smiled at how his face lit up and his little legs pumped in excitement. He was getting fuller in the face, its shape changing daily. A flood of affection filled her. Despite everything – the sleepless nights and hallucinations, the terrible forgetfulness – the fear of going through all the stages again – Louisa was glad she had him. In a funny way, he was actually helping her to keep her shit together now.

As Louisa drew close to the church, she wondered how the event had gone. She hadn't been up the church tower since she was a child, when her father had climbed the steep, spiral steps with her, behind her every step of the way, encouraging her with a gentle push when she slowed. She'd been afraid that when she reached the highest point, a strong gust of wind would push her from the top, sending her hurtling to the ground, her small body splattering on the concrete. She'd seen danger in everything. A trait she seemed to lose during her teenage years.

Louisa had to admit, Tiff's idea about using the drone was actually really good. She hadn't told Brian about it in the end – no doubt he'd see the footage of the church event posted somewhere like Facebook, and go mad at her for lending it out without his permission. He hadn't even used it properly yet – he'd be pissed off that someone had played with it first. She hoped Tiff hadn't crashed it.

Louisa was surprised to see Tiff's car was in the drive – she must've popped out earlier when Oliver had driven past. Louisa swung the pram through the open gate and proceeded around the back. She hesitated at the patio door, her clenched fist about to knock on the glass. She couldn't bear to get the brush-off again, couldn't cope with the questions that would throw up. The paranoia – as Oliver would put it – that would ensue. If someone else was in there with Tiff, she wasn't sure how she'd handle the situation. Barge past, rush inside and see for herself who her visitor was? Or leave with her tail between her legs, annoyed and upset by what she'd see as another snub?

She leant her forehead against the cold glass. She had to make a decision. Knock – or walk away.

She knocked.

With her breath held, Louisa waited. There was no movement. She hammered on the door again, her knuckles smarting from the force. She stood, rubbing them, watching for Tiff to come to the door.

Damn her. Louisa knew she was in there, hiding, waiting for her to leave. Perhaps she wanted to avoid further confrontation or, as was the case last time, someone could be in there with her and she didn't want Louisa to see who. Anger surged through her veins, a dark veil cascading down over her eyes.

Louisa stomped down the decking steps and, turning back to the house, looked up at the top windows. No sign of anyone watching her. She took her mobile and rang Tiff's. Straight to voicemail. She'd obviously turned it off – which proved Louisa's theory: Tiff knew she was here, outside her house, and was avoiding her.

As she took another step backwards, a sharp pain shot through her calf and she tripped, losing her balance, but with arms flailing, managed to keep herself from falling to the floor. 'Shit.' She rubbed her hand over the area on her calf that had struck the object. Louisa's mouth slackened as she realised what she'd walked into. *Bloody hell.* Tiff *had* crashed the drone. It lay, partly concealed by a circle of shrubs in the middle of the garden. How irresponsible to borrow something then not look after it.

Louisa pulled it from its resting place, brushing off loose soil, and walked back up the steps. After placing it on the patio table, she banged on the door once again. She'd trusted Tiff with Brian's new gadget and now it looked as though it had done a round with a plane. He really was going to be mad at her for giving it to Tiff, however much he liked her friend.

'Tiff! Tiffany! Open the door, I need to talk to you.' She banged on the glass again. 'I know you're in there.' Perhaps the damaged drone was the reason she didn't want to answer the door. A sudden ringing in her ears, high-pitched – almost a screech – made her lower her hands and cover her ears. A dizzy sensation washed over her. She turned and leant her back against the patio doors, her breaths coming in short bursts. Was she having a panic attack?

It took a few moments to regain control over her breathing; she felt tired, drained, as if she'd had a migraine and was now suffering the after effects: the heavy feeling, the foggy head, the inability to focus. She would have to give up, go home. Rest. She gave one more look in through the glass doors before taking the drone, propping it awkwardly on the top of Noah's pram, and leaving. She had to get it home, hide it in the garage before Brian came back. She couldn't face the fallout today, too much else had stressed her out.

She'd deal with Tiff tomorrow.

37

THE DISCOVERY

The battered drone, the way Tiff had avoided her, the visits from Oliver – it all rattled around in Louisa's mind every waking moment, like bees buzzing around the queen, haphazardly and noisily. As soon as Noah had finished his morning bottle, Louisa bundled him in his pram and she left to walk to Tiff's. She'd decided to stage a 'sit-in' – literally park herself and Noah on Tiff's driveway until she had no choice but to see her. She'd refrained from sharing this plan with Brian or Emily, leaving them to have their Saturday lie-in. Hopefully they would sleep for hours yet and then when they woke, they'd find her note telling them she was out on a 'long walk' to settle Noah and they'd be oblivious to her using the baby as a co-conspirator.

Even more hopefully, Brian wouldn't decide that this was the weekend he'd like to try out his drone. Louisa still hadn't been brave enough to see if it worked after its apparent accident, instead, shoving it in a box and hiding it behind the old dressing table in the garage. She'd check out the damage after the weekend, but thought it highly likely she'd have to go onto Amazon and buy a replacement.

She packed up Noah's changing bag and popped in a few drinks for herself. As mad as it seemed, she felt sitting it out was the only way she'd gain answers *and* have the opportunity to apologise for her erratic and neurotic behaviour if the need for that arose.

She strolled through the open gate at Tiff's house and stopped in front of the Audi, pushing the pram brake down with her foot.

'Sorry, Noah – but you'll be safe, baby. She's not going to drive off with you in her way.' She tucked the mint-green knitted blanket, the only thing her mum had given him when he was born, around his body, and headed for the front door. Louisa hoped that Tiff might think it was a delivery at the door, this early on a Saturday, and open up willingly. Louisa kept her finger on the bell, the insistent noise echoing inside the house.

Nothing.

Surely Tiff couldn't have seen her coming into the driveway. *For God's sake, this is ridiculous.*

Stretching her neck up to see over the Audi, Louisa checked Noah's pram was still in situ, then proceeded down the path at the side of the house. Like yesterday, there was no sign of movement when Louisa looked through the patio door. She whacked both her palms against the glass, sending a stinging sensation across her hands and pain shooting up her wrists. The glass wobbled in response, sending light rippling across the surface. No movement came from inside.

She gave her hands a quick rub, then banged against it again.

The door shifted. Louisa saw a gap appear. *Yes.* She slowly and quietly slid it open then stepped inside. She thought about shouting out but decided not to announce the fact she'd managed to gain entry uninvited. Pausing at the threshold to the kitchen, Louisa held her breath and strained to hear noises.

Tiff may well still be in bed – it was relatively early, and it wasn't like she had children to wake her, or get up for. At least she knew it wouldn't be Brian lying next to her as he was snoring loudly in their bed. But would Oliver be there, curled up beside Tiff?

Louisa slipped her shoes off, then padded into the kitchen, the icy-cold tiles taking her breath away.

As she was about to take another breath, that too was stolen from her lungs.

Louisa's hand flew to her mouth, stifling the scream that threatened.

Red.

The white tiles were red.

Blonde hair, spreading outwards, tipped with red.

Blood.

Tiff's face, drained of colour, stared unseeing up at the ceiling, her unblemished porcelain skin almost shimmering under the light coming in from the Velux window above her.

The tile grout was stained red, the course of the spilled blood tracking in squares across the kitchen floor.

The scream found its way through Louisa's fingers.

Followed by vomit.

She'd backed up, banging her shoulder against the doorframe leading out to the patio doors, but collapsed before she reached them. Her legs had lost their feeling and could no longer hold the rest of her body upright. Now she leant unsteadily against the wall adjacent to the back door – the kitchen no longer in her eyeline – gasping, heaving. Sobs intermittently broke through the breaths; tears stung her eyes.

She hadn't checked for a pulse. Should she have checked? She hadn't wanted to go that close, but the reason for that – Tiff's wide, staring eyes – also justified the fact that resuscitation would've been futile. It was blatantly obvious all life had left Tiff's body.

Shit, shit, shit. She's dead. Tiff's dead. How?

God. The realisation that Tiff might've been lying on the kitchen floor bleeding out when she'd been there yesterday hit her. No wonder her knocking, the ringing of the doorbell, went unanswered.

Tiff hadn't been ignoring her.

She'd been dying.

Louisa's mouth widened, a high-pitched wailing emitting from it. She'd been right outside when her best friend had needed her most, and what had she been thinking? That Tiff was inside, ignoring her, or hiding Oliver. If she'd pushed the patio door open yesterday, Tiff might still have been alive.

She could've saved her life.

Another wave of nausea crashed over her and she retched. More bile forced its way into her mouth. She swallowed, again and again, her throat burning with more ferocity each time. She needed water.

Pulling her legs up with both arms, Louisa forced them into a kneeling position, then attempted to stand. Her whole body shook, her legs like rubber – bending and wobbling, threatening to give out again. With her hands on the walls to keep herself steady, Louisa took small steps and shuffled back towards the kitchen. Now she was over the initial shock of seeing her friend on the floor, blood oozing from her head, Louisa took a closer look at her surroundings. A thick smearing of blood was visible along the rolled edge of the granite worktop, which covered the centre island, the feature Tiff had wanted most when she'd had her kitchen redesigned. A one-litre plastic bottle lay on its side, the lid off, and the water that had evidently spilled over the edge had mixed with, and diluted, the blood, making an obscene pinky puddle to the side of Tiff's head.

Louisa tried to take it all in; figure out what had happened. It looked as though Tiff might have slipped on the wet tiles, fallen and banged her head. How tragic something so trivial could end a life. Water. Something essential in keeping us alive. Louisa pressed her fingertips to her eyes to prevent more tears escaping. It seemed Tiff's obsession with only drinking bottled water because she was afraid of getting cancer from tap water had ultimately been the reason she'd died. If the situation wasn't so dreadful, Louisa might have laughed at the irony.

With her legs still shaking, Louisa walked to the sink and ran the tap. Bending over she put her mouth to the running water and gulped a few mouthfuls to dilute the bitter taste of bile and to lubricate her dried throat. With her hands on the side of the sink steadying her, she took some long, slow breaths. An icy sensation swept over her skin as she stared out of the kitchen window, knowing Tiff's lifeless body lay behind her.

What had made her drop the bottle? Why didn't she just step around the water?

Oliver's face popped into her mind – his words from earlier in the day reverberating in her head:

'*I wouldn't bother with Tiff.*'

He'd been adamant that Tiff was out, that she'd be wasting her time going over there. Because her car wasn't in the drive.

But it must've been.

Louisa shook her head, trying to rid the thought that he somehow knew about this. It was just an accident – an awful, stupid accident. Oliver couldn't be involved.

But the niggle at the back of her mind didn't fully agree.

Without looking at Tiff again, Louisa skirted around the side of the kitchen and walked out of the house.

Noah.

She'd left her poor baby parked in front of Tiff's car. What kind of mother was she?

223

He gurgled happily as she poked her head around the pram. She ran a finger across his cheek and forced herself to smile. This wasn't how the sit-in was meant to end.

Louisa let out a long sigh, then took her mobile from the changing bag and with trembling fingers dialled 999.

38

THE AFTERSHOCK

'Are you going to be all right getting home from here?'

Louisa lifted her head to see who was speaking. The paramedic, a stocky woman who looked to be in her mid-thirties, with the bluest eyes she'd ever seen, was bending over her offering a lopsided, sympathetic smile.

Louisa hesitated, not because she wasn't sure if she was all right, but because she couldn't process the words she needed to use; they failed to form on her lips. She stuttered random noises instead, drawing a frown from the woman.

'You need to get checked out – you've had a terrible shock. Have you any history of heart problems, or any other medical issues?'

Louisa silently shook her head and watched in a dazed bubble as the paramedic jumped inside the ambulance and came out with a small black bag.

'I'm going to take your blood pressure,' she said as she pushed Louisa's sleeve up and began folding the blood pressure cuff around her upper arm. Louisa stared back at Tiff's house. The perfect show home now cordoned off, with numerous police officers coming and going.

'How? Why?' The two words somehow squeezed themselves from Louisa's mouth as she continued to watch the unfolding scene – wondering how she'd got caught up in this surreal moment.

The paramedic let the air expel from the cuff, removed the stethoscope from her ears and gave Louisa's arm a rub.

'Accidents in the home, particularly in the kitchen and bathroom, are among the top reasons we're called out,' she said. 'It's tragic when the result is a fatality. There's nothing you could've done, love. Such a severe bang to the head, I don't think there'd have been any coming back from that. I'm so sorry.'

Louisa tore her eyes from the house and looked up at the paramedic. She was just being kind, doing her job. Did she really think there was nothing Louisa could've done, even if she'd realised the previous day and been able to call the ambulance straight away?

Because the feeling in her gut was telling her it *was* likely that Tiff had been lying on the kitchen floor for over twenty-four hours.

'If you're so sure it was an accident, why are all these police here?' The amount of police presence seemed incongruent for the situation.

'It's procedure, love. A sudden death, like this one, has to be investigated and the police do have to consider whether, well, you know, whether there was . . . third party involvement, let's say.'

'You mean they're treating it as suspicious?'

The woman shrugged. 'Yeah, well – they have to do it all properly, don't they? And until they're sure that the circumstances indicate otherwise, yes, they will have to approach the scene as potentially requiring a homicide investigation.'

It was a good thing Louisa was already sitting because the

strange flip-flop her insides performed caused her to wobble.

Pain throbbed at her temples as questions bombarded her shocked mind. What happened now? Who would inform Tiff's family, her friends? Should she? She ran her fingers through her hair, catching them in the tangles where the breeze had whipped it up. She suddenly realised she was cold. Really cold – her skin rough with goose bumps.

'Can I call someone for you?' The uniformed officer she'd first spoken to when he arrived at the house appeared beside her and crouched down to her level. Her bum was numb from sitting on the ground, but she didn't have the energy to stand.

'Brian, my husband, please?' she said weakly, handing over her mobile phone without making eye contact with the officer. 'It's unlocked, his number is in the recent call history.'

His voice seemed to be far off in the distance, not coming from right beside her. She assumed he was speaking with Brian, but she couldn't make out the words he was saying – it was as if he was talking with cotton wool in his mouth, the words muffled and incoherent. Louisa felt as though she'd been sat on the driveway for hours. Time had stood still.

Once the officer had stopped talking, he handed the mobile back to her. She took it from him and asked about what would happen next. The coroner's officers were at the scene, he said, and Tiff would be taken to the hospital morgue to await a post-mortem. Once the police had carried out their investigations and the coroner his, if the cause of death was confirmed as accidental, the death would be registered. Although the officer's words mingled in Louisa's head, she did get the impression his initial considerations of the scene, together with Louisa's statement and the paramedic's observations, hadn't indicated that Tiff's death was suspicious. However, they couldn't know for sure yet.

'Lou!' Brian's voice penetrated her bubble. 'Darling, are you okay?' She felt his hands on her shoulders, then his arms were around her, pulling her upwards.

'Tiff's dead.'

'I know, I know. I can't believe it; the police told me on the phone. Where's the baby?'

Louisa turned and pointed to the side of Tiff's Audi where Noah's pram had been parked since she'd called the ambulance. Brian steadied her against the fence, then left her side and she watched as he wheeled Noah's pram out of the open gate. A few moments later he came back for Louisa. A few words were exchanged between him and the police officer, then she was inside the warm car, her teeth chattering together noisily.

'We need to warm you up.' Brian drove past the church and then took the left-hand fork in the road to go down through the middle of the village. For a Saturday it was remarkably quiet. There hadn't even been a gathering outside Tiff's house, and given that there were police cars, crime scene tape and an ambulance, Louisa was surprised. But even if there'd been a crowd gawping, she wouldn't have been aware of it.

All she was aware of at this moment was that she'd let her best friend down. Not only that, but she'd allowed her to die before she'd apologised.

Something else she was now going to have to live with.

With one of Noah's large cot blankets draped over her, Louisa sat, legs tucked beneath her, in the corner of the sofa. She'd been grateful for the hot tea Brian made as soon as they returned home from Tiff's and, finally, she was beginning to feel warmth radiating from her insides to her skin. After he'd given her the tea and placed the blanket around her shoulders, Brian had left the lounge and gone upstairs. Louisa checked her mobile for the time. He'd been up there for almost an hour. Her heart pounded, her upper body pulsing along with it, its rhythm –

steady, but fast. She not only felt it, she could hear it inside her head as well.

Like a ticking bomb.

Brian obviously wanted to be alone. Louisa wondered what inner battle *he* was having right now. Was he grieving her loss? What exactly had he lost – a friend? A lover?

Another sob burst from her. She shouldn't even be thinking that. Why was she still assuming her husband and best friend were up to no good? *Had* been up to no good.

Noah began crying. Louisa sank further down on the sofa, laying her head on the arm. She was so tired. Emily would respond to Noah's cries, take over for a bit. Louisa was in no fit state.

She closed her eyes, trying to replace the images of blood, blonde hair soaked red, pale skin and a lifeless body, by screwing them up tight, causing blackness to take over, then colours and patterns to swim behind her lids. She used to press hard on her closed eyes when she was a child, enjoying the kaleidoscope effect it had. Now though, she knew it wouldn't last – that the hideous images would return and would never leave her.

The last image she'd seen of her best friend would haunt her almost as much as their last conversation.

39

THE GATHERING

Sunday p.m. – Day 16 post-party

As they all stood in the kitchen, Louisa couldn't help but think of Tiff in hers, of what the paramedic had said about it being one of the rooms in the house where an accident was most likely to occur. She'd been told that the other was the bathroom. It was obvious, really.

Louisa eyed Oliver as he spoke about his shock to hear that Tiff had died. Brian had insisted on informing him, despite Louisa arguing against it. 'It's nothing to do with him, Brian; he hardly knows her.'

Brian had countered that with: 'He's our friend, and what affects us, affects him.' Louisa had laughed, much to his apparent annoyance. He had at least given her a day – waiting to tell Oliver until a few hours ago, but it had clearly been a difficult decision – now they were best buddies, Brian felt compelled to share the devastating news with him.

After Brian's call, Oliver had immediately rushed over to the house to give his support. He was currently feigning shock and disbelief, and Louisa watched as Oliver's right eye flickered, like a twitch was pulling at the corner. While she couldn't quite let go of her suspicion he'd had something to do with Tiff's death, she also had to consider that he *wasn't* pretending – after all, he'd already suffered one major shock and although he'd not admitted it, he had also been spending time with Tiff.

So had Brian.

She turned her attention to her husband. His face was drawn, his mouth turned down to such an extent it seemed like it'd slipped further down his face and was closer to his chin. He really *was* upset. He stared off into the distance, out the back window and into the garden. Quiet contemplation. She wished she could tap directly into his thoughts.

'Have you put anything on Facebook, Mum?' Emily's voice sliced through the atmosphere in the kitchen like a knife through butter. Louisa jumped at the sudden sound breaking the silence.

'Er . . . yes. I posted on her timeline. Not until I knew her family had been informed, obviously. I waited for the go-ahead from the police first, too. I just wrote something brief as I didn't want to go into detail, then added a lovely picture, the one of her at the school fete last year being given flowers by the kids. It was one of her favourite pictures of herself.' Her voice caught, tears pricking at her eyes. 'People are commenting with their memories of her. There are hundreds already.'

'She was so popular, always had been,' Brian mumbled, his attention remaining outside. He'd said it like he'd known her all her life, rather than for the past eight years through Louisa. She bristled. She was the one who was going to miss her most – she was the one who'd lost her only real friend. She hated fake mourners.

'I'm going upstairs for a lie-down. Excuse me.' Louisa pushed away from where she was leaning against the worktop and brushed past Oliver as she headed for the door. A hand reached out and grabbed her upper arm.

'If you need me, don't hesitate to call. I know what you're going through,' he said.

Louisa shot Brian a glance. He was oblivious, still staring blankly out of the window. But Emily was glaring right at Oliver.

'I'll be okay. Thanks.' Louisa snatched her arm from his grip and walked out. Before she went into the bedroom, she paused on the stairs. She could hear voices, speaking in hushed tones, Oliver and Brian in full conversation now she'd left the room.

She wondered what they were talking about. Hopefully Emily would relay the details to her later. In the meantime, she sat on the bed, her phone in her hand, scrolling through the memories people had left on Tiff's Facebook page, tears spilling down her face.

Blood, pooling.

Grass, cool and tickly beneath her feet.

'Can I blag one of them off you?'

Icy cold.

Fear.

'She knows.'

Louisa sat up, her hands flying to her throat as she gasped for air. She sucked in huge mouthfuls, her lungs filling, painfully tight.

She waited until her heart rate stabilised, then stood up. Her head was woozy, like she'd been asleep for hours. She may well have been – the shock of finding Tiff like that had hit her hard.

Louisa turned to grab her phone, but it wasn't on her bed. She'd had it though. She was looking at the memory page before she drifted off. She ran a hand along the underside of the bed – beneath the drawers there was little gap – but it wasn't there. She threw up the duvet, checking under it.

'For God's sake, where is it?'

'You looking for something?'

233

Louisa swung around at the sound of his voice.

'What are you doing up here?' she snapped at Oliver. He had a cheek, wandering about the house as if he lived there.

'Brian wanted me to check on you, that's all.'

'Why couldn't he check on me himself?'

A memory sparked as she said the words. At her fortieth party, when she'd supposedly gone off without telling anyone, Brian had said he hadn't worried because Oliver had told him that he'd seen her stumbling into the accommodation block. And she'd questioned it then as she was doing now – why had Brian taken his word for it? Why hadn't he checked on her himself?

'He's sorting people with some drinks.'

'What? Sorting what people with drinks?'

'A few people popped over. I think it's because they know you and Tiff were such good friends and they want to pass on their condolences.'

'Who?' Louisa began ushering Oliver out of her bedroom, but he stopped at the top of the stairs to continue the conversation.

'I thought I recognised a couple of them from your party, but I've no idea who they are really. Anyway, I'll be off now. I don't think you particularly want me here.'

She knew her facial expression would give away the fact that he was right. She didn't want him in her house. But she didn't want to outright tell him that, not now. It felt callous – and she'd experienced enough regret over the past few days to last her a while.

'I've got questions to ask you, Oliver. I—'

'Call me tomorrow,' he said as he descended the stairs. 'We'll talk properly then.' When they reached the bottom, he leant in close to her. She felt his breath on her neck as he inhaled her – then kissed her on the cheek. 'You're not alone. Remember that.'

She shrank back, away from his touch, and nodded without saying anything more. After letting him out the front door, she turned towards the kitchen, and the gathering that had occurred while she'd dozed.

This, she could do without.

It felt like her birthday party all over again, only with far fewer people, thankfully. Couldn't they have waited for Tiff's funeral though – her wake? That was the time people reminisced, passed on their condolences, not by showing up at someone's house, imposing on them at such a difficult time.

'I can't believe it, Louisa. I was just saying to Brian, you never know when your time is up, do you? She had so much going for her, poor love. I can't get my head around it – slipping on those tiles!'

'No, Bridget, me neither.' Was all Louisa could contribute to the conversation. She didn't want to speak at all, let alone to the one person she knew was a busybody and would be sharing any nuggets of information gained from Louisa at the Co-op as soon as she could. Clearly Brian hadn't informed her of the police's initial investigation – that they'd had to look into the possibility of Tiff's death being suspicious, otherwise she would already be embellishing the 'slipping on those tiles' theory.

Had Bridget been at Louisa's party? She didn't remember seeing her at all. Oliver had just said he recognised a few people from the party, but as far as Louisa could tell, none of the seven people currently standing in her kitchen had been there – these were all neighbours. God, that man was full of shit.

However, Arthur *was* there, and that seemed a more likely explanation as to why Oliver had the sudden need to rush off. Perhaps he'd clocked Arthur and was afraid that he'd be recognised from loitering in his car, and awkward questions would be asked.

Excusing herself from Bridget, Louisa sidled over to Arthur.

'Hello, Arthur. I'm sorry, I was upstairs when you arrived, having a bit of a lie-down.'

'Ah, my dear.' He put his hands to Louisa's face, tears shining in his yellowing, old eyes. 'How are you doing?'

He was the first person to ask her that, and she responded by promptly bursting into tears. Arthur put his arms around her and gave her a squeeze. She dropped her head onto his shoulder, hiccupping sobs muffling in his Aran-knit jumper.

'Let it all out, dear.' He patted her back, just like her dad used to do to comfort her when she was little. More regret tore through her. She made a silent promise to make sure she went to see her mum and dad this week. Life was too short to have family feuds ruin what time she had left with her parents.

'Sorry,' Louisa said pulling away and swiping at her eyes with her jumper sleeve. 'It's been a long weekend.' It'd been a long few weeks, but she refrained from telling him that.

'Losing people close to you is devastating, and I'm afraid nothing I or anyone else tells you is going to change that. You just have to remember to let things out – don't bottle up your feelings; that doesn't do you any good. The hurt, the pain, it *festers* if you don't let it out.'

She smiled at him, thanking him for his kind words. Then she poured herself a large glass of wine and downed it in a few, large gulps.

Pain wasn't the only thing that could fester if you didn't let it go.

Guilt and lies – they'd do the same.

40

THE FOOTAGE

Monday a.m. – Day 17 post-party

When Louisa had climbed into bed just after midnight, she'd been so exhausted both mentally and physically that she hoped she'd sleep regardless. But Noah had other ideas. He'd been more unsettled than ever before and Louisa's ability to soothe him, whilst it had never seemed to be great, was particularly useless. The thoughts, the worry, the grief, all added to her own stress levels – and together with her current dark mood, it was obviously enough for Noah to pick up on.

And then there was the guilt.

That would eat through her consciousness; *that* would prevent her being able to come through this latest trauma the same person as before. Two weeks ago all she'd had to worry about was the difficulties that came with being an older mum, coping with endless sleepless nights. A short space of time later, she had a murder on her conscience, a missing person, and the death of her best friend – a death she was convinced she could have helped prevent. Adding to that the fact Louisa had accused Tiff of having an affair with either Brian or Oliver, and it became clear to her that so much had happened, so much had changed, the life she knew was never coming back.

237

It was whether she could adapt to the one she'd created that was the big question. Louisa thought she knew the answer, but it was very depressing and not really an option.

Louisa's head was heavy, her eyes puffy. She was desperate to get back into bed, close her eyes and sink into oblivion now Noah was finally sleeping solidly. But it was nearing six o'clock and soon Brian and Emily would be up and about, banging around getting ready for work and school, so there was little point. Brian had offered to take sick leave so he could be with her over the next few days, but she'd convinced him there was no need. She'd rather just be with Noah, not have anyone there fussing over her, watching her every move.

Despite knowing the futility of it, as Louisa reached her bedroom door and noticed that Brian was already out of bed and in the shower, she went in and collapsed onto the mattress, pulling the duvet up to her neck. The gentle rhythm of the water from the shower was hypnotic; she felt herself drifting.

She woke with a start.

For a moment she was disorientated, couldn't get a grasp on where she was, what time it was, or what was happening. The house was eerily silent. She must've slept through Brian and Emily getting ready and leaving for the day. The vision of Tiff's motionless body, the blood on the tiles, shot into her mind. She moved to the edge of the bed, rubbing her hands over her face to try and rid herself of the images. Her stomach contracted violently, nausea clawing at her throat. Bolting to the toilet, she got there just as the bile forcibly evacuated her body. Last night's drink burned her oesophagus as it reversed its journey.

Louisa watched herself in the mirror as she brushed her teeth. The woman there was unrecognisable, loathsome. She'd buried her past; put it so far to the back of her mind she'd forgotten almost everything relating to it. To protect herself and Oliver. They'd carried on their lives without thought of the consequences. Or Oliver had – she really had suffered from the trauma – her dissociative amnesia *was* real. What was Oliver's excuse for why he had buried the truth for so long?

But knowing she had a condition that meant she didn't remember the events didn't make it right. And especially now she *did* know what had happened, now she had some understanding of what she'd done, to continue to blank it and attempt to put it back in its box and close the lid again, was unforgivable. The knowledge of it was going to be the biggest burden, and if they weren't going to tell the police, then it was one she'd have to bear alone. The only person who Louisa might've had the guts to tell about what she'd learned about herself was now dead.

Noah was still asleep when Louisa popped her head around the nursery door. Good. She'd have some time to eat a bit of breakfast, if she could tolerate it, and peruse Facebook on her laptop. She still hadn't found her mobile despite a frantic search when everyone had left the house yesterday evening, which meant only one thing as far as she was concerned. Someone had taken it. Her money was on Oliver. She couldn't fathom why he'd bother taking it, unless he was afraid she'd told someone about their secret and wanted to check up on her. But even then, he could've just asked her outright. She'd turn the place upside down later to double-check it wasn't in the house before accusing Oliver of theft.

Searching through Facebook, Louisa found the village page, *Spotted Penchurch*, and asked to join the group. She'd never bothered before, even with Tiff's near-constant moaning to do it so she stayed 'in the loop'. She couldn't understand why there was a need for a Spotted page for a small village. You only had to visit the local shop or Post Office to find out about everything going on, and events were always pinned up on the notice board in the window, so why have a Facebook page? Plus, it annoyed her they had dropped the 'Little' – if they had no pride in the full village name, they shouldn't bloody be living in it.

Here she was, nonetheless, requesting to join because she remembered Tiff telling her, prior to their argument, about the fact they'd post pictures of the church tower being open and people walking to the top to see the view. She was hoping Tiff had put photos up herself from Thursday's event.

Two minutes later she had a notification to inform her she'd been accepted, so she went straight to the page to check the latest updates. For Sale posts littered the feed, in spite of the pinned post requesting no adverts. As she scrolled further down the page, there were ramblings from disgruntled horse riders about the speed that cars drove through the village, and various posts about the archaeological dig taking place on the outskirts of the village where Roman artefacts had been found.

At this rate she'd be there all day, so she clicked on the sidebar tab: photos, to bypass the rubbish. The first batch of pictures had been put up by Eddie, one of the church wardens. Louisa clicked through them quickly. They were mostly shots taken from the top of the tower of the landscape and houses of people he knew. She continued scrolling. Tiff hadn't posted any. Disappointed, she was about to shut the laptop, but then remembered the drone. Tiff had wanted video footage, mainly, to get one up on Sarah. Clicking back on the shortcuts, Louisa chose 'videos'.

Her heart rate juddered, missing a beat.

The latest video was one posted by Tiff. Louisa opened it and watched in awe at the height the drone had gained above the church, then how it smoothly swept from one side to the other, taking in the people at the top of the tower. She'd done it. Clever bugger. Louisa smiled. Sarah must've hated that, which meant Tiff had enjoyed every moment.

Even if they were some of her last.

The tears started again, and Louisa blinked them away so she could continue watching the footage. All in all, there were seven separate videos of the drone capturing different groups at the top. And, as Tiff had mentioned when she asked to borrow it, she'd also done several 360-degree shots, moving all around the church and the people. She had to admit, it looked amazing. Brian would be thrilled it worked so well.

Although it probably *didn't* work anymore.

Now might be a good time to tell Brian about its fate. He surely wouldn't be angry, not after what had happened. Louisa kept the Spotted page open at the video and went straight to the garage to retrieve the battered drone. What had Tiff done to it? The footage from the church had been so good, she'd clearly not had any problems learning how to fly it and operate the camera and recording. So how come it was abandoned in her garden?

With the drone sitting on the kitchen table, Louisa stared at it, wondering if she should test it to see if it did work. But then, even if it did, it still looked dented and scratched, so it wasn't as though she could pretend she knew nothing about it. She'd have to come clean. Fiddling with the camera, Louisa managed to unlock the casing that housed the SD card and she popped it out. Tiff may have wiped the original church videos as she uploaded them onto Facebook, but it was worth checking.

She double-tapped the icon when it popped up on her laptop screen.

There was footage still on the memory card, but it didn't appear to be of the church, or the event. Louisa was watching Tiff's own garden from at least one hundred feet up in the air by the look of it. Tiff was practising, learning how to fly it prior to using it on the Thursday. A strange feeling washed over her. She was watching video footage her dead friend had taken. The drone must've been positioned above the foot of the garden, as Tiff's decking was visible.

So was Tiff.

Sadness overwhelmed Louisa. There was her friend, standing with her back to the patio doors. Alive. How long before her death was this shot? Louisa moved her head closer to the screen to see the time stamp. She frowned. It must be wrong; it said it was Friday – so, *after* the church event. That couldn't be right.

Before Louisa could question it further, she saw Tiff make a sudden movement towards the wooden table on the patio. The distance from the drone to where she was standing was quite far, so it was difficult to make out what she was doing, but it appeared she'd placed something on the table and then turned towards the alley at the side of the house. The one Louisa always used to get to the back and into Tiff's house.

The picture wobbled slightly, the drone dipping. But it remained in focus and Louisa could still make out Tiff, standing in front of the open patio door, her back to the drone as if she were about to walk back inside. Had she forgotten the drone was still in the air? Louisa tutted. This *could* be Friday then, after the church event had taken place, and Louisa was about to witness the crash.

What was Tiff thinking walking off and leaving it hovering?

Then Louisa saw a shadow emerging from the side of the house, where Tiff's attention had turned moments before. She'd obviously heard someone coming. Tiff probably thought it was her again and that's why she was heading indoors, to hide from her. Louisa squinted – *was* it her? She *had* been to Tiff's on Friday, had been banging on the door, ringing the doorbell. Was she about to see herself? But she couldn't recall hearing the drone, but could well have mistaken it for a neighbour's lawnmower.

Louisa watched and waited for herself to appear on the screen.

But she didn't.

Someone else did.

A woman, of similar build to herself, walked towards the back door and put an arm out. Louisa couldn't make out what exactly she was doing, but she could tell that Tiff was blocking the door preventing whoever it was from entering. And then in an abrupt movement, the woman propelled herself through the door. It was too dark inside the house for Louisa to see what was going on, but then a flash of light shone off the patio door as it was suddenly whipped closed. The footage took a violent dip, then seemed to judder for a few seconds before dropping altitude. Fast. This was obviously going to be when it crashed.

Louisa sucked in a long breath. If this *was* filmed on Friday, it must've been just before Louisa herself had gone to Tiff's. When she'd stumbled across the drone, it might've only just crashed. Had the person who she'd just seen barging her way into Tiff's been there when Louisa was banging on the door? Perhaps Tiff hadn't been lying on the floor bleeding to death when Louisa was there after all. She felt relieved in one way; she was beginning to piece together the puzzle, and it would take away some of the guilt she'd been experiencing, thinking she'd been feet away from her friend and not done anything to help. This woman, if she could see who it was, might be able to give more information that would help them construct an accurate timeline of when Tiff slipped and fell.

Louisa re-watched the footage again from the point at which the woman came into the picture and focused totally on the woman's features. She was wearing dark-blue, possibly black trousers and a dark hoody. When she turned towards the back door, Louisa noted her hair was long, flowing down her back. It was fair, but she couldn't make out the exact colour – could be light brown, dark blonde, possibly even red.

Louisa pitched backwards, slamming into the chairback.

She took the footage back a few frames then paused it.

Louisa could make out long, spiral curls.

She was looking at Melissa Dunmore.

41

THE THEORY

For the fourth time, Louisa rewound the footage and checked again, unsure whether her conclusion was to be trusted. She blinked hard, trying to keep her eyes focused. She saw no new evidence to suggest she'd been mistaken.

The woman going into Tiff's house was Melissa.

Oliver's missing wife was, apparently, no longer missing.

Louisa screenshotted the paused image. She should call the police immediately, but a niggling voice in the back of her mind told her not to. If Melissa was in the area, why hadn't she contacted the police herself? Surely she knew they were looking for her. There must be a reason why she didn't want to be found. The question of why on earth she'd have turned up at Tiff's in the first place was a baffling one. Something wasn't right – Oliver, Melissa – they'd *both* been to Tiff's house. On separate occasions, or at the same time, she didn't know. Either way, it was a hell of a coincidence and raised alarm as well as more questions. Louisa reconsidered her earlier theory of this being some kind of life insurance fraud. What other possible reason could there be for what was going on?

But if that was the case, then Tiff must've known – even been in on it.

And now she couldn't ask Tiff.

Therefore, she *needed* to speak to Melissa. She couldn't trust a thing Oliver told her now, so there was no point in speaking to him. She'd have to make sure she didn't let on that she knew his wife was alive and well and sneaking around Little Penchurch if she saw him before managing to find Melissa. *If* she managed to find her.

That was the biggest snag. How *was* she going to find Melissa?

'How have you been today, love?' Brian kissed her on the top of her head as he sauntered in, dropping his prison officer belt, the key chain rattling, onto the worktop.

'Ah, you know – it's been weird. It's like I'm caught in another dimension or something. I feel apart from everything – like I'm existing in my own bubble – weightless, numb.'

Brian lowered his head. 'I still can't believe she's gone, Lou. How could this have happened? It's off the scale.'

Louisa filled the kettle, more for something to occupy her hands and mind than to refresh her husband after his long day at work. She had to be careful not to let anything slip – not even mention the drone, let alone the footage she'd found. It would only be a matter of time before Brian went to the garage to retrieve the drone, though. For the moment at least, it was obviously the last thing on his mind. Tiff's death had knocked him sideways.

It was apparent to Louisa he was suffering – and more than she felt he should. Not that shock and grief didn't affect people in different ways, but it felt disproportionate somehow. Tiff was *her* friend, and while she was sure she'd feel shock and sadness if one of Brian's friends were to die, she was fairly confident she wouldn't be taking it as badly as he was responding to Tiff's.

Further adding weight to her suspicion that he'd fancied her or even been in love with her.

Louisa's heart ached, the knowledge that she'd not trusted Tiff still lingering on her conscience. It seemed better to mistrust her husband now, rather than her friend, who could no longer defend herself.

'I feel so useless too – I haven't done anything to help Tiff's family. Is it rude, do you think, to phone and ask if I can help with any of the funeral arrangements?'

'No, not at all. You were her best friend,' Brian said, his voice catching at the end. He gave a cough – a poor attempt at covering it up. Louisa turned away from him and began pouring the boiling water into the mugs.

'I don't know – it might come across that I'm intruding during a difficult family time.'

'It's better to ask, though, Lou. Imagine if you get to the funeral and you find you're the only one of Tiff's friends who hasn't contributed anything to the service or something?'

That was a good point. She would be gutted.

God, what if Sarah does something? Tiff would turn in her grave!

'You're right,' she said firmly, handing Brian his tea. 'I'll ring her mum this evening.'

'Do it now. You'll have talked yourself out of it by then otherwise.'

Yes, again he was right. That was the most likely outcome if she waited. She went to move past Brian, but stopped short.

'Shit. I still haven't found my phone. I can't ring her. Her number is saved to the SIM; I don't have it written down anywhere.'

Brian put his hand up, his mouth to the lip of the mug. 'It's on the coffee table,' he said, swallowing quickly. 'I assumed you'd found it.'

Louisa frowned. 'No. I've been looking all day.' She eyed Brian cautiously. The mobile had not been there earlier. Had he been the one who'd had it? Had he been searching through her texts? The thought seemed ludicrous. Brian had never done that before. She let the thought slide; replacing it with the other, more likely scenario that she'd forgotten what she'd done with it. Louisa walked back into the lounge and, after grabbing her mobile called Shirley, Tiff's mum.

42

THE HOUSE

Tuesday a.m. – Day 18 post-party

Oliver's car was parked along by the trees at the end of the road. The opposite end from Arthur's house this time. Louisa stepped back inside the hallway, yanking Noah's pram backwards up the step. She hoped he hadn't seen her before she'd beaten her hasty retreat.

What was he doing hanging around again?

Arthur had reported him loitering before. He was taking a risk by being anywhere in their road. Louisa ran to the lounge window and pulled back the edge of one curtain. She couldn't make Oliver out; the car was a little too far away for her to be sure if he was behind the wheel. He could've parked up and was out walking somewhere. She needed to go to Tiff's. She'd arranged it with Shirley last night – she was to make a start packing up some of Tiff's things because her poor mum couldn't bring herself to do the task.

Shirley had received the news yesterday that Tiff's post-mortem had been carried out. The coroner reported it as an accidental death. Louisa had felt a strange mix of relief and sadness and she'd immediately envisaged Tiff rushing around, going from one task to another without giving enough attention to each one – knocking over the water without realising then slipping on the floor. Louisa shut her eyes tightly, fat tears squeezing out. It was still so unbelievable to think Tiff was gone. It was hard to consider what her family must be feeling, but she was glad the funeral home was releasing Tiff's body now. At least her family could begin the agonising task of arranging her burial.

Louisa certainly didn't want Oliver following her to Tiff's, making a nuisance of himself. He was bound to offer his assistance, and Louisa wanted to do this on her own. It was going to be the most difficult, heart-breaking thing she'd ever had to do, and she didn't want an audience.

It was *her* time with Tiff. *Her* memories. *Her* apology. It was private.

But with Oliver just outside, the likelihood of carrying this out without interruption was slim.

Binoculars. She ran to get them from the garage. At least then she'd be certain if Oliver was in the car. If he wasn't, she'd take her chance and leave. If he was, well then she'd have to think of another plan.

Louisa's gaze passed over the box containing the battered drone. Just seeing it made her breath catch. She still hadn't had any idea how to find Melissa, but she held some hope that while she was sorting out things at Tiff's today, she might come across something – a clue as to why Melissa, and Oliver, had been visiting her. And whilst she'd been pleased the coroner had concluded Tiff's death was accidental – Louisa couldn't shake the uneasy feeling something was amiss.

Dusting off the binoculars, Louisa took them back to the front window. She angled them in the right direction, then twiddled with the dioptre adjustment on each eyepiece. She hoped none of her neighbours were watching. As she turned the central focusing wheel, Oliver's car came into clear view.

She gave a sigh of relief. No one was inside it.

Louisa flung the binoculars on the sofa and snatched up her bag, pushing Noah back outside. She turned left to avoid Oliver's car, just in case he came back to it as she passed. Although she was glad he wasn't inside the car, it did leave the question of where the hell he was. Why park it there and walk off? His behaviour was increasingly concerning.

By the time she'd reached Tiff's she was out of breath, her lungs struggling, chest tight – from walking so quickly, or from anxiety, she couldn't tell. Louisa punched in the code Shirley had given her to release the key from the small metal key safe on the outside wall, then, with a huge intake of breath, opened the front door.

The stale air hit her. The house had only been closed up for a matter of days, yet it already had the faint smell of must – an 'unlived-in' scent. She stood on the threshold, her legs heavy, feet refusing to move her inside. The stillness, the unnerving peacefulness the house held, made Louisa's skin turn to gooseflesh.

Come on, Lou. You said you'd do this – you can't back out now.

As she pushed Noah in ahead of her, she became aware of a lightness inside her head – a dizziness consuming her.

Breathe slowly.

She'd been taking such shallow breaths she was now hyperventilating to compensate. She had to slow her breathing down or she'd faint.

And bang my head and die.

The thought made her shiver.

The urge to call out 'hello' was overwhelming. Tears pooled at the corners of her eyes. Eight years she'd been coming here, and this was the first time she'd been in the house without Tiff being there. She felt as though she were trespassing. That feeling

251

would become even stronger once she began rummaging through Tiff's belongings.

Why had she agreed to do this? She should've offered to help with arranging the service seeing as Shirley had decided Tiff was to be buried in Little Penchurch because it was a place close to her daughter's heart. Louisa could've happily organised Tiff's favourite songs, photos, anything. Something less obtrusive. Less like she was a stalker. But, on the other hand, if she hadn't agreed to this, she wouldn't now have the opportunity to find evidence. Not that she knew what evidence she was looking for or what form it would take. Or even if there was any to be found.

She meant to begin in the kitchen, wanting to get it out the way first, but as she approached it a squirming sensation rippled through her and she backed away.

Spilling water
Head hitting granite
Blood-covered tiles
Lifeless body

As the unwanted vision flashed in her mind, her whole body began to shake. She needed to settle her nerves first, before entering the scene. Had the blood even been cleaned up? It wasn't only where Tiff had died, but also where the majority of their time had been spent when Louisa had gone over for a chat and coffee. It was the hub of the house – where most of her memories had been made.

She cast her eyes into the lounge as she passed back through the hallway, but didn't go in. Tiff barely used that space. She might check back there at a later date. It would take a while to sort the entire house, and Shirley said she had family who could help with that; she just wanted a friend of Tiff's to do the personal stuff. Louisa wheeled Noah to the foot of the stairs.

Although he was quiet, she couldn't bear to leave him downstairs alone in his pram.

Why not? What am I afraid of?

She lifted him out and carried him upstairs. Each foot on the stair caused a creak – an eerie groan, as though they'd forgotten the weight of the many footsteps that had gone before, the imprints left now mere ghosts. A chill shot up her back. It wasn't really that she didn't want Noah to be left alone downstairs; it was because *she* didn't want to be alone upstairs.

The stairway curved to the left before it reached the landing. Three rooms and a bathroom went off from there, each door closed. Louisa hesitated on the top stair as she caught sight of the boxes. Shirley had told her there'd be some there for her to use. One for personal things to keep, one for charity, one for the dump. Louisa screwed her eyes up tight. She should've asked someone else to come with her. Her plan to carry this out on her own, to 'spend time' with Tiff, had been ill-conceived. This was an awful task to do alone. Forcing herself to move forwards, Louisa padded to the far door on the right.

Tiff's bedroom.

As she didn't have anyone else living with her, it was obviously the biggest – the one with the luxurious en-suite where, on a number of occasions, she and Tiff had got ready for a night out. Louisa balanced Noah in one arm as she lowered the door handle and, inhaling deeply, gently pushed the door open. The room was in general disarray: clothes flung onto the bed, where she supposed Tiff had been deciding what to wear that day; make-up products littered the dressing table, a book lay open, face-down on her mirrored sidetable – Louisa raised her eyebrows at the title: *Gone Girl.* Her throat constricted, tears threatening again.

She had to do this. She had to start packing things up. Laying

Noah in the centre of Tiff's king-sized bed, she went to the landing to retrieve the boxes.

There was a certain melancholy to the scene – the culmination of Tiff's life stacked in cardboard boxes. Louisa stood staring at them and a sadness engulfed her. It had been one of the things Tiff had mentioned once – the fact that she had no children meaning that her things wouldn't be 'passed on' to another generation when she died. It had frightened her, Louisa realised. The knowledge she would completely cease to exist, and that there would be no evidence – not in a lineage kind of way – that she'd once walked this planet.

Louisa had laughed at the time, saying that of course there would be evidence, and even with no children, her family and friends would continue to talk about her, share their memories of her. She'd be alive in people's minds.

Now, sitting among her possessions, Tiff's response to that came back to her.

'Yes, Lou. I have lovely friends, but eventually, their memories will fade, the reminiscing, the daily thoughts about how terrible it was to lose me, will diminish. I may be thought of on anniversaries – like my birthday, day of death – but soon enough life will move on. My friends will remember me less and less. I'll be a random thought one day when something else sparks a memory. It's not the same for you. Your kids will always remember you, will think of you often, not just once in a blue moon. And you will continue on *in* them, your bloodline. I won't.'

'I won't forget you, though, Tiff. I'll think of you every day, I promise,' Louisa had said.

'Oh, fab – so you're assuming I'll go before you then!'

And they'd both collapsed into fits of laughter. The dark, sombre moment broken.

'I promise, Tiff,' Louisa now said aloud in the silent bedroom, 'I won't stop thinking about you. And I *will* find out what the hell was going on before you died.'

Because Louisa had a terrible feeling she'd missed something important.

43

THE FIND

Having spent considerable time looking through Tiff's posses-sions, trying to decide what she might've wanted Louisa to keep, what she'd have liked to go to charity, then placing them carefully into the designated boxes, Louisa felt drained. The thought of searching through the kitchen seemed an impossible task now. She was exhausted and would no doubt do a poor job. But, if she put it off, it would mean returning tomorrow, or Wednesday – and that thought was equally tiring.

Noah pushed his clenched fist into his mouth, then began to grumble. Finally, Louisa checked the time on her mobile and realised he should've had his bottle an hour ago. She could make it home in minutes; he could wait until then. Or, she could warm his bottle up here, feed him and then finish the job. The lounge definitely wouldn't take long – there was only one unit in there and it was mostly filled with books. All of which Tiff would want to go to charity as that's where she'd got the majority of them from in the first place.

The kitchen was a different story – some of the drawers in there were stuffed with letters, personal papers – Tiff's habit of shoving everything in them meant anything could be in there. She'd find renewed energy once she saw the light at the end of the tunnel. Gathering Noah into her arms, Louisa made her way back downstairs. She popped her vocal baby in the pram and rummaged in the changing bag for his bottle.

'Stay there, darling – Mummy won't be long.' The thought of wheeling him into the kitchen didn't feel right. Her tummy rolled as she entered the brilliant-white room. The light streamed in from the side window and Velux, making the room feel less scary than she thought it would. Ridiculous to find a kitchen scary just because someone had died in it. Nonetheless, that's how she felt. Without looking at her surroundings too much, she opened the microwave and placed the bottle in it. She knew she shouldn't microwave the milk because of hotspots but she really couldn't face boiling the kettle, watching the blue light and water bubbling as she'd done just last week. How different things had become in such a short space of time.

As Louisa watched the seconds flash by on the microwave LCD her mind wandered to Friday – to what had taken place in this very kitchen. What could Melissa have possibly wanted with Tiff? A sudden thought crashed its way into her brain. She hadn't come across Tiff's mobile phone while she'd been packing things up. She cast her eyes over the worktop surfaces. They were spotless, uncluttered. No phone. The microwave dinged and absentmindedly, Louisa shook the bottle with one hand as she went around the kitchen opening drawers and cupboards with her free hand. Unless it'd been buried beneath the other items, which was very unlikely, then it wasn't here.

She put the bottle on the island, ignoring Noah's cries, then used both hands to sort through the final drawer. She flicked through the paperwork and miscellaneous crap that Tiff had obviously decided to sort at a later date. No phone. That was concerning. Had the police not found it odd her phone was missing? Or maybe they'd taken it – perhaps it was standard practice.

Louisa pushed the drawer back in, but it jammed. She opened it again, bending to look inside. There was something caught at the back of the drawer preventing it closing properly. Louisa ran her hand along the inside, using her thumb and finger to catch hold of what was blocking it. When she withdrew her hand, she was holding a photo.

Louisa studied it – it seemed old. There was a yellow tinge to it, the quality not great. It was good enough to tell who the people depicted in the scene were though. It had been taken on a beach, of a group of people all in swimwear – tanned, young. All smiling, bar one.

Tiff.

Louisa's mouth dried.

This changed everything.

Standing next to Tiff, with her arm around her, was a younger woman. One with curly auburn hair.

'What the hell is Melissa doing in this photo?' Her words echoed around the kitchen. Louisa looked up, half expecting to see Tiff at the opposite side of the island. She had wanted her to answer the question.

But she was only met with icy silence.

Had she been focusing on the wrong questions, the incorrect theory? Louisa had assumed Melissa had merely paid Tiff a visit, leaving her alive and well. But what if she hadn't left Tiff alive? The police may have been happy with their findings, that it was a tragic accident with no evidence of foul play, but then they didn't have the drone footage. Melissa, a missing woman, forcing her way into Tiff's house moments before Tiff landed up dead did throw a different light on the situation.

Now she really thought about it, the fact that Tiff had never mentioned having met Melissa seemed odd, suspicious even.

Louisa had assumed up until this point that Tiff had never set eyes on Melissa Dunmore. She certainly didn't appear to know her and didn't let on to Louisa that she'd known her from years ago.

But, although that was strange, it didn't go far in answering the question of why Melissa would want Tiff dead. Why *had* Melissa visited Tiff that day?

44

THE DARKNESS

'Can you take Noah, please? I need to shower.' Louisa pushed Noah into Emily's arms.

'Well, yeah – I guess. And yes, Mum, I've had a good day, school was great, thanks for asking,' she muttered under her breath as Louisa turned and ran up the stairs. Louisa called back to her, saying she'd chat afterwards. It was a bit harsh to immediately hand over Noah as soon as Emily came in from school, but Louisa had to wash away the remnants of the stale smell of Tiff's house. More than that, she needed headspace; time to process and arrange her thoughts more coherently than they were currently.

She had no one to talk to about this latest development. No one she could *trust*, anyway.

She allowed the hot water to pound her body, her skin prickling as though a hundred tiny needles were perforating it – it was painful at first, until the numbness came.

Now both her mind and body were numb.

She cupped the water in her hands, then swished it over her face.

Blood, pooling.

Grass, cool and tickly beneath her feet.

'Can I blag one of them off you?'

Icy cold.

Fear.

A face at the window.

SHE KNOWS.

The last two words screamed inside her head. Had they been *her* words, ones she had spoken? She was sure it was her knowledge, her fear she felt when the images came to her from that night, the night of her party.

Shit.

Tiff had said she'd seen her from the window, talking to someone in the beer garden. Now Louisa had a flash of memory of seeing *her* at the window, followed by the words: she knows.

Louisa stepped out of the shower and, grabbing a towel, gave herself a brusque drying and then sat on the bed, shoulders slumped. Her mind had been allowing these brief visions; memories, whatever they were, yet they weren't enough – it was like trying to do a dot-to-dot in the dark with half the dots missing. Impossible. She understood that her brain had been keeping things in another compartment, protecting her from the atrocities of her decisions, her actions. But why couldn't she remember everything in its entirety now, when she needed to – *wanted* to?

She'd have to delve into the darkness, to the depths of her consciousness to find the memories, rearrange them. Make sense of them. But that was easier said than done. How was she going to achieve that, when for so many years she'd tried and failed? She hadn't tried hypnosis before. It was a thought – although it would have to be some kind of self-hypnosis. She couldn't very well go to a professional, allow someone else to unlock her past, from back then, *or* more recently. It'd have to be done alone. Louisa made a mental note to search the internet later on, to find guidance on how to perform self-hypnosis. At this point, nothing was off the table.

The burning question for the moment was why Tiff had a photo of Melissa and how they'd ever managed to know each other without Louisa's awareness.

'Mum! Mum!'

Louisa jumped off the bed and ran to the bedroom door. 'What's the matter?' she called down the stairs. She didn't need an answer. Standing just inside the hallway was Oliver.

'I wanted to check how you were doing,' he said, the smile faltering as he took in her towel.

For fuck's sake, leave me alone! Louisa pulled the towel tighter around her, backing away from the top of the stairs. 'I've just got out the shower – can we do this another time? I'm fine, though, so no need to worry.'

'I won't stay long, but I really need to touch base with you.'

'Why? Has something happened? Has there been news on Melissa?'

There most definitely *was* news on Melissa, Louisa thought, which was why seeing Oliver right now was not a good idea. She didn't know how much he knew about Melissa's past, whether he knew that she and Tiff had been friends, or at least known each other. It could be he knew all of that, which was why he'd been visiting her too, because he thought she might know where Melissa was. Why hadn't Tiff mentioned any of this to her? It seemed crazy, given the circumstances, not to say anything. And she'd even said, 'you never told me about Oliver', insinuating Louisa had kept that quiet from her. And all along it was *Tiff* keeping things from *her*.

'The police came to see me, yes.'

Louisa clenched her fists, her knuckles turning as white as the towel she was gripping. 'Hang on, then.' She ducked back into the bedroom. Her hands shook as she tried to pull her jeans up over her still-damp thighs. The anticipation of what Oliver was about to tell her pressed its weight down in her stomach, the resulting dragging sensation causing nausea. Was there a possibility that something had happened to Melissa since Friday? Just because she was alive then, didn't mean that Oliver hadn't found out where she was and done the unthinkable to her in the meantime.

She shook her head. She had to stop jumping to conclusions about Oliver – yes, he'd been capable of covering up a terrible act when he was younger, but he was an adult now. Had learned from that experience. And he'd felt as though he was protecting her by doing it. Louisa knew the lengths Oliver would go to in order to protect the ones he loved. He'd done it for her, as his girlfriend. So why would he have any reason to harm Melissa – his *wife*?

Oliver was sitting at the kitchen table, his head bowed, when she walked in.

'You smell nice,' he said as she sat beside him.

'Clean.' Was all she could muster. 'Go on. Tell me.'

His deep-brown eyes, shiny with tears, settled on hers. She could feel her heart galloping, was sure it must be literally jumping from her chest.

'They've scaled down the investigation. Right down, so they say. And I knew that already, really. But it still kills me to think they've given up.'

Louisa blew out a breath. It was the relief rushing out of her, but she hoped it would come across more as a shocked expulsion of air. 'Scaled down, Oliver, not given up. They'll still be looking—'

'For a dead body, yes. No evidence has been found that suggests she's alive – no proof of life. So that's it. She's another statistic. A missing person who'll never be found.'

Louisa stared him straight in the eye. 'Do you think this is karma?'

'Yes.' He nodded. 'I think it is.'

'I'm sorry,' she whispered. *Sorry for you, sorry for what we did. Sorry that I know Melissa is alive. That she was at Tiff's just a matter of days ago. Sorry to not be telling you.*

But you might already know it all.

You might be telling me a pack of lies.

I can't trust you.

'What should we do?' Louisa asked.

'About what? Melissa?'

'Melissa, Tiff, the woman in the lane. All of it, Oliver. Where do we go from here?'

'Nowhere.' He shrugged. 'I've exhausted all possibilities with Melissa – either she doesn't want to be found, or she's dead in a ditch somewhere. And Tiff *is* dead – there's nothing to do there, sadly. Apart from give her a good send-off – a party she'd have been proud to have organised herself. And the other thing – well, that stays buried. It has to. If that comes out now, Lou-Lou – I'll be done for. If I was capable of burying a body when I was nineteen, then they'll assume I did the same to Melissa. They don't need bodies to charge you with murder you know.'

No, no they didn't. She felt a pang of guilt knowing he hadn't harmed Melissa, but that the police, loads of the general public – even her family – would think he had. She had also questioned it, before she'd seen the drone footage – even questioned it again just moments ago. If after a certain number of years they still hadn't found proof of life, Melissa would be presumed dead and could be legally declared as such. As must've happened with the woman in the lane. But Louisa knew the woman in the lane *was* dead. Melissa, on the other hand, was very much alive. And surely she couldn't stay hidden, undetected forever.

She'd have to come out of hiding at some point.

But what bothered Louisa most was who was she hiding from, and why?

45

THE TRUTH

Wednesday a.m. – Day 19 post-party

The lack of sleep Noah had caused was now replaced with lack of sleep due to worry, guilt and sadness. Even curiosity plagued her. Louisa's mind wouldn't hush – the constant questions, theories and concerns over what was to come, all bashed against each other inside her skull. She'd also come up with various permutations of the same basic conversation that she could have with Oliver to try and dig further to get to the truth. Because there was a truth, buried somewhere, and she felt sure he hadn't been straight with her up to this point. Not about everything.

The bedroom was dark. She lay with her eyes wide open, but seeing nothing. The streetlights had gone off at 1 a.m. – a recent council policy to save money that she'd welcomed because the one right outside their house managed to infiltrate their room despite the blackout blind's attempts to block it. However, now, after being awake for two hours past the switch-off, she realised there was a certain safety about that glowing light – its absence and the resulting pitch-black surroundings now added to Louisa's sense of insecurity and dread.

'Can't you sleep?' Brian rolled over, placing his hand on Louisa's arm.

'Jesus! You could've given me some warning you were awake.' Her shrill tone filled the room. The suddenness of his deep voice had encroached on her thoughts, setting her nerves jangling.

'Sorry. Just been lying here for ages, waiting for sleep to take me. Clearly it's not going to.'

Louisa turned her body towards him. 'You thinking about Tiff?'

'Yeah,' he said. 'Amongst other things.'

Louisa felt the mattress shift as he turned, flicked on the bedside light and then propped himself up on one elbow to face her.

'A lot has gone on – too much to process, really,' she said.

'Do you trust me, Lou?' His eyes crinkled and, in the lamp-light, Louisa could see tears shining. Her eyes prickled too, the question catching her off-guard. Did she? She had done. Right up until she'd given birth to Noah. He'd never given her reason not to. It was only the texts to Tiff that had sparked her concern. But who was she to question him, to question whether he should be trusted? She was the one with the dark secret – hiding the skeleton, quite literally. Trust went both ways.

'I've struggled, a bit. Lately.' The honest answer escaped her mouth without much thought. She had to open up the chan-nels of communication, had to at least attempt to sort out the problems. She wondered if he'd be as honest, and whether her honesty would continue if it got into deeper, scarier territory. Like her past. She watched his face, trying to read his expression. It remained pensive.

'I know you think something was going on with me and Tiff. And I realise I didn't allay your fears, or dampen your suspicions, whatever, the other day in the kitchen when I started to talk about her. I was trying too hard to explain myself, and all I did was make it sound like you really did have something to be suspicious of.'

'And there wasn't, then? I mean, nothing at all to warrant me feeling as though something was wrong?'

He pursed his lips; closed his eyes. 'There was a moment,' he said, breathing in deeply. 'A very brief one. Fleeting.'

Louisa swallowed, her throat dry in anticipation of what he was about to admit to. 'Go on.'

'It was when you were carrying Noah, about six months in. Tiff put something on Facebook, a "call-out" if you like. Needed help with putting up shelves. I simply liked her post, then, when there were no offers forthcoming, commented to say I was free to give her a hand.'

Louisa recalled that day. Him telling her that he was popping up to Tiff's to help with a bit of DIY, then he said he'd be partaking in a swift half at the pub on the way back down the road. He'd said he wanted to catch up with some of the lads he hadn't seen in a while, and they'd texted that they were going to be watching the football on the big screen there. Louisa also remembered how Brian hadn't returned until almost midnight that night. Now she wasn't sure she wanted to hear the rest of this story. What you didn't know couldn't hurt you. At least, in some situations. It had certainly been the case with what she'd done. How could she tell Brian now?

Her silence gave Brian the go-ahead to continue his story. The one where he was about to tell her he'd betrayed her by shagging her best friend. She couldn't believe she felt bad for mistrusting Tiff now. It seemed she'd been bloody right to do so.

'She was really grateful, said it was hard being on her own when things like that needed doing. She felt awkward asking her male friends to help out in case it looked dodgy to their wives.'

'Hah! She always did think highly of herself.'

'Don't, Lou. You don't mean that.' He rubbed his hand up and down her bare arm. 'She wasn't like that, and you know it.'

'Then what? What the fuck are you trying to tell me?'

'Shhh, calm down, you'll wake Emily.'

'I'm just not sure where this "chat" is going, Brian,' she whispered.

'I know.' He pushed himself up and sat cross-legged in front of her. She did the same. 'I'm making a hash of this.'

'You need to spit it out, whatever it is, say it. Please.'

'I wanted something to happen. Wanted to make . . .' He gulped in a huge intake of breath. 'Wanted to make a move on her, I guess.'

'And?' Her insides felt shaky; adrenaline coursed through her veins.

'And I did. Stupidly, in a moment of utter madness, I did. I'm so sorry, Lou. I can't even remember consciously making the decision to kiss her.'

Louisa's sight clouded; a tingling sensation swept through her body. It wasn't anything she hadn't thought about, but hearing Brian say it crushed her. She'd been carrying his baby, and he'd been out trying to get his leg over with her best friend. Bastard.

'Was that it?' She couldn't look at him, didn't want to see his lying eyes. 'Was it just a kiss?'

'Yes. And I regretted it immediately. I felt like a complete fool.'

'What did she do?'

'She pushed me away, then gave me a good, hard slap across my face. I deserved it, of course.'

There was an element of relief hearing about Tiff's response. But it was brief. 'What if she hadn't? Pushed you away, I mean?

I'm guessing you wouldn't have felt a fool then. I'm also betting you wouldn't have regretted anything instantly? You'd have gone for the full thing – a shag on the sofa, her bedroom – then worried about your infidelity at a later point. Like now. And are you sure? Because if I remember correctly, you didn't crawl home that night until the early hours. It's not like I can ask Tiff to back up your story, is it? You can say what you bloody well please and there's no one to go against your version of events—'

'Louisa . . . Lou, please, calm down,' he said, grabbing both her hands and squeezing them. 'It's the truth. Really. She pushed me away, and I left with my tail between my legs, panicking about the whole thing, scared she'd call you right away and tell you what a twat I'd been. I went to the pub to drown my shame. I stayed there; they had a lock-in. That's why I was late, like I told you back then. I wasn't with her, I promise.'

'I – I'm not sure whether I can believe that. I hate the thought of not trusting Tiff—'

'Oh, but you're fine with not trusting me? That's perfect, that is.'

'Hang on a minute.' Louisa propelled herself up and out of the bed, turned, and with both hands flat on the mattress pushed her face up to Brian's until it was almost touching. 'Don't you dare turn this around on me. I'm not the one who made advances on *your* best mate. And the reason I'm upset about not trusting Tiff is that, one – if you're right then she did nothing wrong in this scenario, and two – she's bloody dead, Brian.' Hot tears tracked down her face. 'She's not here to shout at, not here to talk to, ask for her version of this cringeworthy event. That's why I hate not trusting her, because I've *lost* her. I shouldn't be angry with a dead person. But you? Well I can be as angry as I damn well please with you. And I think I have every right to be, don't you agree?'

Brian's silence meant she had time to compose herself. Exhausted, she pushed away from him and walked into the bathroom, the coolness of the tiles welcoming to her hot feet.

'And what about you and Oliver then?'

Louisa heard Brian's deflated voice as she sat on the toilet. She contemplated his question for a moment. There had been a fleeting moment on a few occasions where Louisa had felt an urge to lean in towards Oliver, kiss him. She'd been wise enough to realise they were old feelings, though – ones that belonged in the past with a couple that had long since grown up and apart. You couldn't rekindle something from so long ago. Not when both people had changed so much.

'What about us?'

'Well, weren't you tempted?'

'Tempted? Tempted to what?'

'Oh, come on, Louisa. You can lie to yourself, but not to me.'

'I don't know about that.' She regretted the words as soon as they were spoken and she hoped Brian had not caught what she'd said. The last thing she wanted to get into was a deep discussion about what she was holding back from him. She was a hypocrite. But at this point in time, concentrating on Brian's shortcomings was the only way she could possibly move on from the devastating truth of what *she'd* done.

'What?'

'I said, I don't know if I can talk about that now.' Louisa made her way back to bed. 'I'm tired. Can we resume play in the morning?'

'It *is* morning. But whatever.' Brian flung himself over to face away from her.

Louisa got the impression that he didn't really want to hear her answer.

46

THE HYPNOSIS

Breakfast had been strained. Neither Brian nor Louisa spoke more than five words to each other, and Emily left for school earlier than usual. Louisa bet it was to take herself out of what must've seemed like a toxic wasteland. Brian got ready for work, but then hung about in the kitchen watching Louisa – a worried look fixed on his face.

'We really need to make more of an effort in front of Emily, Brian. It's not good for her to experience our pain.'

'I know. I'm sorry. I'm tired is all. It's nothing for her to worry about – she'll be okay.' He walked over to where Louisa was sitting and planted a kiss on the top of her head – his usual move before leaving for the prison.

'We don't know that. It's been a really unsettling time for her, and she's a teenager; she doesn't tell us the half of it. We should be keeping our stuff to ourselves. Put a brave face on it when she's here.'

'Right. Sure. Will try harder.' The sarcasm was evident. The fact he was trying to make her feel as though *she* was the one in the wrong annoyed her. He plonked his travel mug of coffee on the coaster and sat down opposite her. Louisa felt compelled to broach the subject of last night's late-night chat despite knowing it'd be uncomfortable and she'd make him late.

'So, I guess I should answer your question.' Louisa waited for Brian to make eye contact with her. He gave a small shrug. Louisa took a deep breath.

'Unlike you, Brian – I didn't, and wouldn't, make a play for anyone else. As for Oliver, well it's *you* who invited him into our lives. Not me. Remember that.'

He raised his eyebrows. 'I know.'

'Well, to be fair, you *and* Tiff did. I would never have gone looking for him. Oliver is my past, as I told you. I have never been unfaithful to you, not in any way.'

Brian lowered his head, avoiding her eyes. 'I'm sorry. It's all I can say, all I can keep saying.'

'Good. I'll never be able to forget that the only reason things didn't go further was because Tiff put the brakes on, though. That hurts, Brian. But we all make mistakes.' Louisa swallowed her pride and decided that in fairness, her secret from him was far worse than his secret from her. At least he'd had the guts to come clean about his. Eventually.

'I'll make it my mission to never hurt you again. I promise.'

Louisa nodded. 'We'll try and put this behind us, then. I also have something I need to . . . confront. Something from years ago.' Louisa noticed the slight tremor in her hands as she held her mug. She wasn't sure how much to say, now, to Brian. But if she wanted to carry out her plan, then he'd need to be in on it, to some extent. 'You know about the dissociative amnesia – the episodes where I've no memory of events in my teens?'

'Yes, sort of. You didn't really ever explain fully – you never wanted to talk about it so I didn't push you.'

'Well, stuff has been coming back to me. It's patchy, but I know it's important. The memories that are trying to reveal

274

themselves – they are key to something. I need to capture them.'

'Okay, But how?'

'The only way I can think is by self-hypnosis. I've been looking online and have found some guidance and I think I can do it. But I need quiet. Space to myself.' Louisa looked questioningly at Brian. He gave a gentle nod.

'I'll phone in sick.'

'Oh, I wasn't meaning right now, necessarily.'

'I'd suggested I take a few days off to be with you anyway, hadn't I, so now is as good a time as any. I haven't pulled a sickie in, like, ten years. I'm pretty sure no one is going to bat an eyelid.'

'If you're sure, that would be really helpful. Now seems the right time to do this.'

'Absolutely.' He sat up straighter, as if he'd been given orders and was ready to execute them; glad of a distraction. 'I'll take Noah out for the day. I think I'll take him to your parents', actually. It's about time they got involved in their grandson's life, don't you agree?'

Louisa hesitated for a moment. 'Yep, okay,' she said. It would suit her plan to have them gone for the day, despite her not really wanting them to go crawling to her mum and dad. But, needs must. 'That's a great idea. Better coming from you, too. You've always been good with my parents.'

'Sorted then.' He got back up from the breakfast bar and walked to the window, his phone to his ear as he informed the prison gate he wouldn't be in to work. Then Louisa watched in silence as he paced around the kitchen, then in and out of the lounge, collecting what Noah would need for the day. Having a purpose, something to make him feel as though he was being useful was clearly helping him to feel better about what he'd done.

She hoped the same would happen for her now she had the

goal of doing the hypnosis. If it worked. Her heart sank at the thought it might not. She had to be positive. Believe it was going to work. The key thing with hypnosis itself was positive, not negative, statements:

Today I'm going to remember everything from those missing months.

I am going to remember the missing parts from the night of my party.

As she finished her cup of coffee, apprehension hit her. She was about to embark on something that might put an end to the blocked memories.

And that could only go one of two ways.

Was she prepared for what she might learn?

Louisa lay in the middle of the mattress, the pillows tucked comfortably under her head. She'd carried out all the preparation work as stated in the online resources she'd found. She was comfortable, all distractions had been removed: no phones were on, she'd taken the batteries out of the doorbell, the windows were all closed. Although the instructions she'd found didn't mention anything along the lines of having a clock, Louisa felt sure monotonous ticking would help her relax, so she'd pulled the one off the kitchen wall and now placed it beside her on the bed. The tinny-sounding tick-tocking was surprisingly loud and echoey in her now peaceful bedroom.

Concentrating on the clock's rhythm, Louisa began the process of relaxing her muscles, step by step, moving from her toes up towards her head. Then her breathing became the focus. Deep breaths, in . . . and out. She visualised a large body of water with stairs going down into it, and began stepping down. Ten, nine . . . breathe in, and out. Lowering herself further: eight, seven . . . she was almost touching the water. Six, five . . .

her toes dipped into the cool, blue ripples. Four, three . . . deeper and deeper. Two, one . . . she was submerged.

She felt calm, relaxed under the water, weightless – and she knew she could still breathe deeply despite being below the surface of the cool liquid.

There were three boxes beneath the water.

She knew she had to swim to each one in turn.

Each one held a memory from a different time. The first was from 1997. The second was from her fortieth birthday party. The third was unknown, unmarked. She knew nothing about its contents, but she had an awareness that this box also needed to be opened, its contents spilled.

She took a breath as though she'd literally been holding it whilst underwater and sat up abruptly. What had happened? Had she done it – remembered everything? Her head swam for a few moments, her thought processes floundering.

Relax.

Yes. She had done it; she'd revisited the memories in each of the boxes. She envisaged them again, frame by frame. It was tough, and her psyche still fought against it. Initially, the boxes had been easy to open. During the hypnosis she'd visualised them, then imagined herself placing the key in the padlock, flipping the latch and lifting the lid. She did this for boxes one and two, but the third box had been the most difficult to open; its lock stiffer, resistant. Once she'd succeeded in opening it, it was also the most challenging to close again. But close it she did. She'd had to. The other two were the ones that needed her full attention at this time. They were the ones that required action.

The last one could wait. Maybe forever.

47

THE GHOST

As Louisa showered and dressed into jeans and a jumper – her only remaining clean ones, she noted – she let the contents of the first two boxes come back to her. Since the hypnosis session Louisa's adrenaline levels had abated, and the retrieved memories had settled and fixed themselves firmly in her conscious mind. She realised, though, that the session hadn't been entirely successful. They were all so close – she could almost touch them – but they were not altogether coherent.

The solution to this was crystal clear to her now: she had to revisit the pub.

Go to the place where this nightmare began and retrace her steps.

Back to her fortieth birthday party.

She had to be in the right place.

Although the woman in the lane had happened twenty-two years prior to her birthday, both events were inextricably linked. She knew that now. It was a case of returning to the scene of the crime, so to speak.

A dull ache began in her head. At one point she'd considered that there *was* a crime. The way she'd felt the day after the party, the visions, the subsequent revelations – had all added to the hideous feeling that something bad, very bad, had happened that night. Now, she at least felt less worried that she'd done something then, but she did know there was a hidden horror. One she felt compelled to uncover.

The hypnosis had only lasted for an hour. An hour of her life that had changed everything. Brian was still out with Noah – which was hopefully a good sign, in that her parents were finally keen to spend time with him. She couldn't therefore ask Brian to drive her to Abbotsbury. She'd walk out of the village and get the bus from the main road. If she was quick she'd be able to catch the 3 p.m. Totnes to Newton one. Then she could jump off at the turning to the village – it wasn't too far from there to the centre of Abbotsbury.

The bus had stopped at the top of the road leading to the village – to the pub – and Louisa had walked briskly. In her mind, now she was walking down the path to the pub, she was retracing hers and Tiff's steps. If she'd realised it'd be her last time properly spending time with her best friend, she'd have made more of it. The lateness of the afternoon meant it was getting dusky and as Louisa approached the pub its stonework appeared dark, unwelcoming. She had to continue, had to 'relive' their actions and pull to the front of her mind what she remembered from that night. It was important to fill in some gaps by being in the same venue – the hypnosis had made her realise she had to be here.

Tiff had been on her mobile as they'd approached the pub from the accommodation block. Louisa remembered the feeling of indignation at the time, and afterwards she'd assumed Tiff was texting Brian, letting him know they were there – so the birthday surprise could be executed without a hitch.

It hadn't been Brian she'd texted though.

The thought propelled itself into her head and left her puzzled. How did she know that? She couldn't remember ever asking Tiff. Pushing it away as an unnecessary distraction at this point, Louisa carried on walking towards the pub door, then stopped short. Could she retrace her steps, the night's events, without physically going inside the pub? She didn't want to draw attention to herself, have to face any people who might ask her questions. Instead, she headed around the side of the pub to the beer garden, which she felt would be equally sufficient in helping to draw out the memories.

Sitting down on the wooden bench beside the table, Louisa pulled off her shoes, then stood.

Cold grass.

She walked up and down in a small circle, the grass tickling her feet. She stopped and closed her eyes, taking a deep breath in through her nose. She visualised the box from her hypnosis session. Visualised herself opening it here, now. A vivid image of the woman she hit in the lane twenty-two years earlier flashed up, inside the darkness of her closed lids.

'*Can I blag one of them off you?*' The voice caused fear to surface again.

And now, Louisa felt a presence; she could sense she was no longer alone. A chill shot through her as she opened her eyes, and slowly turned around.

The woman she'd run over was standing in front of her.

Louisa blinked hard several times but the apparition remained standing, staring at her – an expression that was part amused, part disgusted.

Her mind was confusing the memories, mixing up the images.

It hurt her to take a breath; the pain seemed to crush her ribs, restricting her lungs.

It's not her. She's dead. Your mind is playing tricks on you.

Louisa's legs felt cold, weak. This wasn't real. It was one of her hallucinations and she'd come of out of it in a minute, if she didn't panic.

The dead woman could not be standing with her in the beer garden. It was impossible.

There's a rational explanation for this.

Louisa closed her eyes tightly again. When she opened them, the dead woman would be gone.

'I've been trying to get to you,' a voice said.

Louisa felt a shift in her bowels. This wasn't the same as the other hallucinations.

It seemed very real.

She opened her eyes to face whatever was in front of her.

48

THE REVELATION

'I've been trying to get to you,' the woman repeated. 'Without Oliver catching me.'

Louisa's cheeks filled with air and she blew it out slowly, recovering now that she faced the woman. Faced the truth.

Melissa Dunmore.

'Where have you been? How come the police haven't found you?'

'I've been careful. Not used my mobile, not bought anything with any of my cards, no withdrawals. I've done nothing that would offer any proof of me being alive and well.'

'You wanted people to think you were dead? How could you put your family, your friends through that?'

'I have my reasons. One in particular that you should be familiar with.'

Louisa wasn't sure which specific reason she was referring to, but it was safe to assume it could be related to running away from something in her past, or hiding from the reper-cussions of a bad decision. Or could she be alluding to something else? Had Oliver told Melissa what Louisa had done all those years ago? But if she did, what could she do about it now? It wasn't as if Melissa could threaten her with the police. Firstly, she had no evidence. And secondly, Louisa did. *She* had evidence that put Melissa at the scene of a death – even if the police were yet to realise it had been a crime, she would bet that if she showed the police the drone footage, they'd look at the circumstances again, investigate further. Louisa held the cards here.

'I don't know what you mean,' Louisa said. 'But I do know about Tiff. That you were there, at her place the day she died. I've seen the evidence – Tiff had a drone, and you are clearly visible on the footage. It was you who hurt her, wasn't it? *Why?* I don't understand.'

'I didn't hurt her.' Melissa shook her head, spiral curls bobbing around her face. 'What happened to Tiff was not my fault. I just went there because I always felt sure she knew more about my sister's disappearance than she said at the time.'

'So, you *did* know Tiff?'

'I knew of her, yes. Knew her type.'

'I'd say you knew more than that. I saw the photo. The one on the beach, the happy group of friends all together. You with your arm around Tiff. I need to call the police – sorry, Melissa.' Louisa turned to the table, taking her handbag and rummaging for her mobile.

'Wait.' Melissa reached forwards, laying her hand on Louisa's arm. 'Aren't you interested in knowing the truth?'

Louisa hesitated, a squirming sensation rippling up her arms. Of course she was interesting in knowing the truth. 'Go on,' she said, her eyes narrowing.

'Tiff must've slipped. She was alive when I left. That's the truth. We'd talked, finally put some ghosts to rest. It must've just been a terrible accident; it was nothing to do with me. Well, not directly. She'd been trying to protect you.'

'Protect *me*?'

'She said Oliver had been hassling her, telling her she had to be careful of you. He told her what you'd done.'

Louisa gasped. After everything he'd said about keeping quiet for both of their sakes, why would he then tell Tiff? It didn't make sense. Annoyance pressed her lips together tightly. She stared at Melissa, trying to deduce if Oliver had told *her* what had happened too. Told her how Louisa had killed a woman and asked for his help to cover up what she'd done. A heat burned her cheeks.

'What I'd done?' Her mouth was dry, her throat raspy. The question hung suspended in the air for a moment, unanswered. But Melissa's face darkened, her features losing their sharpness. She looked as though her mind had wandered some place else. When she spoke again, even her voice had altered, had lost its sweetness.

'Oliver had always been so supportive.' An abrupt burst of laughter snorted its way through Melissa's nose. 'So understanding. Helping me through my grief.' The garden lamp suddenly illuminated, and the light caught her eyes, the tears sparkling just before they dropped down her cheeks.

'Grief?'

'Yes. He knew what we'd gone through when Helen ran away. The thought that she couldn't talk to us, confide in her family, was always tough. Never finding her was excruciating. It killed my mum.'

Louisa's stomach rolled; a darkness encroached her vision from the edges, moving its way across her eyes. She put a hand on the wooden table to steady herself – her legs twitching, the bones feeling as if they'd been liquefied.

'Your sister looked just like you,' Louisa said, her voice barely a whisper. It wasn't a question.

She knew.

'Yes, even though she was older by a few years, everyone

always mistook us for one another. Thought we were twins.'

'It was her in the photo with Tiff, not you,' Louisa said aloud, the reality dawning on her – Tiff had known Melissa's sister, had worked with her. It was her Tiff had referred to when she'd told Louisa about her experience of being involved in a missing person investigation. 'Did you ever find out what happened to her?' She realised her question was futile, knowing the answer before she'd even asked it.

'No. Oliver convinced me to stop looking, said it was destroying me, and that moving on would be what Helen would've wanted. And I had moved on. As much as I could. But when he wanted us to come back to Devon to branch out the business, I wasn't happy about it. I couldn't understand why he'd want to do it here, of all places. Why go backwards when it was he who had encouraged me to move on?

'It was because of you, though. I know that now. You are the reason he came back. But he never banked on me meeting you.'

'Now? He knows you're meeting with me now?' A surge of panic seized her.

'No. He has no idea about this, or where I've been. No, I mean at your party.'

'Oh, right.' Louisa's muscles relaxed a little, but then she realised what Melissa had said. 'You weren't at the party. No one saw you.'

'Oh, yes. I was there. Not that Oliver knew at first. But Tiff saw me. Talking to you right here.' Melissa cast her eyes around the beer garden.

So, she'd been right. She *had* seen Melissa. It just wasn't the woman who'd been standing by Oliver on the stairs. 'Tiff said she couldn't remember,' Louisa said, shaking her head. 'She knew I was talking to someone, she remembered that, but she couldn't say who and I was too out of it to remember.'

'Obviously I wasn't to know. I assumed she'd recognised me, so that's why I dragged you away from the garden. Out of view from your guests.'

The memory now came easily – filling the gap that the self-hypnosis had left. She remembered Melissa pulling at her arm, felt the coldness beneath her feet as she was taken into the grassy area behind the pub, then to the cobbled road running adjacent to it.

I need my shoes.

No. You don't. Just come with me.

But the stones. Ouch.

Stop whining.

'How come Oliver didn't know you were there – and why did he allow everyone to believe you *were* there?'

'It suited his plan. He wanted to keep me at home. To keep me from meeting you. But I was too curious. Jealous, I guess. I wanted to meet you, so I followed him. When I saw you here, in the garden, and spoke to you, everything fell into place.'

The sudden clarity hit her. 'Yes, for me too.' The reason she'd been plagued by the images and visions from the beer garden were alarmingly clear to her now – that repressed memory too, now forcing itself to the forefront of her mind. As soon as she'd seen Melissa on the night of her party, she'd realised who she must be.

Louisa looked away, not wanting Melissa to see the guilt in her eyes.

'I know. The look on your face when you saw me – like you'd seen a ghost.'

Louisa's breathing shallowed. God, this was it. Melissa knew what she'd done.

Louisa had killed Melissa's sister.

'I can't begin to explain. I have no excuses, Melissa. I'm so very sorry. I was young, I freaked out. I didn't even know what I'd done until Oliver told me – I know it'll sound like a cop-out to you, but I've suffered dissociative amnesia since it happened. I started getting flashbacks after the party – after seeing you. But even that I didn't remember – I only had fleeting memories of the evening.'

'But now you remember.'

'Most of it, yes. I . . . I can see . . .' The words caught in her throat; tears burned at her eyes. She shook her head, a part of her now wanting to displace the images that were so easily appearing. She shouldn't be telling Melissa this. It would be too much for her to cope with.

'What? What can you see, Louisa? Tell me exactly what you think happened.'

Louisa hesitated, stumbling on her words. 'I can see . . . your sister; I can see Helen, on the ground in front of my car. I can hear the engine idling, the music from my radio cassette blaring out of the speakers: the words from that song, which has been in my head recently; I can feel the bile rising, my whole body shaking as I slowly get out of my car to see what I've done. I feel the sheer panic when I see she's completely still. I realise I can't drive past her. There's no room in the narrow lane. I—' Louisa retched, her upper body folding over her thighs. 'Oh my God,' she gagged. 'I got hold of her arms, and pulled her to the side of the lane under the trees. Then I somehow drove home and rang Oliver. I was in such a state. He helped out, came over then drove the route I'd taken. He told me she was dead. That I'd killed her.'

'Oh, Louisa.' Melissa's brow creased, her expression a mixture of anger and sadness. 'Oliver did a good job on you, too, then.'

'What do you mean?'

'You did hit my sister, knocked her down. She was badly

288

injured. But she was alive when you left her. *You* did not kill her. Oliver did.'

'What? No. Poor Oliver, it was *me* who'd made him drive out there. He did what he thought was best for me. He disposed of her body. For me. I was drunk, had been taking drugs. He said I'd have gone to prison . . .'

'Louisa. Listen to me. It was *Oliver* who killed Helen. Not you.'

'What are you talking about?' Louisa took a step back, pressing both hands to her chest, her breaths suddenly shallow.

'After I saw you in this garden, and we talked, you told me your history with Oliver. You told me how he'd left you back in 1997, that he'd said he was doing it to protect you after your accident – you got so upset and I knew something big had happened. So, some things fell into place for me. I confronted Oliver after the party, said I knew the reason he'd come back as I'd spoken to you, and he flipped. He must've assumed you'd told me everything about the accident in the lanes, thought I'd added two and two together. He lost it, tried to strangle me, Louisa. Look.'

Melissa pulled at the silk scarf around her throat, revealing a yellowing ring of bruises.

'I tell you, it was like he'd become possessed. I couldn't understand it. I fought him hard, kicked him in the balls. He backed off then, unable to carry on his attack. When he'd got his breath back, he began rambling an incoherent explanation about what you'd done. He was trying to blame you to start with, saying you'd killed her and that his only crime had been in trying to clear up *your* mess. But then he crumpled, like all his strength left him and he was finally defeated, his lies too heavy to bear; he fell apart. He sat there, crying like a child. Then it all spilled out of him, the truth, like a long stream of hot guilt that he'd carried with him for over twenty years.'

'But . . . he told me. Said it was me who'd killed her. He went to where it'd happened and when he came back, he said he'd taken care of it. For me. To protect me. And after a while he left the area – again, to protect *me*. That's what he said. It's what I believed.'

'It's the way he'd have liked to believe it happened too. But it didn't. He said when he got to the location you'd specified, my sister was propped against a tree trunk. Battered and bloody, but very much alive. She looked at him, begged him to call an ambulance, to call *me*. He said he was doing it for you. That's how he'd justified strangling the life from her, then burying her body.'

'He couldn't have done that, Melissa. Oliver is a lot of things, but not a murderer. He took the flak for *me*. And anyway, he wouldn't have had time to kill her *and* bury her – he was back at my house less than . . .'

'Less than what?'

'I – I'm not sure exactly, but he hadn't been gone long. I was beside myself with worry, but I would remember if I'd been waiting ages for his return.'

'And you have a clear memory of everything that happened that night, do you? You weren't panicked? Confused?'

'Well, I . . .'

'So you might not remember the time he came back. An hour, two, may have passed. Can you be one hundred per cent sure he was back within half an hour? And anyway, I'm sure it didn't take long for the sick bastard to end her life.'

'No. I guess you're right.' Louisa's head shook involuntarily with shock, yet also an element of relief, as she attempted to assimilate this new information. 'I just can't believe it. I thought it was me. That I'd killed her. I can't understand why Oliver would tell you now, though.'

'Guilt. It's what made him seek me out in the first place.

290

He'd murdered my sister, with his bare hands, and then dumped her body. Covered it over with earth, leaving her to remain undiscovered for however many years – forever if he was lucky. Ensuring her family never got closure. It wasn't until the night of your party, when I finally confronted him, that he dropped the pretence. He never really loved me. I was just his act of atonement. He tried to make amends for his actions by being there for me, supporting me, but of course, he couldn't have ever told me the real reason he'd asked me out before – the reason he'd asked me to marry him – or he'd have lost me. I was his only source of redemption. He'd been willing to keep his hideous secret, the real reason he was with me, from everyone. And if it wasn't for me coming here, meeting you, he'd likely have succeeded.' She tutted and looked away.

'Why would he make me believe that it was me?' A surge of pain, hot, seared inside her stomach. 'Did his feeling of guilt not reach as far as me?'

'He saw an opportunity I imagine. Thought he could finally offload the guilt onto you. Then he'd finally be able to get on with his life. With the sister of the woman he murdered. Makes me sick.'

'So your disappearance . . . ?'

'I was angry, hurt. Mentally and physically. I had to get away from him. But I wanted to make him pay. Make you pay as well.' She smiled thinly. Louisa opened her mouth to speak, to put up some sort of defence, but no words came out.

'Don't worry, I'm not going to hurt you,' Melissa said, as if sensing Louisa's fear. 'I've had time to think, and I can see that he took your life too, in a way. He didn't know you couldn't remember that night, and he left you here to face it all on your own while he went looking for redemption through his victim's family. How warped is that? He could've saved Helen, Louisa. But he chose to let you take the blame for ending her life instead. What you did is unforgivable, but it was an accident. You were young and you turned to someone you loved and trusted to help you. He let you down too.'

'What are we going to do now?'

'There's not a shred of evidence that will link Oliver with Helen's disappearance, and without a body . . . well, there's very little we can do. And trust me, Oliver is never going to say where she is; I tried and failed. I've even considered the possibility he doesn't *remember* precisely where he disposed of her. We have nothing that can damage Oliver. But you, Louisa – you have evidence that can damage me. The footage on that drone doesn't prove anything other than I was at the scene the day Tiff died – and don't forget you'd been there too – but as *I'm* the one faking my own disappearance, questions will be raised. Links made. I can't afford that to happen.'

'He tried to kill you. Isn't that evidence enough?'

'He'll say it was an argument that got out of hand, one spawned by my jealousy of finding out he'd come back here for you.'

'But he didn't come back *for* me, he came back to offload his bloody guilt!'

'It's his word against ours.'

'He could still be charged with actual bodily harm—'

'It's not enough, Louisa. Not nearly enough. He has to be punished for what he's done. To Helen, to me. And to you.'

'Don't you think your disappearance is punishment enough? The police feel he's behind it, so do a lot of people. He's lost you and he's under suspicion.'

'Knowing what you do now, do *you* think that's enough?'

'No. No, it isn't.' Something was still niggling her about Melissa's story, though. 'Why were you bothering with Tiff, after all the years that had passed?'

'You don't need to know the full story, Louisa. It's best you don't. Like I said, I was trying to find out more about Helen's disappearance, and seeing Oliver going in and out of hers made me think she knew more than she was letting on, that she'd been in on it too. She'd known Helen and she was your best friend. I saw red when all she did was deny everything. She said you couldn't know anything, that what Oliver was saying about you was malicious and unfounded, and you'd have confided in her if it were true. That's when I knew everything was falling apart all over again – my belief that I was beginning to pull things together shattered in that moment. I was never going to find where my sister's body was. So, I wanted all of you to suffer.'

Louisa realised she'd been gullible up to now and had absolutely no reason to trust the woman standing in front of her. All that came from her mouth could be lies. But against her better judgement, she believed Melissa. What she was saying made sense now, given all the facts, the supposed facts, the fragments of memory, the way Oliver had come back into her life and manipulated her.

'I get that. I know I should suffer. I'll hand myself in to the police, tell them everything I know.'

'No. It won't stick. You may well get arrested but they will only have your story. Once they speak to Oliver, he'll give his account. And I'm not being funny, I don't know you, but from what you've said about the amnesia, a good lawyer would take you apart.'

'Then what? What do you want from me?'

'I want Oliver to suffer. I want him to pay for what he did then, and for what he's been doing since. He's destroyed my life whilst being beside me, holding my hand while he's doing it. He's evil, Louisa. He's spun all these lies for years and now made complete fools out of both of us.'

'I'm not sure where this is going . . .' Although her twisting gut informed her otherwise.

'We need to confront him together,' Melissa said firmly. 'Tonight.'

49

THE TRAP

'I'm planning on going out with some of the old crowd tonight, would that be okay?' Louisa held the mobile phone so tight to her ear that it hurt. Every muscle in her body was taut, like a coiled spring awaiting its release.

'Of course. I think it's great that you've hooked back up with them.' Brian's voice sounded far away, despite only being down the road at her parents'. She wondered if they were making it awkward, whether they were as hard work as they had been the last time Louisa visited them. 'You could do with some company, a bit of fun,' he added.

'Not sure how late I'll be, though, so don't wait up or anything. I'll take house keys.'

She waited as Brian's muffled voice relayed this information to her mum and dad – why he felt the need to do so was beyond her.

'I'll get takeaway for us all and stay here then,' he said finally. 'You go – and try to enjoy yourself.'

As much as Louisa felt the urge to question what on earth her mum and dad would eat from a takeaway, she let it go so she could get off the phone. He'd obviously been far better at building bridges than she'd thought, and her parents *wanted* them to stay. That had to be a positive thing, she guessed.

'Thank you. See you when I get back.'

Louisa ended the call then got dressed into an outfit that would look as though she were going out to the pub, not to the common on the edge of the village. She couldn't dress down too much, or Brian might query it when she got home later. If he was still awake of course. She put her flat shoes on – she had to walk for about ten minutes to the back lane running out of Little Penchurch to reach the common where she was going to meet Melissa.

And Oliver.

When Louisa had returned home from Court Farm earlier, she'd felt exhausted, confused, conflicted, angry and full of indecision about what to do. Melissa had been clear, though. She had talked Louisa into setting up a meeting with Oliver. And then, as planned, Melissa was going to ambush him. A bizarre 'surprise' she was imagining to be even more awful than her fortieth party. Louisa's stomach twisted with nerves just thinking about it. The two of them, confronting Oliver about what he did. Her confusion came from why Melissa seemed prepared to overlook the fact it was Louisa's irresponsible and dangerous behaviour that had caused the accident in the first place, and was instead wholly intent on making just Oliver suffer.

The most worrying aspect to Melissa's 'plan' was not knowing the outcome. Once they'd confronted him – what was going to happen then? She had no idea how, exactly, Melissa intended to make him suffer. That part of the plan hadn't been discussed, and that's what set Louisa's heart rate soaring. The unknown. She was walking into this with her eyes only partially open. Melissa could be operating on a completely different agenda to her.

What if her plan all along was to get her and Oliver together so she could punish them both at the same time?

She shouldn't go. The best thing would be to leave well alone. She should go to her parents', join in on the takeaway evening instead.

But at the same time, she wanted to see Oliver's face, wanted to hear Melissa's rage hit him full force. She wanted to hear his side of the story; find out why he'd purposely sought out the sister of the woman Louisa had hit in the lanes, years after it'd happened. The thought he'd done that – gone as far as to marry her, too – made her skin crawl. Oliver really wasn't who she'd thought he was. He'd lied to Melissa. Lied to Louisa. Lied to everyone. Melissa was right: he'd be unlikely to be found guilty of Helen's murder – unless her remains were found. And Melissa understandably believed he shouldn't get away with it. Louisa knew if she could help that process a bit, she had to take that opportunity. And besides, she'd told Melissa she'd do it now, so she owed her. Justice for Helen, for her family, had to prevail.

Was the truth, and confronting Oliver, justice enough for Melissa though?

The evening was crisp, and Louisa pulled her black mac tightly around her to keep the chilly air from sneaking through the gaps. She set off at a brisk pace, but slowed as she passed the church, an ache causing her to clutch her tummy. Tiff's funeral was tomorrow – she'd already seen the plot that had been dug in preparation when she'd walked through the churchyard with Noah. Was that yesterday, or the day before? She'd lost track.

All she knew was she wasn't ready for it; it seemed too soon to be burying her friend. But it's what her parents wanted – Shirley had said she needed to get that part over with, so they could begin the grieving process properly. The newly dug grave was against the far wall of the churchyard, next to the meadow that stretched on for acres and backed onto Tiff's house. Her final resting place would be next to one of the oldest graves in the cemetery. A lovely spot, if there was such a thing in a graveyard – under one of the two huge oak trees. Tiff would have been happy with that. The reality had hit Louisa when she'd seen it, though – the hole in the ground signifying the end. The end of Tiff. The end of their friendship.

Louisa gave her arms a rub and, head down, carried on to the meeting place. A few minutes later, with the darkness beginning to envelop her, she came to the entrance of the common. She gave a furtive glance around her. The road was quiet and the small tarmacked area on the opposite side where people often parked their cars whilst visiting the common was empty – a chain looped across its narrow entrance. She slipped through the kissing gates without any hesitation – the time for that had long passed – and took the right-hand path that led to the top of the disused quarry.

Why hadn't Oliver asked the reason she wanted to meet him; queried the location?

Louisa knew he'd taken many walks at the common since Melissa's disappearance, which was one of the reasons she'd suggested it – that and the fact it was most likely to be deserted in the evening. Since the quarry had been totally fenced off, even the teenagers had abandoned it as their favourite drinking spot and started using the back end of the park behind the skatepark as their meeting place. The quarry no longer held the sense of adventure and danger, so walking that far just to be out of sight had lost its appeal to them.

Louisa held her mobile out in front of her and used the flashlight app to guide her along the bumpy, muddy path to the fenced quarry. As she turned and began to ascend the incline, a figure came into view – a dark shape motionless against the fence. If it wasn't for her phone, she'd be unable to make out anything but the trees; the light was fading fast, the night stealing it.

Louisa didn't like it; she'd never felt so vulnerable. Unsafe.

'Hello, Oliver,' she said when she reached him, her breathing shallow from the excursion. From her nerves.

'This is all rather cloak-and-dagger, Lou-Lou.' He grinned. 'I think I like it.'

God, did he think she was there to have an illicit encounter with him? Perhaps that was why he hadn't questioned the meeting place – he'd naturally assumed she'd chosen it as a good place where they could get up to no good without being caught. The thought both horrified and excited her. If it hadn't been for Melissa hiding somewhere close by, would she allow something to happen between them – to punish Brian's attempted infidelity with Tiff by doing the same with Oliver? She had to admit, she would've been tempted once. But that was before.

Before she knew what a low-life liar he was.

'Don't get too excited. It's not what you think.'

She could see disappointment hit him first, followed by confusion.

'Why are we meeting here then?' His brow lowered, making his eyes appear even darker than usual.

'I didn't want to be overheard. Wanted to be somewhere away from my family. Common ground, so to speak.'

His smile wavered. 'Riiight. So, what *did* you want to discuss?'

'Don't pretend you don't know.' Louisa's voice caught. She felt sure he was playing with her.

He shrugged. 'There's been rather a lot going on lately. I'm not a mind reader.'

Louisa swallowed down the urge to yell at him and took a

slow, deep breath to remain in control. 'Yes, there certainly has, but I mean, you know – the thing you told me—'

'Oh! Of course. The woman in the lane . . .' He gave a wry smile.

'Yep. Her for starters,' Louisa snapped.

'I know it was a terrible shock for you, to hear from me what you'd done after you'd buried the memory for so many years. You've always got me to talk to about it though – you know that. We are the only ones who know what you did. What I did to cover it all up. It's our secret.' He reached forwards, taking hold of her upper arms. 'As I said before, the guilt is a huge burden, but now we've found each other again, we can share that weight. We can be each other's support.' His confident smile sent a sharp shiver down her back.

'Yeah, about that. I'm not sure we *are* the only ones who know. And I think you are well aware of that.'

'No, Lou-Lou,' Oliver said, taking her in his arms and holding her tightly. 'I promise, I haven't told a soul, never would. I'll protect you until the end.'

'Protect me?' She pulled out of his embrace, so she could look directly into his eyes. 'Are you sure about that, Oliver?'

'Yes, I'm sure. What you did was something many people have done – drinking, smoking dope, then driving – you won't be the only one who's done that. You were unlucky that night.'

'No, Oliver – I was *wrong* that night. Wrong to get behind the wheel, wrong to drive through the lanes, wrong to call you for your help. Wrong to go along with you.'

Louisa watched as the words sank in – catching Oliver's expression as it hardened, his jaw tightening.

'That hurts,' he said, taking a step back. 'I put myself on the line for you! Don't be so selfish and ungrateful now. My life is in tatters – because *you* killed that girl and I covered it up for *you.*'

The shift in Oliver's mood and the way his voice was suddenly thick with malice scared Louisa. She took a step back, lowering her phone light so she couldn't see his face. But he walked forwards, clearly not finished.

'How different do you think your life would be now if I hadn't done that for you, Lou? Eh? No lovely marriage to the safe and dependable Brian, no children – you'd have been locked up for life!'

'No, Oliver, she wouldn't have.'

The voice, loud and strong, came from a little higher than where Oliver and Louisa were standing. Louisa lifted her mobile and shone it in Oliver's direction, in time to see his face pale; it looked like a perfectly white oval against the night's blue-black backdrop. He lost his footing as he turned abruptly to the direction the voice had come from.

'What the fuck?' His words escaped his mouth like a weak hiss of air leaking from a deflating balloon.

'Surprise!' Melissa emerged from the bushes, a look of determination set on her face.

Oliver's mouth gaped as he looked from Melissa to Louisa – the reality dawning on him.

He'd been caught in a trap.

50

THE FORGIVENESS

'Melissa?' Oliver's voice was weak, his posture stiff. But he recovered quickly. 'What's going on here? I was so worried about you.' He moved forwards, his hands held up towards his wife.

'You were worried about me? Or about yourself?' Melissa stepped down the pathway, avoiding Oliver's outstretched arms, until she was standing beside Louisa.

'You, darling. Obviously you. Why did you disappear like that? How could you leave me knowing that I'd be beside myself wondering if you were okay – whether you were alive or dead?'

'I'm guessing you rather hoped I was dead.'

'Why would you say that? Tell her, Louisa, tell her how frantic I've been.' Oliver turned to Louisa, his eyes wide, pleading. 'Lou, you know, don't you? How I've been searching every day, worried sick that something bad had happened to her.'

'Yes,' Louisa said, 'you do seem to have been worried. But I'm not sure if it was for everyone else's benefit. And really, you needed to build up an image, didn't you? One where you were the concerned, loving husband. One where you were the innocent party in all this. You needed me, and Brian, to embellish the clever picture you were painting.'

'That's not true.' He shook his head vehemently. 'I came to you because my wife was missing, and I needed a friend. Being in Devon, away from everyone I knew, was awful. I was so lonely. You were the only person who would understand, the only one who knew me.'

'I don't know you at all, Oliver. And probably never did.'

'Look, this is ridiculous. Why are you two here, now, doing this to me?'

'I wanted to teach you a lesson,' Melissa said. 'Wanted you to hurt as much as you hurt me.'

'I have never hurt you – don't you dare lie like this.' Oliver's arms hung loosely at his sides, as though all his energy had been sucked from him and he didn't have the strength to hold them up anymore.

'I know you didn't set out to. Not at first. But *you* orchestrated this trip to Devon; *you* got yourself an invite to Louisa's party. It's because you wanted her, needed her. That's why *I* wanted to meet her – to find out why. And boy, I found out all right. You needed her to help cleanse your guilt, you sick—'

'Please, don't listen to her, Lou-Lou, she's bloody lost it.' Oliver lurched towards Melissa – she sidestepped and backed up behind Louisa. 'This is what she does, Lou, you have to believe me. Why would I lie to you? She's jealous of you, that's all. That's the only reason she wanted to meet you. This whole stupid disappearing act to try and pin it on me – it's pathetic. You won't win, Melissa.'

'I already have, Oliver. Don't you see? Your precious Lou-Lou knows everything. You can't hide the truth from her any longer.'

'You're deluded.'

'It's great, isn't it, how men pull that line when they know they're trapped?' Louisa suddenly felt more confident, furious at the game Oliver had played. Was still playing. 'It's mind games, manipulation. Make the woman out to be deranged, put the onus on her to prove she isn't. It won't work now, though. I've figured it all out and I think it's safe to say you know that. You lied then, and you're lying now. Nothing you say will make me waver. Melissa is telling the truth, I'm one hundred per cent certain of that.'

'Oh, dear, dear Lou. How on earth can you be certain of anything? You couldn't even remember feeding your own baby.' Oliver's facial expression changed from the concerned, worried look to a smug, menacing expression in an instant, the sudden flip making Louisa's muscles tense.

'Is that why you were happy to make me believe I was the one who'd committed murder? Because I was a soft touch and you were confident you could convince me it was all my fault?'

Oliver closed his eyes and sucked in a large lungful of air. 'I have no idea what you're rattling on about. I'm getting a little fed up with this circus now.'

'Are you? Ah, that's a shame because we're only just beginning the show.' Melissa turned to Louisa and smiled widely before placing one arm around her shoulder.

'Bloody women, sticking together like a pathetic women's union – fucking feminism has such a lot to answer for.'

'Tut-tut. Keep it calm, don't want you losing your shit and attacking people again, do we? Look, I'm here to help you. You have the opportunity to purge yourself of your sins, Oliver,' Melissa said.

'And if I don't want to?'

'Oh, you will. You've been desperate to rid yourself of the guilt for years. Well, now you can. You owe it to us.'

Oliver's shoulders slumped, his usual height diminishing. He backed away from them and slid down the fence, crouching with his elbows on his bent knees. A defeated position.

'What do you want me to say? That I'm sorry?'

'That would be a start.'

He shrugged. 'Then, I'm sorry. Are we done now? I'm so tired.'

For a moment his pained expression pulled at Louisa's conscience. She almost pitied him. But then the anger flooded back in. This too, was clearly an act. He was trying to manipulate them again. 'That's it? All you're going to say?'

'You wanted an apology. You got one.'

'You've got more to offload though, haven't you? The weight of the lies must be crushing you. If you tell us the truth, here and now, the *whole* story of what you did and why, *then* we'll be done. Then we'll let you go,' Melissa said.

'Let me go?' He laughed – a snort so loud it made Louisa jump. 'That implies that if I don't tell you what you want to hear, that you *won't* let me go. I know there are two of you, but surely you don't think you could prevent me from leaving?' He shifted, getting to his feet again, and Louisa knew it was because he was suddenly concerned about his subservient position on the ground – the two of them above him taking a far more powerful stance. They'd rattled him after all.

Melissa moved away from Louisa's side and walked over to the fence, looking over it. 'There's a perfectly good quarry there – a few good pushes from us, and you'd go over.'

Laughter filled the space between them. 'Ah, that's very humorous, Melissa.'

'I'm pretty sure you wouldn't be laughing as you fell.'

Louisa shifted her feet. They were getting numb from the lack of movement; the discomfort at the turn the conversation had taken now making her jumpy.

'Well, we'll never know, will we? You haven't got the strength. Or the *guts*,' he spat.

Louisa's breathing shallowed as she scanned the fence – there were no gaps; it was too high to push Oliver over. She tried to relax. It was just scare tactics, that was all. Melissa couldn't really carry out her threat. Oliver knew that too, and that's why he was relishing the fact, and now taunting his wife. Louisa hoped Melissa wouldn't snap; she didn't want to witness, or get involved in, any kind of scuffle – she was already regretting being talked into doing this.

'Say it, Oliver. Tell us the truth. Let Louisa off the hook.'

'And what? You've got your phones recording and will go to the police with your "evidence"?' Oliver shook his head. 'I'm not fucking stupid.'

'I haven't used my mobile, obviously. I've been missing – remember?'

Oliver turned to Louisa – the light from her mobile's flashlight app still illuminating the quarry fencing. 'And yours?'

She held it out towards him. No apps were running. No voice recording activated.

'Hmmm.' Oliver crossed one arm and put his other to his chin, stroking it, mockingly. 'You want me to believe you'd be that naive?'

'I don't care if you think we're naive, Oliver – it's about hearing the truth, not about catching you out, or grassing you up.'

Even Louisa didn't believe what Melissa was saying now. The uncomfortable feeling she'd had was growing – the purpose for which Melissa had got her and Oliver there was becoming more ominous by the second. Yes, she wanted the truth too, and if she was honest, she also wanted Oliver to suffer for everything he'd done. She'd have preferred to have gone through the proper channels, though – police. Justice in the way it was meant to be carried out. While she understood Melissa's reasoning and knew she was right, that there was no evidence to convict Oliver of any wrongdoing – here and now, she wanted to back out. Retreat. Go home to her family. Forget everything about the last few weeks.

But Melissa wasn't done. She couldn't forget – Louisa got that. Oliver had murdered her sister and disposed of the body. Then he'd actively sought Melissa out, manipulated a meeting, and shoehorned himself into her life, the same as he'd recently done with Louisa's. Had he pretended to love Melissa for all that time? Is that what she was thinking now, that for the entire time she'd been seeing Oliver it had all been fake, his feelings for her fabricated? Or, Louisa wondered, had he been so torn about his actions that being with Melissa and marrying her was his only way of redeeming himself.

A niggling feeling deep in her gut also offered the possibility that finding the dead girl's sister, infiltrating her family, was his warped way of seeing first-hand the damage he'd created – like when murderers revisited the scene of their crime – only he'd taken that one step further. Whatever his twisted reasoning, the betrayal was obviously way too much for Melissa to endure and when Louisa had drunkenly given her details about her and Oliver's relationship, the accident that had caused him to leave her, she'd given Melissa the missing jigsaw pieces that she was now acting upon so ruthlessly.

This whole situation was her doing.

How will it end?

Louisa had been lost in thought, the words being spoken now bounced around her, unheard.

'Did you hear him, Louisa?' Melissa shouted inches from her ear. 'Say it again, Oliver. Tell her.'

Louisa's eyes settled on Oliver's, her focus now back on the moment.

'I'm sorry, Lou-Lou. I don't know why I lied, back then. I guess I couldn't bear to lose you, even though that's what ended up happening. But if I'd told you, if I'd come clean about what I did, what would you have done? You were already beside yourself, verging on hysteria – you looked to me to solve everything. To save you. It was easier to keep the details of how I'd managed that to myself – it was better for the both of us. Surely you can see that?'

Louisa couldn't find her voice, couldn't respond with anything other than a strangled noise emanating from her paralysed voice box. Oliver took her silence as indication he should continue – the voice inside Louisa's head was silently screaming for him to shut up.

'All I've thought about since then was *why*? Why did you drag me into it? If you hadn't called me that night in such a state, I'd never have done what I did. I did it for you; that's God's honest truth. I thought if she survived, she'd be able to identify the car, and you. I panicked, and she was shouting at me to call an ambulance, but I froze, couldn't think where the nearest phone box was – the lanes weren't the ones I drove. I didn't really know where I was.' He stopped speaking, breath-less.

'Go on. Tell me what you did. Tell Louisa how you ended my sister's life.'

Oliver took a juddering breath in, releasing it in a slow hiss. 'I knew she was hurt badly; she couldn't move her legs, blood was oozing from her broken body. I knew it wouldn't take much. I've snapped a rabbit's neck before – I didn't think it would be so different.'

'Oh, Jesus, no!' Louisa covered her mouth with her hand.

'It *was* different, though. Tough. Much harder to do on a human. Bigger throat, tighter muscles, more resistance.'

'Stop. Oliver, please stop,' Louisa said.

'You can't have it both ways! You wanted the truth, so now you have to listen. Don't we all follow the path of least resist-ance? I did what was easiest for us in the long run, Lou.' His eyes glared, as though a film had appeared over the retinas. Dark, as though his pupils had swallowed his irises. Louisa's stomach churned with acid. She looked to Melissa, afraid of her reaction. But she was standing still, no emotion showing on her face.

'Where did you take her?' Melissa's voice a whisper in the silence of the night.

'Oh, come on. You expect me to tell you that? I'm not going to prison for your stupid runaway of a sister, Melissa.'

The shriek seemed unnaturally loud. There was a waft of air as Melissa rushed past Louisa, causing her to step back in shock.

The hoarse grunt that followed confused her for a second.

Then, with a surge of panic, she knew.

She hadn't noticed Melissa reaching into the bag she'd held under her arm.

Hadn't noticed the blade.

And Oliver hadn't noticed it quickly enough to move out of its way.

Now, Louisa looked on in horror as a dark patch appeared on Oliver's shirt, and spread outwards like deep-red ink on blotting paper. Her eyes focused on the handle protruding from just below Oliver's ribcage and her legs gave way. She fell to her knees on the stony ground, watching on helplessly as Oliver slumped back down to the sitting position he'd been in moments before, gasps of air the only sound she could hear.

'Melissa . . . what the fuck have you done?'

Melissa was standing over Oliver, staring, saying nothing. Then she crouched down, and with one hand she reached for the knife.

Louisa closed her eyes, waiting for Oliver's scream as Melissa removed it. She couldn't bear to watch.

'I guessed you would never tell me, so there was no point holding this off. The only way I'm ever going to feel better about what you did to Helen, to me, to Louisa, is to punish you myself.'

Louisa opened her eyes, and swallowing the acid liquid that had erupted into her mouth, she directed her gaze towards Oliver.

'Oh, God.' She couldn't keep her stomach contents in any longer. Retching to the side of where she was kneeling, Louisa brought it all up, coughing and spluttering like Noah did when he gulped his milk too quickly and choked. She wiped her mouth with the back of her hand and tried to stand. She had to get away from the scene, as far away from the common as she could. She couldn't have anything to do with this.

'Lou-Lou . . . come . . . here—' The voice sounded alien to her, the words bubbling, as though they were being spoken under water. He was drowning in his own blood.

Oliver was going to die.

Louisa went to him, warily stepping around Melissa. Despite wanting him punished, she didn't want this. This was going to have serious repercussions. *I'm going to be next.* Was Melissa going to make sure she shared the same fate as Oliver, given they shared the same crime? Where was the knife? Louisa cast her phone light around as she approached Oliver, but couldn't see it. She stooped so she was closer to Oliver, but made sure Melissa was still in her line of sight. She didn't trust her now. She shouldn't have trusted her in the first place.

Too late now.

'What do you want to say, Oliver?'

His hand reached up and grabbed the collar of her coat and with what must have been his last ounce of strength, pulled her towards him, causing her to drop her phone. The light went from Oliver's face, but now she was so close, she could see it clearly. See the fear in his eyes.

'I did it because I loved you,' he said, the sounds of the words light, quiet, like tiny puffs of air. 'Forgive me.'

Louisa opened her mouth to speak, but Melissa pitched towards them.

'Don't you *dare*, Louisa. *This* is his punishment. He dies without forgiveness.'

'But, Melissa, he shouldn't die at all,' Louisa said, brushing away Oliver's hand from her coat and straightening. 'His punishment should be life behind bars, not the release of death!'

'I've told you. Don't you listen? He won't go to prison.'

'But *we* will. If we let him die, we will.' Louisa could hear her own begging tone. 'Do you want that? To let him win? He'll have taken your sister's life and yours and mine. Why should we suffer for him?'

'We won't. Because no one will know what we've done.'

Louisa wanted to argue the what *'we've'* done part, but the sudden cessation of gurgling brought her attention back to Oliver. Melissa's gaze followed hers as they both stared over at him.

'Oh well, I think it's already settled,' Melissa said as she bent to pick up the fallen phone and pointed the light directly at Oliver.

The light shone onto his face – his open eyes.

He didn't blink; his pupils didn't dilate.

'Fuck's sake, Melissa, he's dead. Now what are we going to do?'

51

THE PLAN

The two women faced one another other, their postures mirrored: legs apart, hands on hips, each mind silently and rapidly attempting to process the scene, work out their next move.

'Between us we can lift him over the fence, roll him to the edge of the quarry and just let him fall. It's a fair drop, isn't it?'

Melissa's carefree, upbeat tone shocked Louisa. She'd killed a man, and here she was calmly stating how she was going to dispose of him in the disused quarry.

'Yes, it's a four-hundred-metre drop if I remember rightly. But, no, that's not an option. He would be found easily, and it's clearly murder as he has a stab wound!'

'I thought you said it was disused? And it's fenced off, so no one—'

'People climb it. From the other side – there's another way to get to it from the bottom; he'd be found within a week, easily.'

'So, what do *you* suggest?' Melissa swung the phone light around, right into Louisa's face.

'Jesus, lower that, will you?' Louisa shielded her eyes from the glaring white light. 'I don't know, Melissa. It's not like I knew you were going to *kill* him, is it? I didn't come with a plan.'

'Sorry. I didn't come here with the sole intention of killing him, you know.'

'Oh right. So that's why you brought a kitchen knife with you?'

'That was for protection. He tried to kill me before, remember? I wasn't going to come here unarmed. I didn't want him to hurt me or you. He's caused enough pain.'

'I wish there'd been another way.' Louisa sunk down to the ground again, her head hanging down. 'My brain won't work. I can't think what to do.' Her eyes prickled with tears. She rocked back and forth, her head in her hands. 'I can't believe this has happened. I can't believe any of it has. I want to go back to before I was forty. Before Tiff hacked into my Facebook, before Oliver turned up and turned my life upside down, before Tiff went and bloody died. *Shit.* It's her funeral tomorrow and here I am the night before trying to figure out what to do with a dead body.'

'I'm really sorry about Tiff. I was wrong about her; I don't think she did know anything about Helen's disappearance. It was just a massive coincidence that she was your friend and you were the one who hit my sister. You can see how that looks, right?'

'Yes, of course I see how that looks. But until you went "*missing*", Tiff had never mentioned Helen. It was only then she happened to say in passing that she'd known someone who disappeared years ago, someone she'd worked with.'

'I know. I can only blame Oliver. Well, and you.'

Louisa froze. The uncomfortable feeling that Melissa had unfinished business lay heavily in her gut. But she needed Louisa now, needed her to get rid of Oliver's body so they could try and escape going to prison for the rest of their lives. Unless she didn't care. It could be that she wanted to exact her revenge on them all, and to hell with the consequences for her personally. Life in prison may well be worth it in Melissa's mind.

Louisa had to play this carefully.

'If I'd had any idea, any whatsoever, that Helen was still alive, I'd have called an ambulance, The police. I promise. Oliver said she was gone. That I'd killed her. Everything from there was a blur for twenty-two years, Melissa. I'm so very sorry for the part I played.'

'I know you are. I don't blame you anymore, I told you. It's Oliver who needed to be held to account for everything.'

'Okay, okay.' Louisa paced, her nerves on edge. 'Look, it must be getting really late.' She took her mobile from Melissa and checked the time. It was nearly midnight. She hadn't realised they'd been at the quarry for so long. The adrenaline had kept everything going, but now it'd dipped, Louisa was feeling tired and cold. 'We have to think about how we're going to move him, and where we're going to take him. I'm guessing you didn't bring anything like plastic sheeting, blankets, or anything?'

'No. Nothing.' Melissa raked her fingers through her hair. 'Like I said, I honestly only brought the knife for protection. I wasn't planning on killing him.'

'Great.'

'Oh, hang on. The car I've got. There might be something we can use in there.'

'Whose car is it?'

'Mine. Sort of. I did a cash deal with this dodgy guy before he was going to crush it – it's not exactly legal, but I wasn't planning on using it much; it was to follow you, really. I've been careful not to go anywhere where there are cameras. I think, anyway. Don't worry, once I'm done with it, I'll set it on fire.'

Louisa screwed her eyes up. This was sounding more and more bizarre and less like they could possibly get away with it

315

with every passing minute. But now wasn't the time to question Melissa's thinking.

'And where is it now?'

'I parked about five minutes from here and walked. Didn't want to be seen. I could drive it as close to the entrance as possible.'

'How the hell are the two of us going to get a dead-weight body back down the path to the entrance though? It took me a few minutes to get here on my own; it's a bit of a climb.'

'We can drag him? It'll be easier to do as it's downhill all the way. I know that'll leave a trail, but no one will query marks like that, will they?'

'No, possibly not. These are well-worn paths – but we'd have to be careful because of the blood. This is the dog-walkers' paradise – a sniff of blood might get them all going, draw unwanted attention to this part of the common. We're going to have to clean up as best we can.'

'Okay. I'll go and see what's in the boot, and bring whatever I can back here.'

'Don't leave me here with him!' Louisa didn't want to be with a dead body, but more than that she didn't trust Melissa not to do another disappearing act, leaving her to clean up the mess, or take the fall for what she'd done. That would be ironic – Oliver and Melissa each carrying out a murder and then pinning it on her.

'You should stay here, just in case anyone comes.'

'And what in God's name am I meant to do if someone does!'

'You can somehow make sure they go the other way, tell them there's a . . . tree fallen . . . or something, that the path's blocked and they can't get through.'

'And I'm doing what, exactly, here at bloody midnight? I've no dog, I'm not a reckless teenager up to no good – it will look really suspicious. And what if I know them?'

'The more we stand here debating it, the more likely someone *will* come. Let's get on with it, shall we?'

Time slowed dramatically. Louisa felt as though she'd been waiting for an hour by the time she heard rustling. *Please be Melissa.*

'It was useless, I'm sorry. I've just got this rank towel.' Melissa's breathing was laboured as she stopped in front of Louisa. She stared at the item in her hand with a sense of defeat.

'Well, that's great, Melissa. That's not going to wrap around him, is it?' Louisa banged her palms against her temples.

Melissa sighed, dropping the towel at her feet. All Louisa could think about was the wealth of fibres, DNA, and footprints they were going to be leaving at the scene. They may as well give themselves up now. Tell the police that Oliver had drawn them to the common then attacked them. That in self-defence, Melissa had stabbed him. That was a better plan than trying to hide his body and hope for the best for ever more that it wasn't found.

Had that been how Oliver had felt for all those years? Louisa glanced at his motionless body. Melissa had done him a favour, really. She'd released him from his guilt.

Now that guilt was hers for the rest of her life.

'You've got that belt on your mac,' Melissa said brightly. 'We could at least tie the towel around the wound, stop some of the blood from leaking everywhere as we drag him.'

Louisa's lips parted, an objection ready to trip off her tongue, but before it materialised she realised they had nothing better to work with. 'Well, let's try it, then.'

Louisa whipped her belt from the loops as Melissa picked the towel up. Now they'd have to touch him. Louisa's stomach flipped over. Holding her breath, and not looking at his ashen face, she took hold of Oliver's upper body, pulling it up until there was enough room to slip the towel beneath him. Melissa tugged it, bringing it up around his torso, and together they manoeuvred him so they could secure the towel with the belt.

Louisa stood and yanked her coat off – the effort it'd taken just to get that far had made her sweat.

'It might stop the blood, but without him being completely concealed it's obvious it's a body. I wish we could've rolled him up in a rug or something. It'd be slightly less conspicuous if anyone did spot us!'

'You could tie that around his head,' Melissa said, pointing to Louisa's mac.

'No, Melissa. If he's ever found that'll link him straight to me!'

'Louisa. If he's found, there will be far more than your mac linking you to his death.'

'Fair point. It would stop us having to look at him at least. And I can take it off and burn it when we get to wherever we're going. Where *are* we going to take him?'

'I don't know the area. This bit is up to you.'

'Oh. Fantastic. The time it's taking us, it'll be light before we've even figured out where to ditch him. I may as well take him to Tiff's funeral.' Louisa let out a sharp laugh. Hysteria was setting in.

'That's brilliant!' Melissa stood up and began pacing. 'That's a good idea. It could work.'

'What? In what world is that—' And then she caught up with Melissa's thinking.

'Shit. Yes, that *could* work. It's risky, but genius.'

For the first time since Melissa's rash action, Louisa felt a glimmer of hope.

Perhaps they really could get away with murder.

52

THE LAST TIME

Thursday – early a.m.

'We'll need tools. And different clothes to change into afterwards.'

'You sound like you've done this before, Melissa.'

'Of course I haven't. But I've seen enough crime documentaries to know we have to take precautions. Can we go to yours and get a shovel?'

'No! Shit, no. Brian will hear me. I can't involve him in all this. And anyway, I've got a neighbour who is literally up all night, sitting at his front window. He would see the car and, not recognising it, would most definitely report it to the police. He's done it before. We can't chance that.'

'Okay. Well, could there already be a shovel at the graveside? If Tiff's grave has been dug, they might've left tools?'

'No, they used a mini-digger thing. I saw it when I walked through the other day.' Louisa stared out of the car window, wishing she were anywhere but sitting there with Oliver's wife – her dead husband squashed up in the boot. They'd had to sit for the last twenty minutes recovering from the task of dragging Oliver's body down the pathway. Louisa's arms shook, the ache from the weight and awkwardness of their load tracking up into her shoulders. She'd be stiff in the morning. 'Tiff has tools in her garage,' she said, her mind suddenly alert again.

'Can you get into it?'

'I know the combination to the key safe by the front door, and you can access the garage from inside her house – there's a connecting door.'

'Great. We can take some of her clothes, too. You can't put your coat back on now, and we'll need fresh clothes after all this.' Melissa looked down at herself – her jumper and jeans were caked in mud from the numerous times they'd stumbled over with the body.

'No. That's just . . . weird. Wrong.'

'Really? I think we've gone beyond that already.'

'Fine. I bagged everything up the other day. If it's still there, and no one has taken it to charity, we should be able to find a change of clothes.'

The engine rumbled into life, and Melissa slowly drove in the direction of Tiff's. The weight of Oliver in the boot had lowered the rear of the car, and as it bumped over the stony ground leaving the common, the exhaust grated on the ground. If they managed to get the car to Tiff's and then to the church, without someone clocking them, it would be a miracle.

Louisa had been right about Tiff having tools in the garage. They took a bucket shovel and a spade, then got a change of clothes and some trainers for each of them. They made two trips to the car before driving along the road to the church.

The churchyard was eerily quiet as Louisa walked in first through the gate at the top entrance. Melissa's car was parked as close as she could get it. The nearest houses were far enough away that even if someone looked out of their window, they shouldn't draw too much attention – the streetlamps had gone off, so it would be difficult to make anything out with clarity. As it was two in the morning, Louisa hoped that would afford them the luck they needed in order to carry this out undisturbed.

The church itself was illuminated on one side, the floodlight casting an orangey glow. Once they passed by this side of the church to get to the prepared plot, they would be in relative darkness. Louisa's phone battery was on its last bar, so they wouldn't have the torchlight for long. They had to work fast.

Louisa pulled at the plastic sheeting over the open grave, while Melissa did the same to the sheet covering the pile of excavated earth. Giving a desperate look to Melissa, Louisa took a deep breath then lowered herself to the ground. Sitting with her legs dangling over the edge of the hole, the reality of what they were about to do hit her.

'I can't do it. Melissa, this is mad – stupid. We have to think of something else,' she whispered.

'This is the best plan there is. Don't overthink it, just do it,' she hissed, giving Louisa a nudge with her knee.

'Hey, don't! I'll do it in my own time.'

'Time is a luxury we don't have. Jump.'

Pain reverberated up her ankles into her calves as she hit the ground hard. But she was in the grave now – there was no going back. She just hoped she could get out again.

Louisa turned and looked up at Melissa. 'If we are both in here digging, how will we manage to climb out?'

'We'll have to take it in turns. Once we've dug more earth out, I think we'd struggle to get out if one of us wasn't up here to help. And if we're both found in here when the sun comes up . . . well. That's the end, isn't it.'

'Okay. Pass me the spade – I'll use that first and then we can swap, and you use the shovel to get rid of the loose earth.'

'Don't forget – put your back into it,' Melissa said as she

lowered the spade down. Louisa grimaced, snatching it from her and beginning to dig.

They'd swapped several times before deciding they'd displaced enough extra earth to cover Oliver's body and still leave the grave looking as deep as when they'd started.

'Right. Let's do this.' Melissa pulled Louisa back out of the grave, both of them collapsing at the edge, their breathing rapid, chests heaving. Louisa's hands were blistered, but thankfully the skin hadn't broken. She rubbed them gently together, wincing at the sharp pain. The hardest part was yet to come. They had to get Oliver, carry him in, carefully roll him into the grave, then pile enough earth over him and make sure they compacted it so it didn't look as though the grave had been disturbed.

With the boot up, Louisa took the head end, Melissa the other. With a coordinated effort they tried to lift Oliver's body up and out. They moved it an inch or so, but no more, dropping him back down, the car rocking with the weight.

'Shit!' Louisa turned her back on him, sitting on the edge of the boot. 'We're not going to be able to do it. All that digging, and dragging him from the common beforehand, my arms are numb – I haven't got the strength.'

'We have to. There's no choice. We'll try both taking the leg end and move that part out first. Come on.'

The effort to get him out of the boot, then carry him to the grave was so great that it came as a relief when they got him to the edge and the burden was released. It would only take one more heave to roll him into the deep hole. Louisa's adrenaline had got her this far, and she knew once it wasn't needed, she'd crash.

'After three?'

'Yep, after three,' Melissa agreed. 'One . . .'

'Two,' Louisa said, preparing herself.

322

'Three,' they said together.

Louisa pushed the top end and as she did, the mac covering Oliver's head slipped off, exposing his pale face, his wide-open eyes. She let go, muffling a scream with her hands. Luckily her push had been enough, and together with Melissa's, gave the force needed to propel the body into the hole.

'Calm down, Louisa. We're on the home run.'

'I can't believe you're making light of this. Don't you feel any remorse? Any ounce of guilt?'

'No. And after you've recovered from tonight, once you get your life back on track, nor will you. You'll go over all that he's done to you, to Helen and me, and will be glad we did this.'

'Maybe.' Louisa shone the light down inside the hole to make sure he'd fallen right. The glare of the light catching his eyes made the whites shine as though an ultraviolet light was on them. It was freaky. 'Let's hurry up and cover him, shall we?' Louisa sank to her knees and began pushing some earth into the grave with her hands.

'It'll be easier with the shovels?' Melissa said, her voice full of sarcasm.

'Yes, obviously. I just had to cover his face.' Louisa couldn't bear to look into those eyes anymore – eyes that had once been so hypnotic, now lifeless. She got back to her feet and snatched the shovel from Melissa's hands. They both winced, the friction sending a burning sensation across their palms. 'Sorry,' Louisa muttered.

There was excess earth left over once they'd covered him. And one of them had to get back into the grave and flatten the loose earth.

Louisa hesitated.

'Don't worry, I'll do it,' Melissa said, immediately jumping back in.

Louisa watched numbly as Melissa walked back and forth in the six-foot hole, pressing the earth down with each small footstep.

Then she told Louisa to throw in another shovel-load from the mound. This continued until the bottom of the grave looked flat.

Louisa pulled Melissa from the hole, using what little energy remained. She was so exhausted that despite the macabre surroundings, despite the knowledge of what had just taken place, Louisa was sure she could sleep right now, right there.

'We've done it,' Melissa said.

They helped each other up, and standing side by side at the edge of the grave, Louisa pointed the phone downwards. It looked good – the ground sufficiently compacted, no sign of a body that didn't belong in there. A bubble of anger at everything she'd been put through erupted to the surface. How could Oliver have done this to her? The anger wasn't entirely focused on him, though – Louisa was also angry about her own actions; then and now. But there'd been no other way, had there?

'Claw your way back from that, Oliver,' she whispered.

'That's the last time you'll ever have to see that lying bastard. We've done everyone a favour.' Melissa grabbed Louisa's hand.

Guilt burned in her stomach, like acid was slowly eating through the layers. Melissa might be right, but who was she to decide someone's fate?

'What's done is done, I guess,' Louisa said. 'We have to live with this.' Like Oliver had lived with the knowledge he'd taken someone's life, supposedly for love, if his dying words were to be believed.

Only he hadn't managed to live with the guilt, had he? Will I?

'Seriously, Louisa. This has to be the last time Oliver has any control over your life.' She squeezed Louisa's hand. 'The last time you even *think* of him.'

'Yes. The last time.' Louisa closed her eyes, forcing the tears to remain in them. She couldn't change what had happened, however much she'd like to. But if she was to have any kind of future now, after all this, she knew Melissa was right. Oliver had to be deleted from her mind. They re-covered the dug grave with the plastic sheeting and replaced the stones that had secured it there. 'Let's get out of here.'

Once they got back on the path, they took off their mud-caked shoes, placing them in the bin liner, and put on the fresh ones. Tiff's. A strange sensation passed through her as she walked in her dead friend's shoes. They left the church via the small, rear, stile-like stone that led to the steps on the other side, rather than pass the illuminated side of the church again. The road was dark, with the moonlight only revealing a small area in front of them. They backed against the high wall as they moved cautiously away from the church.

At the end of the lane, which opened up to the road leading to Tiff's house, they went in separate directions. Louisa walked towards home. Melissa, carrying everything they'd used, walked back to the top entrance of the church where the car was parked. She was going to drive the car along the back lanes to Torquay to avoid any CCTV cameras. Not that there were many, but it was better safe than sorry. At some point, she was going to set fire to the car, and its contents: the bin liner, the shovel and spade – and that's as far as Louisa knew about the next step of the plan.

They didn't speak when they left each other. There were no words that could convey the desperate act they'd both played a part in. Louisa didn't know what Melissa would do now. Go home to Yorkshire? Stay and make a home here? She wondered how she was going to explain her disappearance. There were so many questions remaining, but Louisa didn't have the strength to contemplate any of them right now.

Letting herself in the back door, she crept inside and sat at the kitchen table to gather her thoughts before sneaking upstairs. She hoped Noah had stayed asleep, that no one had heard her come home. If they did, she had the excuse of staying out late with one of Tiff's friends, reminiscing and trying to come to terms with her death.

Not that she could even imagine being able to come to terms with the events of the past month.

Or with what had been in box three, when she'd unlocked that padlock in her mind.

The thunking sound of a head hitting granite.

Blood-covered tiles.

Desperate for a shower, but aware that would wake everyone, Louisa undressed downstairs and bundled Tiff's clothes into the washing machine. She quickly pulled a nightie over her head and made her way up the stairs. A gentle snoring greeted her as she reached the top stair. She sneaked inside her room, gently pulling open the drawer beneath the bed. She listened for movement from Brian, but he was dead to the world. One less worry. Louisa took out the mobile phone that lay next to the photos of her at college. The light glowed as she pressed the button to bring up the texts. The battery icon flashed – it was going to run out soon. That was good. But she had to delete the message dated the day of Tiff's death first.

> You'd better have a fucking good explanation. I know you've lied to me – you and Brian disgust me. You're meant to be my best friend, but I'd be better off without you. I'm coming over now. Be there. Be ready for the repercussions.

She pressed delete, but before replacing the phone in the drawer alongside the packet of photos – her lost memories – she used the glow from the screen to illuminate the top photo. Oliver and her. She flipped it over and read what she'd written.

Don't trust Oliver.

She'd been right to be wary.

A shiver ran the length of her back when she saw the words

she'd scrawled beneath that. Ones she didn't remember writing:

Don't trust yourself.

She quickly replaced the packet and slid the drawer closed, and then crept back out of the bedroom. Emily's door was shut, no light showing beneath it as she passed. She tiptoed into Noah's nursery and took a seat in the chair. Noah's soft puffs of breath relaxed her.

She'd done the right thing, hadn't she?

As she thought about Tiff's upcoming funeral, her eyelids fluttered closed.

I'm under water – box three ahead of me now.

I swim to it, and after several heaves, more than it's taken to open the first two, the lid opens . . .

This box contains the newest lost memories, those I've only just secured in a separate compartment, there to be buried along with the others that might harm me:

I'm walking up the side of Tiff's house. There's a fogginess in my head, one that is getting denser as I think about her with Brian. They've been talking about me since Noah's birth. That's bad enough.

But it's what happened before that, that bothers me.

How could she do it to me?

She lied to my face.

It's not all she's lied about.

There she is, standing in her immaculate kitchen, her back to me.

She knows I'm coming, but she hasn't heard me – her attention is elsewhere.

Looking down. At something in her hands.

She drops it as she turns abruptly, both hands flying to her chest in shock as she realises I'm there.

She looks guilty – as though she's been caught out.

But it's her who accuses me. 'I'm glad you're here. I know what you did,' she says, her voice quiet.

'And I know what you did,' I say, anger attaching itself to my words like venom.

'We should chat over coffee.' She takes a bottle of water and unscrews the cap as she has a hundred times before. Only this time is different – and suddenly a dark veil descends over my eyes.

I hear shouting. Words echoing around the room.

An argument.

She's enraged. But not about what I did, back then – it's about now. About Brian.

'I know you're upset, but you're wrong about me!' She bangs the water down on the granite surface. It tips, water pouring out and onto the worktop, the floor. She rights the bottle although there's very little left inside now. 'I have done nothing but protect you, Louisa. More than once, actually.'

'You're a liar,' I scream.

She lurches to the side of the island unit – to calm me down? To grab me?

I step back, and she slips as she moves towards me.

The deep thud sends a chill through my body. My stomach knots. Blood.

Her eyes are wide and blood – viscous, dark – seeps into them, turning the whites red.

Her hands grasp for the worktop, knocking the bottle. Her body falls: limp, boneless, like a rag doll.

Bang.

She disappears from view.

I back further away, and then out of the patio door.

I force the lid of box three closed and swim back to the safety of the surface.

When I wake, it'll be gone.

53

THE FUNERAL

'Hey. I didn't hear you come home last night. What time did you get in?' Brian wandered into the kitchen, a shirt over one arm, the other holding up a hanger with his ancient suit on.

'Oh, I'm not even sure. Lost track of time and ended up going back to Amber's house.' Louisa got up from the bar stool and filled the kettle.

'Amber? Who's she?'

'A friend of Tiff's.' Louisa found the lie came easily, but then her back was turned. Lying straight to his face would've been harder. 'Don't you have a different suit you could wear? I swear you wore that to our wedding,' she said, turning back to face him now she'd changed the subject.

'Ha-ha. I wanted to get a new one, but I didn't get around to it. This is serviceable, just needs a press.'

'Leave it on the side, I'll get to it in a minute.'

'Okay, thanks. Your mum said she'd have Noah today, by the way, so we could concentrate on the funeral.'

'Really? She doesn't even know what to do with a baby, Brian. I don't think that's a good idea.'

'I think you need to go and see her, and your dad. They

were great with him yesterday – not as incompetent as you like to think.'

'I don't like to think that. I'm only going on what I've seen, the actual evidence.' Her hackles were up, an immediate response when Brian tried to take her parents' side over hers.

'Give her a chance, Lou. Life's too short.'

He was right – on every count. And as it was, she was glad that she didn't have to cope with Noah at the church. The entire service was already going to be one of the most difficult things she'd have to go through, and having a crying baby would only compound that.

'Sure. What time are you taking him over there?'

Louisa noted the subtle raise in Brian's eyebrows. '*We*. We are taking him over at twelve.' He smiled.

'Okay. Conceded. We'll take him. But I'm not going in – I'll pass him over at the door. One step at a time.' Louisa handed Brian a mug of tea.

'Thanks,' he said absently. 'Good. That's settled then. Are you doing all right?' He looked over the top of his mug as he took a sip of tea, his eyes doleful.

The question threw her off balance for a second. No. She was nowhere close to being all right. But she knew she had to get through this day. Once it was over, she could make a start on rebuilding her life.

'If I'm honest, I just want today to be over with. We can all call it a celebration of her life and laugh and reminisce about our memories with her, but the reality is, it's going to be a hideous day where all I'm thinking is what a waste of a life, and what I should've done – how I could've saved her. I don't see any reason to celebrate.'

'I know. I'm with you. It's easier when the person is old and had a good, long life. But when they die too young, when they had so much more to give, well, that's a travesty. But you know, she really would want you to celebrate her life, not feel guilty and mourn her.'

'There's so much more to this, though, isn't there – it's not a simple process to work through. Grief, guilt, love, hate, regret – all tied up in a fuck-off-big messy, tight knot. It's going to take a lot of time and effort to undo it.

'Wow, Lou. Deep,' Brian said.

Louisa sighed loudly and shook her head. 'Fine. You take the piss. I'm going for a shower.' She slunk off, away from Brian and his sarcasm. He didn't have a clue about what she'd been through, what she'd done. And despite his mocking, she hoped to God it would stay that way.

Tiff's mum and dad had done a brilliant job with the order of service; the music, hymns and readings they'd chosen were just right. They screamed 'Tiff'. Even though she hadn't been particularly religious, Louisa knew she'd loved feeling part of the church's activities and had always joined in with the children from the school when they did Harvest festival, Easter and Christmas services. She would've been proud to see the turnout. Louisa turned around to take in the congregation – almost the entire village's population seemed to be packed inside the church.

'Here you go,' someone said, pressing a packet of tissues into Louisa's palm.

'Oh, thank you.' She was confused at first, but then realised tears were already cascading down her cheeks. As soon as 'Amazing Grace' started playing on the organ, Louisa felt something give. From her position in the pew nearest the east-facing window, she caught a glimpse of the coffin being carried slowly up the path towards the church door. Her chest tightened, her heart feeling as though it too had ceased beating. A wave of anxiety consumed her.

In that moment, Tiff's death became real. In that moment, Louisa was immobilised by grief, pain and regret. She lowered her eyes as the coffin was brought in by the pallbearers; she wasn't able to face it now it was in close proximity to her. The sound of her galloping pulse whooshed noisily in her ears, drowning out the music.

Hurry up and be over.

She held her hands together so tightly they turned white. She focused on them, not on her feelings, not on Tiff's coffin, and not on Tiff's mum and dad who were walking behind their only daughter. All she had to do was concentrate for another hour and it would be done. Shirley had asked Louisa to read the eulogy but she'd broken down at the mere thought. Realising it would be too much pressure to put on Tiff's best friend, Shirley had asked if Louisa might write some things about Tiff instead, and ask her other friends to do the same, and she'd give that to the vicar to read.

Louisa had been thankful to be let off the hook. Before the events of the past few weeks, she might've had the courage to stand up in front of Tiff's family and friends and tell everyone how amazing Tiff was – had been. Now, it seemed disingenuous, inappropriate.

Brian's arm on hers alerted her to the fact everyone had now taken their seats. Louisa sat down and with the service sheet on her lap, read it through, word for word, front to back. When she finished, she started it again. That was how she was going to get through this service.

The church air had been cool – it was always that way. But stepping outside now, the change in temperature and atmosphere began to rejuvenate Louisa. She'd become drowsy during the hymns and readings, the constant rereading of the order of service causing her to wilt. She was vaguely aware of being guided, by Brian, around the side of the church. And suddenly, like a smack in the face, Louisa was completely alert.

They were heading to the graveside.

Her feet retraced the steps she'd taken twelve hours earlier. In her mind, she watched herself and Melissa dragging the body along the path, across the grass. Her pulse quickened; sweat pricked under her armpits. Brian reached down to take her hand. She snatched it away.

'You okay?' he asked.

She nodded, not daring to attempt speech. She couldn't let Brian hold her hand – he'd feel the blisters and ask how she'd got them. Instead, she balled each hand into a fist, her nails almost piercing the bubbles of fluid-filled pockets of skin. She winced, but wanted the pain. She deserved it.

Finally, after some shuffling of bodies into spaces around the headstones, they came to a standstill. After casting her eyes briefly around the grave and surrounding area, Louisa hung her head; she couldn't make eye contact with anyone for fear they would see behind them, read what was in them – they'd guess what had happened here the night before. She fiddled with her fingers, and as she looked at them, her world turned into darkness as her inner voice spoke, telling her what she was trying not to hear:

I can still feel the mud embedded deep under my fingernails, taste the dirt on my lips. Can still see the eyes: shining like glass, open and staring, deep in their sockets. Dead.

In my mind I watch the earth piling onto the body, slowly blotting out what's been done. Finally covering those eyes, so they can't judge anymore.

I'm confident no trace of it can lead back to me.

Part of me feels regret; a sadness that it came to such a drastic act.

For the moment, my conscience is telling me I'm guilty.

But I know that can be buried too.

333

Louisa swallowed the guilt and blinked the visions of the previous night away. Now, her head raised, she watched as Tiff's light-oak coffin was lowered into the ground.

Lowered on top of Oliver's body.

With her breath held, she waited until the bearers released the supporting straps before she exhaled the held air from her burning lungs. She'd half expected someone to yell 'stop' as they noticed an irregularity in the ground – fingers sticking up from a loose bit of earth. But there was resounding silence.

How would Tiff have reacted if she knew what they'd done? Buried a murderer beneath her. Louisa's body shook violently. An arm came across from her right, then enveloped her tightly.

'I'm sorry, Lou. This must be so terrible for you.' Brian gave her a weak smile.

He'd never know just how terrible.

THE EPILOGUE

*The Mid-Devon Advertiser article
dated 21 June 2019*

Archaeological dig uncovers body: and as one mystery is solved, another begins.

A body found during a local archaeological dig has been identified today as that of a missing woman from 1995. Farmland close to the village of Little Penchurch, the site recently discovered to be an old Roman settlement, has not only uncovered ancient artefacts but also a tragic twenty-four-year-old mystery. Excavation of the land began in early June and two days into the dig, human bones were unearthed. Exeter Archaeology Group immediately suspended the dig as they suspected the bones to be human, and from recent years.

The remains have been identified as the body of a local woman, Helen Herbert, who was first reported missing by her parents in February 1995 when she supposedly ran away following family disagreements. Despite extensive police investigations at the time, no evidence was found to suggest harm had come to Helen, and with no leads, the search dwindled. Her family were said to have tried, and failed, to find Helen themselves, finally giving up hope after fifteen years and coming to the devastating conclusion Helen had committed suicide despite a body having never being found.

Until now.

Helen's sister, Mrs Melissa Dunmore, who herself had been reported missing in March of this year and had returned of her own accord in early April, was said to have been glad to finally gain closure for her and her family.

Helen's funeral took place last week with a private service for family only. Melissa's husband was not in attendance. Mr Oliver Dunmore, who'd initially been a suspect in Melissa's disappearance, has not been seen for over eight weeks. Police say that a letter, addressed to his missing wife, was found at their rented flat. In the letter, Mr Dunmore apologised for his behaviour, which he felt was the reason his wife had 'run off' in March without telling him her whereabouts.

Friends of Mr Dunmore confirmed he'd been experiencing suicidal thoughts since his wife had left. Police investigations have yet to find him, and it's their belief Mr Dunmore has taken himself somewhere remote and may have taken his own life.

The archaeological dig will resume shortly.

ACKNOWLEDGEMENTS

As always, a huge thank you to my amazing agent, Anne, who continues to guide and support me through my publishing journey. My thanks also to Kate from Kate Hordern Literary Agency and Rosie and Jessica Buckman for your hard work on the foreign rights. My editor, Katie – you never fail to encourage me and help make my novels better, and your dedication is second to none! I love working with you. A big thank you to Sabah, Elke, Rachel, Molly, Phoebe, Dom and the rest of the brilliant team that make up Avon, HarperCollins – you are all terrific to work with.

I'm very lucky to have great family and friends who continue to encourage and support my writing. Big shout out to J and San who are fabulous friends and staunch supporters (thank you for sharing my books with literally everyone you know!) I look forward so much to our Wednesday nights!

I had a launch for the first time for *One Little Lie* and was overwhelmed by the love and support – thank you to each and every person who came along (and to those who bought a book!) It was lovely to celebrate with family and friends. I will do it again for *The Missing Wife* and won't be as nervous this time!

Thank you to Doug, Danika, Louis and Nathaniel. My 'little' family is growing, and we've now added Josh and Emily – who both fit into the family perfectly – and by the time this book is published there will be a new baby! I'm so very proud of you, Danika, you are amazing and awe-inspiring. You are going to be a great mum and I'm so excited to become a nanna. Thank you all for believing in me and encouraging me every day.

Grateful thanks to my Psych Thriller Killers: Libby, Carolyn and Caroline – you are all great friends and writing buddies and I couldn't do this without your support, fun and laughter. I always look forward to meet-ups with you. My thanks also to Lydia Devadason, Louise Jensen, Rosina Farley, Claire Hill, Ian Hobbs (Devon Book Club), The Savvies, and The One That Cannot Be Named, who have offered support online or in person and shared chats about the joys and pitfalls of writing! There are many other authors and bloggers who I chat to and who make writing the most enjoyable it can be, so thank you all.

Knowing that my books are getting into the hands of readers is the best feeling and I feel proud and privileged to be able to write stories for a living. I want to thank every reader who has picked up one of my books, read them, reviewed them, and spread the word. I have had some wonderful messages – I do love hearing from readers! This is for you all – I very much hope you enjoy *The Missing Wife*.

Your daughter is in danger.

But can you trust her?

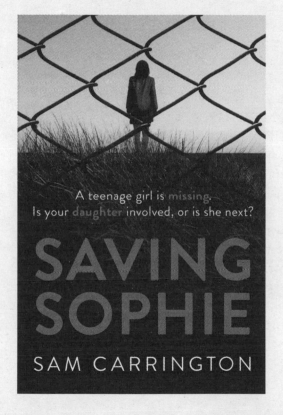

Available now in ebook and paperback.

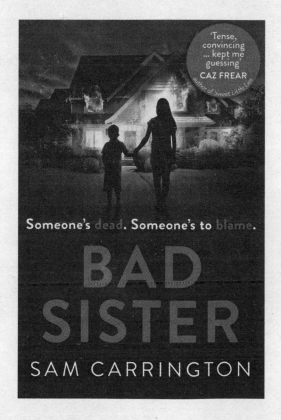

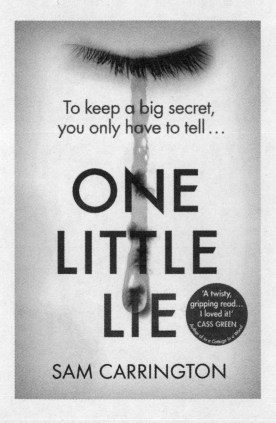